The Best Asian
Short Stories

2020

GUEST EDITORS OF
THE BEST ASIAN SHORT STORIES

The Best Asian Short Stories

2020

Editor
Zafar Anjum

Foreword by
Tabish Khair

Kitaab
Singapore

KITAAB

First published by Kitaab,
an imprint of Kitaab International Pte Ltd
10 Anson Road, #27-15, International Plaza,
Singapore 079903

Kitaab International
Singapore

ISBN: 978-981-14-8042-3

Printed and Bound in Singapore

www.kitaabinternational.com

Contents

Foreword
Why this Anthology Makes A Difference

Growing up in an Urdu-speaking family, I heard various words used to refer to a story or a short story: kahani, qissa, dastan. Sometimes, the word 'afsana' was also used, but not by the purists, who employed it to refer to 'fiction' in general. However, the only word used to describe a 'novel', and only a novel, was 'novel,' pronounced 'naavel.'

Growing up (due to four generations of professional education in the family and my own English-medium 'convent' schooling) to be more Anglophone than 'Urduprone,' I did not consider this to be odd. After all, in English too, one talks of the 'short story' and the 'novel.' The idea of radical newness – novelty – is attached to the genre of the 'novel', not to that of the short story. The implicit Anglophone assumption is that the short story is a version of longer stories written in the past, and Urdu sustains that reading too with terms like 'qissa' and 'dastan,' which have medieval moorings.

It is only when I picked up some other European languages – mostly in bits and pieces – that I realized that this situation was an oddity. In Danish, which I speak with some competence, the word for novel is 'roman' and the word for story is 'novelle.' In French, which I read falteringly, the common option is 'roman' and 'nouvelle.' And so on and so forth. In other words, most European languages provide medieval moorings to the 'novel' – 'roman' is obviously linked to medieval romances – not to the short story.

This difference is important to bear in mind, as both the short story and the novel are 'new' and 'old', depending on what features of the two genres one focuses on. That many Indian languages, such as Urdu and Hindi (which uses both 'novel' and 'upanyas'), associate radical newness with the novel and history with the short story is a record of the trajectory of colonization in South Asia. Despite that, the 'short story' has had a very different history in South Asia – and, from what I can see, given the limits of my knowledge, in Asia. For one, well into the 20th century, the short story was a dominant genre in languages like Punjabi, Hindi and Urdu. The great 20th century writers in many Asian languages – such as Saadat Hasan Manto and Ismat Chughtai in Urdu, Premchand in Hindi, even the more novelistic Rabindra Nath Tagore in Bangla – are sometimes exclusively and always significantly associated with the short story genre.

It is a history that has been largely ignored by global scholarship, especially in postcolonial studies and west-facing comparative literature: the short story played a much bigger literary and cultural role in Asia in the 20th century than it did in UK or even USA. It continues to be vibrant in the 21st, though less visible, solely due to critical and publishing prejudices imbibed from an Anglo-centric reading of the two genres.

That is the biggest reason to celebrate an anthology like *The Best Asian Short Stories*, and to applaud *Kitaab* for bringing it out every year. The fact that the stories in this anthology are all in English should not blind the reader – and the critic – to the *distinctively* Asian provenance of this endeavor: this anthology gives the short story the attention that the genre deserves within the Asian cultural tradition, attention that is often denied to it globally. That this attention is fully warranted is confirmed by the variety, lucidity and vibrancy of the stories – from so many different backgrounds – selected for inclusion in this anthology.

There is another set of reasons to celebrate this anthology: it creates an Asian community of writers. I am not making a parochial point. Let me explain this with reference to the two genres – the Anglo-dominant one of the 'novel' and its poorer cousin, the ignored, but no less crucial, genre of the 'short story.'

As all practitioners of the art of novel writing know (and I must shame-facedly confess that I have written about as many novels as I have written short stories, which I find more difficult as a genre), the novel has often been associated with modernity by many scholars. The most obvious – Anglophone – association was by Ian Watt, who traced the novel form to both individuality and modernity. Though I have a slightly different reading of the novel, Ian Watt's definitions are sufficient for my purpose here: because the novel, by its very length, is 'individualistic' in ways very different from what Watt had in mind. It simply cannot be anthologized!

Yes, you might have a completed volume of the novels of, say, Franz Kafka, but the fact remains that anthologies of novels are not possible. On the other hand, anthologies remain the prevalent form of dissemination for poems and short stories. Hence, regardless of individualism as Watt might have defined it, the *very lengths* of the two genres permit or prevent the creation of a collectivity.

And *because* the short story allows the creation of such collectivities, it is of far more use in marginal, oppressed, ignored and frayed spaces. The novel, due to its very length, which imposes a high level of financial and individual risks, is a monopolistic genre: its 'trends' tend to move towards monopoly, as does its marketing, procurement and even reading. The short story can resist this. An anthology of short stories can include the work of authors who would not be able to get entire collections – let alone novels – published because of financial, cultural, political and other factors. It can contain stories with very different agendas and styles, thus moving the reader out of her/his monopolistic biases. I believe that among the prose fiction genres, it is the short story that is *more enabling and potentially radical* than the novel. The very possibility of anthologizing is an aspect of this.

That is another reason to celebrate this new edition of *The Best Asian Short Stories*! Another year. Another list of authors: some new, some published. Many of them writing from spaces that do not allow them access to the monopolistic publishing of novels – which is not just a matter of getting those 200-plus pages printed and marketed by a house, but also the even more difficult matter of visibility in the crush of glamourous, mainstream novels. This anthology, like all anthologies, brings all of them together. The different experiences, the different styles, the different politics, all of them are not just presented but also, to a degree, protected by being collectively anthologized. It is in this sense that a community is created, and every reader who picks up this anthology, as I hope many will do, helps create this necessary community: a community of Asian writing that stands on its own two – no, its own million – feet!

TABISH KHAIR

Introduction

I was not supposed to be the editor of this volume of short stories that you are holding in your hands. As the founder and series editor of the Best Asian series, I was happy to remain active behind the scenes—curating the content with the help of a guest editor. Over the last three years, we have had three brilliant editors to helm the editions and every time it worked smoothly. It was only this year when we had a situation of a chosen guest editor dropping out at the last moment because of some personal matters. Consequently, I had to step in and play the role of the editor too.

Nevertheless, I wished to have an outsider's perspective on the stories that we had selected for this particular volume and I requested well-known novelist, poet, and critic Tabish Khair to write a *Foreword* for us. Being a gentleman that he is, he agreed to oblige us. And that's why, this year, we are breaking away from our tradition of having a guest editor, and for the first time, we also have an insightful "foreword" from one of the most respected contemporary writers, working out of Europe with deep roots in Asia.

The stories gathered in each volume of *The Best Asian Short Stories* reflect the taste, preferences, and aesthetic proclivities of its editor. In my case, I must admit, my main concern was readability of the story besides the literary levity that it displayed: how uniquely it was told and what it talked about.

Take, for example, Scott P. Salcedo's *Mud-bound Country*. It's a finely crafted story that takes us to a time when the American colonial rule was at its height in the Philippines. In such a time, a man bets all he has on a patch

of untamed and remote land whose bounties he thinks
he will profit from. More than a century later, we see the
remnants of his dreams and his struggles to fetter nature's
wildness.

Similarly, Moazzam Sheikh's *Sunshine* deals with the
perils of parenting in an increasingly racist and violence-
ridden world. It reflects on a father's emotions towards his
young son who he cherishes spending playtime with—nerf
guns and wrestling—in the evening before bedtime; and
yet the father cannot overcome his anxiety or fear, for his
child's safety when he faces the outside world, informed
by the political and economic reality as it exists within a
racist world.

Set in picturesque Thailand, Darryl Whetter's *Turquoise
Water, White Liberal Guilt* is a story of travel and so-called
race. Like COVID-19, the story asks whether we really
need to travel and, more importantly, what love requires.

This time, the writers from Singapore have a strong
presence in the anthology, and many of them have a
connection with the MA Creative Writing programme at
LASALLE College of the Arts. It is very exciting to see a
young crop of writers emerging from this little red dot to
fashion remarkably well-wrought narratives.

One of them is Seema Punwani. In her story, *Spin*,
we enter into the beautiful world of father-son relationship
that gives us a glimpse into a very unfamiliar world of
Singapore.

Adeline Tan's *Babel* is also imbued with the themes of
familial ties and relationships. It introduces us to a situation
in which when a father dies, his three estranged siblings are
pulled back together to deal with the family flat, which

could fetch a tidy sum in land-scarce Singapore. Donna Tang conjures up a dream-like world around a couple in her story, *How She Knew*, that flits between Singapore, Paris, and Batam.

In Kim Phong Huynh's *As Legal As We Get*, we meet Ajay, a gay expat in Singapore, who leads a double life as a meth addict. The story narrates a dinner party where Ajay re-encounters his love interest Aiden, who also happens to be a policeman. As night goes on, his secrets slowly unravel in front of Aiden.

Set against the contrasting backdrops of contemporary Edinburgh and Singapore's bygone kampongs, Sarah Soh's *Lingua Franca* tells the story of a young Singaporean university student who is caught between her past and present worlds. The story considers the issues of language, identity, race, and the things we leave behind in order to move forward.

Kelly Kaur's *Singapore Dreams* yet again engages us with the issues of migration and how one gets torn between the charms of a new land and the emotional pull of the land and people left behind. In this story, the characters are all trapped by their notion of migration, whether by choice or forced upon them.

How can an anthology of Asian stories be complete without a few large and complicated families? Jasmine Adam's *A Women's Place* (there is a reason why the title appears wrong!) spans four generations of women, who are migrants from China and Indonesia. It is a story of how women tackle challenges even though they may not have the upper hand, and how they too can win battles in their own way.

Yap Swee Neo's *In Towkay Lee's Mansion* describes the daily activities of a wealthy Peranakkan household seen through the eyes of Rositawati, a young Indonesian girl whose mother worked for the Lee family. Lee is lecherous and has a complaining wife. We wonder what an educated Indonesian woman is doing in this house? Well, this is a story that carries a sting in its tail.

Farah Ghuznavi depicts a similar world of deceit, skulduggery, and racial cross-connections in her story, *Saving Grace*, which is set in a hotel in a Dubai-like Middle Eastern Emirate, Al-Nourain. It is quite an unusual tale as the story switches narrators after a certain point, making the narrative more layered and complex.

Writing from America, just like Moazzam, Murali Kamma's *Route to Lucky Inn* also reflects on a contemporary theme: migration and the politics around it. In his story, Kamma explores how an immigrant should react to the demonization of undocumented migrants. Weaving a Raymond Chandler–like world of intrigue and mystery, the story brings out many aspects of this human tragedy: borders, inequality, responsibility, grit, compassion, the media, and perseverance.

Among all these pieces, Sudeep Sen's *Gold Squares on Muslin* stands apart like a whiff of fresh air, as a work of imagination, of speculative fiction, of dream tales. It is a very satisfying read on various levels as it beautifully uses filmic devices such as dissolves, inter-cutting back and forth in time, using a varied poetic cadence.

In our *Call for Submissions,* we had mainly invited stories on the themes of migration and climate change for the 2020 edition. We already touched upon the narratives of migration earlier. There are at least three stories in this anthology that highlight the hazards of climate change. Areeba Nasir's *Bench* (set in the mountains of Uttarakhand, a northern state in India, the story revolves around the lives of Rukhsana and Prakash who left Delhi long ago where their marriage was unaccepted), Karen Kwek's *Borungurup Man* (how do we lay claim on our environment, or does it in fact possess us? The story is set in a particular red-gold Western Australian outback), and the closing story, John Gresham's *Dog at the End of the World* (it provides a canine perspective on dystopia).

Besides these selections, we have also chosen three stories (by Eric Wee and Prachi Topiwala from Singapore, and Sohana Manzoor from Bangladesh) as Web specials. You will be able to read these amazing stories at the *tbass. org* website in due time. The website will also feature interviews with all the authors of this anthology, where they will share with you why they wrote these stories.

Each story gathered in this anthology managed to touch me as a reader and did something to my spine (who said that? Nabokov? Or was it Marquez?). They engaged my attention, transported me into their world, and kept me engrossed until I reached the last word written by the writer. Some stories took me to the lands and times I had no idea about, some magically brought immediate concerns and challenges of our lives into a sharp focus, while others amused me either with their mesmerising narration or a clever turn of events. I hope when you read these tales, you too get pulled in into the imaginary worlds that these narrators have so lovingly rustled up.

ZAFAR ANJUM

SCOTT P. SALCEDO

Mud-bound Country

When Simeon Pedregosa reached a valley flanked by hills
on which vines tumbled like unkempt hair and the canopies
of trees that gorged the terrain proved impossible for the
sun to worm through, he thought he stumbled upon a
gold mine. This was in 1907 when William Salomon and
Co. had begun laying down the tracks for the Philippine
railroad that started in the cities of Roxas and Iloilo, the
south and north ends of Panay Island. The tracks would
converge in the middle of the island and would possibly
run along this very hill they were standing on, towards
the municipality of Passi, the town to which these valleys
and hills belonged. This was why Simeon walked twelve
kilometres just to get here with his brother, Romulo, to
survey the location. The news of the train construction and
a flag stop sounded fortuitous, at least for the sugarcane
plantation business he was thinking of putting up, but
looking at the swath of land, too wet even for grass to root
into came as bad news.

"At least there's water. We're never going to run out
of it," he said to his brother as his eyes, dabbed with dark
circles, rested on the contours of the distant hill where the
waterfalls undulated the colour of the last drop of carabao
milk. Sunlight throbbed on his shoulders and his camisa,
glimmering from the wet dots of mud, towards his trousers
which he folded above his soiled feet. Behind him, on
the turquoise palette of the sky, rays of sunlight whisked
white and orange streaks ruffling like his mother's favourite
patadyong. He imagined, below those, a paved road wedged

between the hillsides, a train station around which trade would burgeon and farmers lay their produce and choice crops against the ground on a wraparound skirt, and there would be dried fish and salted anchovies, or freshly harvested pineapples whose scales ripen into fire-orange. The air would be filled with fresh green; vegetables, crisp, would turn dewy and moist on the merchant's tables; his sugarcane, ready to be ferried off to the city, stacked in bundles, would be piled evenly among the grass.

"Looks like a gamble. Are you sure they'll build it right here?" Romulo asked.

"I saw it. The blueprint. This American engineer, he showed it to me."

"I was thinking there'd be people," his brother said.

"They could trickle in once the station is built, I hope."

"I pray it's worth it, Simeon."

They had sold a parcel of their farm back home. And Simeon saved up some money while working as caretaker of a Hacienda, borrowed the rest from his employer. He knew that beyond these hills, other barrios thrived and produced huge crops. He gazed at the clumps of brown at the distance, where the *payag* of wealthy haciendas orbited the plains and inclines. There lay Nueva Union, besides it Mulapula, the biggest barrios in this district.

Simeon thought of the paths that farmers from those districts had carved out of their own hands on the adjacent hill, muddy and webbing with branches of vines and madre de cacao. That was the only way to town. If a road and rail tracks were laid out for the station, it could attract merchants, buyers, and farmers from nearby barrios who needed to transport their goods. He imagined a thriving village on this hill and valley, slopes and higher ground teeming with houses. He'd bring his parents to live here, Roming and his wife and children, their aunts and uncles, relatives he couldn't do without. He gazed once more at the earth plunging and rising, and it began to look more like his promised land.

Simeon conjured up off a magazine, a flag stop that could transform this monochrome of green to something more lively—a building with red gabled roof and truss, concrete, a Cape Cod with a mission bell, out of which passengers spill out with their colourful bags and scarves, rondalla musicians in *baro't saya*, camisa, or *traje,* with instruments playing komposo. Other towns grew and progressed because of the church or the municipal hall which brought to them business. The same development could come with the train station. Maybe a fifteen-minute walk from it, they could build a school. His future children wouldn't have to cross the river to and fro or spend three hours just so they could learn some English. Maybe the government could build it for them when this place got more people. For now, the valley teemed only with insects and weed, mayflies rising from the mud like bits of a burned tobacco, clumps of tigbaw strong enough to bury its base into the still murk, makahiya that had lost not just its pallor but the thorns that constellated its stalk, browning and turning brittle like firewood. Yet, he saw a more ordered future.

During the fiesta in honour of the patron San Jose that same year, Simeon met Herminia at the baile in Pototan, his hometown. That she lived in a neighbouring barrio in which he grew up came as a surprise. Herminia was fairer than other girls in this town. It wasn't this quality that attracted him, however. It was her wide smile and her small face shaped like that of a young coconut shell. She had hair, flowing down to her hips, the colour of roasted cacao and face flushed from the sun which her fair skin had withstood. It was the first time in Simeon's life that he felt excited to touch someone's hand or waist and so, when he asked her to dance and she said yes, he spoke to her about the land he purchased, along which he believed a flag stop would be constructed. He thought he'd call the place Lunoy because, every time the rain came, parts of the lowland would hold too much water that the only way to cross them and reach higher ground was to waddle across with half your body submerged. No one got more excited to talk about farms than Herminia and when talks about marriage came up months later, the couple decided to settle in Lunoy to think of what to do with all the undergrowth on the hills and the sodden waterlogged fields so they could plant sugarcane.

Herminia just turned sixteen and couldn't read the alphabet even if one wrote for her letters as big as a wooden pestle onto which they pound rice to remove its husk.

"But she knew farming like no other," Simeon told his family.

The hill on which their bamboo *payag* stood was flanked by gardens in which root crops and vegetables needed for *laswa* grew. She told Simeon to plant on the slopes banana, coffee, and cacao. She surrounded their nipa hut with bamboo that would grow into groves. These could protect them from strong winds during typhoons. The other slopes, she lined with young coconuts. She raised chickens at her shed and thought of putting up a piggery nearby. Before planting season, she brought in her cousins and neighbours from her barrio to build small canals on the edges of the field to divert water from it. Simeon and the men built them with their bare hands and used young bamboo stalks as pipes to channel water from one area to another. The fields were no longer too wet. And thus, they harvested crops way beyond subsistence. The rest of their produce she took to town, wrapped around in her *patadyong,* which she placed and balanced on her head. She would walk for hours, beginning at dusk, to the town market when Simeon was using their carabaos to till the fields. She had to wait until she dispensed much of her vegetables, and if time didn't permit her to return in the darkness of the night, she would sleep over at the house of her relatives in town. Herminia brought order to a once thicket of chaos, and now, the square fields sprawled and the hills had glinted colours of the fruits that grew on it— not just green, but lively colours one would see in a Malong they covered themselves with when nights turned cold.

When Herminia bore her third child five years later and the train construction whimpered in some rocky highlands outside of town, Simeon felt loneliness creeping like the swarm of night-time mosquitoes in the monsoon season. He thought at first that it was the distance that unravelled such. He had been close to his family. But his brother, Romulo, decided to stay with his wife and children. Their parents were growing old and would get arthritis flare-ups if they thought about living in a new place far from the roads or the church. He thought he inflicted upon himself some penalty, isolation for being callous or cavalier, and they had lost their access to some small joys. But there remained small joys in what he and his wife did. This isolation and inaccessibility, however, dampened some of his optimism. He was used to living in a place where everyone knew each other. Everyone was related. That came with some sense of security and safety, something he couldn't find too easily where he was now. They had no one to leave their children with when it was necessary to journey to town to buy farm and home necessities. And so, they'd store salted dried fish and the meat they'd sun dry when the rains became relentless during the wet season, venturing only to the town market twice a month. But most of the time, mud formed grey clamps around their feet, drying off as they walked. Mud stuck to the crannies of their *karosa* as well as around the ankles of Hangud, the beast they tug along to town on market days.

"I'm no longer optimistic about the railroad, Simeon," Herminia said one day, "we can try other crops, *paray* maybe; what do you think?"

"It will come one of these days and things will get better."

"If you think I'm having a difficult time, you're wrong. We have to make do of what we have."

The sugarcane plantation grew and Simeon owed this to his wife. But there was not much they could do to expand it even if the land was big enough for another crop. They owned a few *karosas*, but they couldn't make more than one trip to town with the carabao as it would get exhausted. They could plant more and produce more if cane was that easy to transport.

"But *leche*," Simeon would say, "that stuff could break your arms and neck."

Both of them refused to relent, however, determined to make the most of their choices. Even when they fought like most couples did, no one packed a bag and threatened to leave. Simeon remembered his mother; whenever she and his father disagreed, she'd leave and

walk to the neighbouring village where her relatives lived
and would come home only after much urging for her to
go back to her children and face the life and husband she
chose. Hence, they busied themselves during wet and dry
seasons as there were babies to tend to and clothes to wash.
They were fortunate to have access to water. There wasn't
a dearth of it. She could find a brook, a pond, a stream
nearby, if not, they dug up a well. The waterfalls spouted
fresh water all year. They'd store drinking water in the jars
Simeon tied on both ends of a bamboo plank. He balanced
them on his shoulders and in her case, on top of her head.
The rest, they'd keep in bamboo culms. Their house got
bigger, sturdier as once a year during harvest, they needed
hand, and people from other barrios would come, needing
a place to sleep. Their cousins would come too and they'd
roast pig. Roming would bring his children. Then, he and
his brother would share tuba and get drunk and talk about
the railroad and the stations and what could have life been
if a flag stop stood on the nearest hill which overlooked
his house. Their voices fluttered with sadness as they
sang songs and recited the *binalaybay*—mostly about the
exploits of their ancestors; a local hero; a young, beautiful
maiden. Their children would listen to them and would
try to emulate the rise and fall of their epic poems. The
rest of the year, they'd be on their own, their humdrum life
interrupted by occasional merchants who'd wander, selling
eggs or chicken or rice cakes, or a few nomadic Ati who'd
offer them their live catch, a wild deer, or a pig.

A few times a month, they'd walk two hours to the
chapel of Santa Ana in the village of Mulapula on good
Sundays, sit in church when the rain had eased, but those
were just a few months of dry season a year. Then, they'd
be back home, skinning root crops, repairing fences and
canals, and weeding out wild grass from the canes, making

ferments, sowing seeds during planting season—the children running about the garden and they, taking turns caring for them.

When their children got sick, Herminia would harvest herbs as medicinal cures, and if she couldn't, she'd fetch help, a *hilot* or a babaylan in Mulapula or another neighbouring barrio. Other than days like those, they'd begin their mornings with the songs of birds and roosters and in the afternoons, they were joined by the harmony of insects and crickets, and the croaking of frogs on rainy days. But Marife, their eldest, turned five and could carry a tune. So they'd let her sing a komposo about Pedro Mendez, a boy who left home, orphaned at ten, watching the reed sway as when he began to feel sorry about his life. Simeon thought it absurd as the boy, too young to be on his own, packed his bags and never came back.

"Didn't he have relatives who could take care of him?"

"It's just a song," Herminia would say.

But it wasn't just a song. Their songs told their ancestors' stories and their courage, the villages they built, and the lands they kept. Marife memorised an impressive number of lines of these songs. And thus, nights became a bit bearable as they put out their oil lamp by seven in the evening, listening to the cicada assault their ears until they fell asleep. Before night fell, he would teach his children how to read. Elias was four and had his father's curly hair and round big eyes and was more curious than his younger brother, Protacio, who looked more like his mother.

A few dry seasons after that, Herminia's cousins and their wives and children had put up huts by the nearby slopes. Produce was good and they required more hand.

They raised enough money to buy more carabao to transport sugarcane to town and purchase their essentials back home. Marife could now sing longer tunes.

It took a decade before Simeon accepted the fact that it would take a miracle for a station to be built in Lunoy, which now grew to seven houses occupied by a few of his cousins and Herminia's. A flag stop had been working in the Summit, the municipality's highest point, for more than a decade now and all their produce had to be ferried a kilometre away. It wasn't that bad except that the mud slowed them down much of the year. Roads were unpaved and he thought it could benefit everyone if they all could start clearing one main path that led to Mulapula where his children had gone to elementary school. The rest of the path and some small access roads could follow. Marife had gone to town to work with a group of musicians, preparing to audition for the zarzuela or the vaudeville in the city. She came back after a year, pregnant with Renato's child. Nato was eighteen, pimpled and lanky with the skin the colour of a free-range chicken eggshell.

"All the more we need the roads. This boy would get buried in mud if he didn't put on some weight."

Marife and Nato built their own hut and farmed rice instead. Nato helped his father-in-law and other men from the neighbouring villages carry sand, stones, and gravel to the road they were working on in the hills. Simeon thought the boy to be good and responsible. The road, a cream-coloured incision among the verdant hills, was used later on by the local government to access the barrios nearby. Sugarcane business had prospered and the whole town profited from it. The stones and gravel helped ease the mud but Simeon felt they all needed one that would link them to town. Simeon turned optimistic that the local government could pave a longer road for them, though the one they built with their bare hands didn't end up unused. Occasionally, a *karosa* would slit through it carrying produce or supplies and quite rarely, an American military truck would collect crops. But the war broke out in 1941, and Protacio, Simeon's youngest, had to serve in the army and joined USAFFE. The Americans liked him as he wrote good English.

Lunoy was spared from looting and pillage as the Japanese forces focused on the accessible routes, using the railroad stations to deliver supplies and stolen valuables from villages to their camps. For a few years, they had limited access to town. The parish of St. William in town, stonewalled and sturdy built, had been turned into a Japanese headquarters and the army took over control of the railways and main stations. But Marife and her mother knew how to be self-reliant and the boys—growing in number after Marife gave birth to five, four of whom were males—helped with raising chicken and pigs. Marife's paray harvest with Nato could last more than a year but the rest of the dwellers in the sitio still welcomed the sowing season, halting the planting of sugarcane temporarily as they focused on growing beans, vegetables, corn, and other herbs. Fish turned scarce but they found a way to catch some in the river. Nato tried his hands at raising catfish and once, almost got drowned in his pond, saved by Marife's cousin who thought a pale-skinned piglet fell in a murk. He peddled the rest to other villages nearby and made good money.

Simeon was getting older and spent his time listening to the radio for the news about his son who had been gone for three years, thinking his boy had forgotten to send him letters from the war zone.

"Could be impossible for them to send anything," Herminia said, "and besides, how is the letter going to reach us? We're cut off from the rest of the world."

"Somehow a blessing, yes?" Simeon would say. The Ink Spots were on the radio singing a song about setting the world on fire.

"Take care of your eyes and you'll be holding one you can read one of these days," Herminia said. Simeon's eyesight was slightly failing him.

"I have sons and a daughter I sent to school. They'd read for their old man."

Three years later, they received a letter from USAFFE informing them that Protacio was one of the missing soldiers in the war and disappeared during the Bataan March. Simeon was heartbroken and barely ate for weeks after hearing the news. Elias took over the farm. He wasn't as skilful as his father but the farm still made good money. Protacio's superior at the US Army sent them another letter nearly a year later. Simeon would receive pension for his son's service. They'd give him a considerable amount after they gave up looking for his son's body.

"Everyone will think our lives got better because of the pension," he tells Herminia one day.

"It's not a better life to lose a son, Simeon. We'll take the money. It won't make our lives better. Because what will?"

Their lives weren't always bountiful but they believed they owed something to their land in that, one shouldn't stop nurturing it. Planting crops was always a kind of ritual and a successful harvest came as a sign of good fortune.

There wasn't always good food on the table but there was food. Simeon hoped his son would find his way home. His children knew hardship like no other. They grew up farming. They'd survive walking for days without food or would have found something edible—a wild gooseberry perhaps—along the way.

Simeon, still waiting for his son to come home, many years later, built the only concrete house outside of town. He thought his son would love the cerulean blue that they used to paint its walls. Protacio loved staring at the skies and dreamed of having his own family. He wanted to build a house with big windows so he could view the open space. Simeon's blue house looked foreign on the peak of the hill, a tiny blue square on a green table cloth.

The changes that Simeon envisioned came to him in slow trickles. Upon his request, a chapel was built on a nearby hill. They called it Ermita. A priest came to officiate mass every Sunday. A few houses stood around it, constructed by no one he particularly knew but farmers with good intentions. But his list of requests was long—electricity, a small post office, more roads, a clinic, a school.

In the 60s, public works started paving a road that linked them to town. Simeon was old; his back hurt but he could still tend to the vegetable garden. He got tired of waiting for a son to return. He'd say, he could die ahead. Herminia thought her husband stubborn but it remained a trait that got him respect. She told herself that acceptance could take time and spent her days looking after her grandchildren as Marife had ventured into business and bought a jeepney which would travel the route to take farmers to town and back. The road wasn't concrete or cement that was laid out and flattened with stones and gravel but convenient enough as it took only one ride to town. Travel was bumpy and on dry season, dust twisted and circled the valleys and hills like miniature clouds hovering and landing on the skin and clothes of the passengers and their goods and their baggage and produce, after which, everything turned grey from dust. Rainy season came with its problems as well. It would get so muddy that the pavements would cave in, carving a parade of potholes and tires would bury themselves in the soil. Passengers would sometimes get off and help push or lift the jeepney out of holes. An hour ride could become two hours as tires would slip off wet, mossy rocks and stones. The jeepney travelled to town only once a day and left very early in the morning at five and would come back at three in the afternoon, avoiding the sunset and the darkness at all cost or else it would get buried in mud or fall in the ubiquitous cliffs and ravine. Marife had put up a waiting shed at the spot where her father thought a flag stop would be built. The jeepney would wait from there and was now called Bantayan.

Sugarcane business crashed in the 80s and Elias thought he'd try corn. There was a huge demand for garlic as well so he tried it but nothing really worked. He had the farm rented in the next few decades. During its peak in the early 1990s, Lunoy grew a constellation of twenty houses among the hills and the slopes. Twenty houses, whose dwellers were all related, came as a great achievement for Simeon although it wasn't a part of his plan. He dreamed of something much bigger.

"Aren't we the foolish couple who waited for a train that never arrived?" he asked Herminia one day.

"No, Simeon, we were the ones who dared to dream and life brought us some surprise."

At the turn of the 21st century, Lunoy's last house was carried to Ermita where electricity existed. Marife's son built it, transported by thirty men who placed it on their backs. They waited for decades for the electric posts and lights that never came. Simeon's descendants had all moved out of their sitio, most of them to Mulapula where the government built a high school, a small hospital, and a barangay hall. They bought TV's and computers for their homes and their children. They said they had to go where the lights were, like moths who couldn't subsist without the flames. Marife's grandson would memorise lines of komposo about his great grandfather and for how long he'd remember them, no one knew. He was moving to the city to study nursing.

Simeon's blue house had been abandoned on top of the hill and it was the only structure left standing, the only other block of colour on the tropical hills, fields, and valleys. As the lowlands began to overflow with water, muddy and murky, at times, a jeepney would whisk through, but no longer picked up, unload, or stopped for passengers at Bantayan. A few rainier seasons and the vines would take over the house's blue walls and red roof. The trees would grow thick canopy. And everything would turn completely green again.

SEEMA PUNWANI

Spin

She is an angel. My girlfriend. Not my wife. The only way my wife could be an angel would be if she were dead.

Ha ha ha. Old joke. But the joke's on me. What do these young kids say? FML. Fuck my life. Would probably be adapted for my epitaph. Jeff Evans. RIP. *Lived a fucked-up life.* Or maybe *Fucked up his life.* Some days dying just seems easier.

Everything's getting out of hand. A man can't go to the fucking supermarket and buy a simple loaf of bread. Gluten-free, sunflower seeds, organic shit to be bought from the farmer's market in Tiong Bahru. Where are the fucking farmers in Singapore? Now a new message from Elsa with two more items added to the list. Fifteen years of marriage and never once have I received a complete shopping list in one go. Flowers. Is that a reminder that I don't buy flowers anymore? Or a demand? The flowers are probably just another must-have item when one is having a dinner party. Damn! My girlfriend is calling now. I let it go to voice mail. Has Anna been taking lessons from my wife in nagging? Elsa and Anna. You got that? Like I said. FML. I couldn't make up this shit if I tried! Wish I could just go play golf.

*

When I get home, I can hear the shrieks all the way from the lift. Thankfully, it's one apartment per floor and we are spared being embarrassed by the almost daily outbursts that erupt. My eight-year-old is having an "episode." Not supposed to call it a "meltdown." And "tantrum" is a total no-no. Joshua's sandwich was probably cut diagonally instead of straight. Or Bobo is nowhere to be found. Who bought that stupid pink elephant, anyway? Yes, that would be me. Thinking that giving my only son a present would make him like me. But he hadn't even looked at me. I had to keep that damn soft toy on the Giving Chair for three hours before my child picked it up.

Yes. We have a Giving Chair. You see, my son does not like to be touched. So, my smart wife, reading some smart book, came up with this concept of a "Giving Chair." Whenever any of us wish to give Joshua something, we have to place it on this damn blue chair. After three hours precisely—no more, no less—Joshua would pick up the item, which would either become a lifeline he can't do without or be placed outside his bedroom at night as a sign of rejection. Guess I should consider myself lucky that not only was my present accepted, that damn elephant even has a name and now is something Joshua cannot live without.

It's not easy to buy gifts for someone who finds most clothes scratchy, most toys noisy, and most books easy. Unless we are talking toy trains! Now that's one item that's always welcome. But still, must be placed on the Giving Chair. And Joshua will still pick it up only after three hours. Though he does run outside his room every fifteen minutes to check that the train set is still there. It's exhausting for us. His therapist told us to think of how tiring it would be for him. I am constantly reminded that Joshua is "special" and has his "unique" way of doing things.

This morning my special child is stomping his feet on the floor and spinning around way too fast.

"What's going on, Elsa?"

"Shhh. Soft. Joshua is upset that Maricel didn't let the intercom ring thrice before picking it up."

"She should fucking know this by now. Stupid cow!"

"Keep quiet, Jeff! It's the twenty-fifth spin. He will be done in three more."

Yeah. Twenty-eight spins. That's what my son needs. Exactly twenty-eight spins. This will be followed by him sitting in the corner of his bedroom, always on the left side, hands clutching his knees, looking straight out of the window, counting to ninety-six. Yes, ninety-six. Why? you ask. No one fucking knows! Not the occupational therapist I pay $500 an hour. Or the behavioural psychologist. Or the school counsellor. Or even his own father. Sometimes I imagine scooping him up in my arms, mid-spin, and hugging him tight till he stops screaming.

Elsa looks weary. She is nervous about the dinner. After Joshua is calm, I offer to take him to his room. I spend the next hour reading him his favourite book about trains. He seems calm now. Not of the first time, I wonder what lurks beneath the surface. But right now, I just enjoy this peaceful moment reading aloud the classifications of steam locomotives based on their wheel configurations.

Elsa goes about preparing for the blasted dinner party, asking Maricel to take out the cheese platter, put out the right cocktail napkins, and make sure there is ice in the star-shaped ice trays. Might as well order a freaking ice sculpture!

Elsa is taking her own sweet time to doll up. Today she wears a classic slip dress which is rather becoming.

Her body belies her middle-age. The new fitness regime is showing effects. Or is it the new hunky fitness trainer? I saw them working out in the condo gym. Is wiping sweat off the client's cheeks now within the job remit of a trainer? Turn a blind eye, Jeff. You don't want her looking closely at your comings and goings.

Guests start arriving from 8:30 p.m. The evening will go like the rest of our parties. We all play our parts. Sipping wine, eating tapas, and swapping stories about the latest Speakeasy on Amoy Street, the swimming coach options that the club offers, the upcoming holiday to Boracay. Bali is passé, apparently. And when the conversation moves to everyone's adorable, precious darlings, my wife will use words like "spirited" and "high emotional intelligence." You see, my son is not the only one who spins.

*

Finally, the weekend ends. Freedom! The security guard outside my office building bows and wishes me a good morning.

"Good morning to you too. Hope you had a good weekend."

"It was like all others, sir. Eat and sleep."

What would I not give to have one weekend like his?

Anna is at her desk. She looks fetching in a pale-pink dress that stops right above her knees. Those glasses! They really add to her appeal. She does not even need them. She wears glasses to look older, so people take her more seriously. She looks up from her screen and gives me a tiny smile. Don't want people talking. As soon as I settle in my office, and my secretary stops fussing with the air-conditioner remote and leaves me alone, I email Anna.

Subject: Lunch?
Tiffin Room at Raffles?
Yours, Jeff.

I delete "yours" and replace it with "cheers." In case nosy IT is reading our emails. I get an instant reply, with a lone "OK." Perhaps some more excitement would be nice? It's lunch at the freaking Raffles. Not chicken rice at Lau Pa Sat hawker centre.

Over lunch, Anna is friendly but distant. She is more interested in looking down at her chicken tikka masala. Midway through lunch, I let her know that I can't come over to her place in the evening. From then on, I only get monosyllabic replies. Joshua has an appointment with yet another specialist. I have already received three reminders from Elsa— a WhatsApp, an email, and a phone call to my secretary. When Anna and I get back in the car, I put my arms around her. Her response is a hurried peck on the cheek. The last time we were here for dinner, I was deemed worthy of a hand job. Women!

*

Elsa is in a buoyant mood as the new therapy seems to be working for Joshua. Fewer episodes. No night terrors. Full night's sleep. Which means Elsa will do her girly nights at CÉ LA VI, dancing like she is still in her 20s. I can finally spend an uninterrupted evening with Anna.

The lift is stinking again. What's fucking wrong with these people? Don't they have a bathroom in their homes? As soon as I enter Anna's flat, Ryan comes running into my arms. Oh, the joy! I lift him up over my head and hear him squeal with laughter. I spin him around and he giggles nonstop. Anna is cooking a pot roast in the kitchen. I have told her a dozen times that I enjoy Asian food, but she always tries to make something special. I go over and give her a kiss while Ryan is fetching his football. Then, I take Ryan down to the park.

"Why didn't you come on Sunday? The picnic was boring with only Mama and me."

"Sorry, pal. I had some important work. But I'm here now. How's school?"

"Fun! Alisha likes me. I told you she does."

"Why am I not surprised! Handsome young man that you are."

"But she is in P1. I am P2."

"Ah! Age difference. I am sure you can overcome that."

"What's 'overcome'?"

The child has a limited vocabulary, but hell, he speaks to me.

Seeing Ryan's radiant face, Anna is animated all through dinner. No demands. Only banter. And laughter. I put Ryan to sleep as he snuggles up close to me. We read his favourite book, Gruffalo. Joshua outgrew this book at four. He was a fast reader, that one.

Anna and I settle down on the couch with some wine and I am hoping to "Netflix and chill."

"My ex missed his weekend visit with Ryan yet again. Ryan was so upset."

"Oh, honey. I am so sorry. Would've been rough on him," I stroke her back, "and on you too."

Anna looks at me. I hate that look. Like a dog who knows he is going to be put to sleep.

"You love Ryan, don't you?"

"Like he was my own."

"And me?"

"You are what keeps me going. My wife is too busy to even notice me. Joshua! Well, you know Joshua. It's like I don't even exist."

"Then you need to make a decision." Anna's eyes are steely now. Like a wolf, protecting its little one.

I put her hair behind her ears and kiss her forehead. She puts her head on my shoulders and we watch some mindless American cop show. After about fifteen minutes of cuddling, I reach out my arm from behind her back to fondle her boob. She shrugs my arm off and moves to the other end of the couch. She switches the channel. One of those sappy Korean dramas come up on the screen. Guess that's my cue to leave.

*

"Two weeks? Two! Elsa, how am I to manage?"

"Speak softly! Joshua cannot be hearing us arguing again."

I lower my voice to a whisper. "It's a freaking fifteen whole days. Just me and him ..."

"And Maricel. And his teachers. And his counsellor. It's not *just* you."

"Can't you take Joshua with you?"

"On a 13-hour flight to London? Can you even hear yourself? Did you forget what happened when we went to Phuket? That was only two hours. Joshua is not good with confined spaces. You know that. And it's my mother! She's going to be in surgery. I have to be with her."

"Elsa … I … I …"

"Jeff. Please, for fuck's sake. Step up for once in your life. He is your son too. He is not my responsibility alone."

Fuck!

Elsa spends the day explaining the situation to Joshua. She takes out the customised magnets with our caricatures—Joshua's, Elsa's, Maricel's, and mine. She plots out the week on the massive whiteboard in Joshua's room. Colour-coded by activity. Every hour carefully mapped out with the Maricel magnets next to them.

*

Elsa refuses to let me drop her at the airport. It's Sunday. Damn! Maricel's day off. Should I pay her the extra daily wage and get her to stay home? Wouldn't be fair though. Six days a week she cares for Joshua tirelessly. She needs her weekly day off. Unlike other Filipina helpers, she does not go sit by the pool and watch TikTok videos on the pretext of taking the kid down to play. Her only focus is our son. And we cannot afford to lose her.

Maricel has got Joshua up, brushed, showered, and dressed in his Sunday clothes. Black tracks, sky blue cotton tee, and a navy-blue hoodie. Other days are variations of the same. Each ensemble categorised daywise in the wardrobe. Blue tracks on a black tracks' day? No, siree. We can't have that.

"Morning, buddy!"

"Good morning to you too," says Joshua, looking worriedly at the whiteboard on his bedroom wall. I take the Maricel magnet off and put mine in its place.

"Today Daddy will be looking after you."

"Maricel told me. I asked her to remove her magnet, but she forgot."

I brace myself. I can't be running into a wall this early in the day.

"Brekkie?" I ask slowly.

"It's Sunday. It's grilled cheese day."

"Yup. I know that," I say, double-checking the whiteboard.

"No butter."

"Only olive oil. And cut diagonally. Coz it's Sunday!"

Was that a hint of a smile curling at the corner of my son's lips?

Joshua eats in front of the TV. Not because it's Sunday. Ah! You thought you were catching on, weren't you? If only it were that simple. Odd-numbered days, he eats in front of the TV. On even-numbered days, it's the dining table. Joshua arrived at this system after consulting multiple calendars. Fun fact. According to the Hebrew and traditional Christian calendars, Sunday is the first day of the week. But, according to the International Organization for Standardization, Sunday is the seventh day of the week. As both one and seven are odd numbers, Joshua concluded that Sunday was an odd-numbered day, hence eat-in-front-of-the-telly day.

"We need to leave soon, Joshua. I have to go to the Polo Club for a meeting. You will have to come with me."

"When is soon?" Joshua's eyes stay glued to the latest documentary on Netflix about the Roman Empire.

"11:00 a.m., 11:15 a.m."

"11:00 or 11:15?"

"Let's make it 11:12 a.m."

Joshua gives me a sideways glance and nods his head. Acknowledgement! I must have done something right.

At the Polo Club, I get Joshua to sit at a corner table furthest away from the balcony, his noise-cancelling headphones firmly attached to his ears, his hoodie covering half of his forehead. He places his backpack on the chair next to him and takes out the latest book from the Greek mythology series by Rick Riordan. God bless that man! Joshua is always so engrossed in Riordan's books that the world around him fades into oblivion. Just what I need.

After my meeting ends, I look at the table behind me. Where is Joshua? WTF! I rush to the waitress serving that area. "Have you seen an eight-year-old boy in blue tracks and black hoodie … no … black tracks and blue hoodie … he was just …"

"You mean that kid there?" She points towards the other end of the room.

Joshua is standing in the balcony overlooking the Club grounds. As I draw close, I realise there is a polo match going on. Joshua is captivated. I stand at a distance observing him. He barely blinks as he continues watching. One of the polo jockeys, in a smooth stride, strikes the ball with the end of the mallet. Joshua inches closer to the railing, still not touching the bars, his hands firmly in his pockets. When the ball hits between the two goalposts, the stadium erupts in loud claps. Thankfully, he has his headphones on. Else the noise would've had disastrous effects. But Joshua is unnerved. He is hand-flapping! A motion where you wave your fingers and twist your wrists with hands up to each side of your face. Autistic and other neurodiverse individuals can find the clapping noise disturbing. Hence, we are encouraged to hand flap. When the counsellor first taught us this technique, I simply refused to indulge. Looked like I had nail polish on my fingers and was trying to accelerate the drying! But today I find myself lifting up my hands and waving my fingers.

Joshua's eyes are still on the grounds where one team is rejoicing, mallets up in the air as they raise themselves from their saddle.

"Joshua ... buddy ..." I approach softly.

He turns back, startled. Like he is being woken up from a trance. I hold my breath. Did I break the spell? Will the spinning start now? Shit! Shit! Shit!

To my complete shock, Joshua looks at me quickly and gives me a half-smile, before looking down again.

"Did you like watching the polo match?"

He nods his head.

"What did you like about it?"

"The horses."

"You know I used to play polo in college?"

Joshua looks up at me. His eyes find mine. I am in uncharted territory here. I don't want to scare him off. But I don't want this moment to end either. *When he wants to engage, do so without creating a fuss,* I remember the counsellor's advice.

"Let's walk and talk," I say.

Joshua picks up his backpack and without a word starts walking next to me.

"In polo, each player is assigned a position with certain responsibilities, but the positions are numbered, not named."

Joshua bobs his head. A good sign.

"I was the hustler, in position two. Someone who is always scrapping for the ball. You need a keen eye to play in this position. The toughest of all four positions."

Joshua tilts his head to the right. He does that when he is organising his thoughts before speaking them out aloud. "Weren't you scared of the horses?"

"Nope. I grew up around them."

He stops walking and looks at my face again, his eyes wider than usual, his lips slowly moving upwards, like they would finally oblige me with a smile.

"You had horses as pets?"

I laugh. "My grandfather lived on a farm on the outskirts of London. He was a horse breeder. Your aunt, Lucy, and I used to go to the farm every summer."

"I remember Aunt Lucy. She took me on the Singapore Flyer. I like her."

"She and I used to take riding lessons. We each had our own pony."

"You had a pony?" Joshua's voice is replete with excitement.

"His name was Ares."

"The Greek God of War!" His voice grows loud.

"The very one. I wanted my pony to signify courage."

"Word." Joshua shakes his head in disbelief, his eyes bright, and his lips curling up more and more. I count this as a smile. I made my son smile. Maybe for the first time in his life.

"Would you like to see a pony up close? The polo coach here is my friend."

His eyes squint together. I recognise that look. He wants to, but is afraid.

I bend down in front of my son. I resist putting my hand on his shoulder. "Horses are usually nicer than humans. And they recognise people who like them. Maybe you can observe from a distance? And if, by any chance, you feel scared, we shall decide a safe word. Like Dr. Halie taught us. If you say the safe word, no questions asked, we will leave."

"Ares."

"Ares?"

"That will be our safe word." Joshua taps my wrist, indicating that he is okay if I hold his hand. Hand in hand, father and son, we walk towards the stables.

*

Two weeks later, Elsa comes to the Polo Club with Joshua and me. She was livid on the phone when I told her that I had registered Joshua for Equine Therapy. She would've hopped on the next plane home had it not been for her mother. Joshua did not spin or scream when he saw the horses at the Polo Club that day. He was serene. Just observing. Admiring. That's when the brochure caught my attention. I started taking Joshua to therapy twice a week. The first few classes were academic in nature, which Joshua loved. He likes to know everything about a situation before getting in. I ordered an equestrian helmet from Amazon for him. To my amazement, the minute the package arrived and I gave it to him, Joshua simply accepted the present and took it straight to his room. Take that, Giving Chair!

At today's lesson, Joshua is taking a step forward. He is touching the horse as the instructor explains how horses communicate with humans. He then, slowly, under the instructor's watchful eye, starts brushing the horse. Suddenly, he erupts in laughter at something the instructor says. My phone buzzes. Anna. I press the red decline button, which I have been doing a lot recently. I look at my wife. She is crying and shaking. I put my arms around her and let my tears flow.

KELLY KAUR

The Singapore Dream

Shaking the snow off his boots, Desmond bent over to remove the cumbersome boots. His nostrils flared with the effort and his misty breath came out in long, hard puffs. Finally free of them, he impatiently tugged at his gloves, scarf, hat, and bulky winter coat. The effort exhausted him. It was chilly in the house, and he walked over to the thermostat and cranked it up. Hot and toasty. Like the Singapore heat he ran away from. As a young boy growing up in Toa Payoh, he used to daydream about picturesque Christmas scenes from those Disney movies. Soft and sexy snow. What he didn't bargain for when he moved to Calgary was the complex array of snow and days that no immigrant could ever prepare for. Today, when he looked out the window, he shuddered at the sight of the harsh, ugly flakes of snow that blanketed the world outside. The cars in the neighbourhood were barely chugging by— thick, voluminous clouds of smoke billowed from their exhaust pipes as drivers carefully inched down the street, slipping and sliding on the black ice that had formed in the most unexpected places. Desmond shuddered at the winter stress.

He closed his eyes and heard the gentle waves of East Coast beach. He could feel the sun's burning rays leave a mark on his skin and the green tress doing the beautiful Malaysian dance - *joget* on the beach. His flicker of confusion was momentary as he opened his eyes and saw the giant snowman the neighbours' kids had built in their driveway. With a sigh of relief, Desmond heard the other car enter the whirring, opening garage door. He could stop worrying about his family on these treacherous roads. His two children, Wendy and Weilin, burst through the door and immediately began removing their winter wear. The living room looked like a combat zone, with all the items strewn everywhere. His wife, Hwee Ling, stepped in, her face puffy and red from the biting cold. Desmond locked eyes with Hwee Ling and smiled in relief. She nodded, aware of his apprehension.

Desmond helped Hwee Ling prepare dinner. "Wen---dyyyyy. Wei---lin,' hollered Desmond. The girls ran down from their rooms on the second floor. Weilin had been furiously preparing for her last exam which was on the next day at the University of Calgary. Yes, one more course and she would receive her Mechanical Engineering degree. "One more exam only *lah*," said Hwee Ling. "Then, engineer. Not like in Singapore. Remember: cannot even pass your exam. Cannot go to University. Desmond nodded at his wife. He felt sorry for Weilin as she looked tired but the wave of pride rose in him as he remembered the long way she had come from her days in the Singapore education system. They sat around the table and looked at the Canadian spread—steaks, baked potatoes, and Caesar salad. "Good stuff, Mum," said Weilin in her Canadian accent. "Perfect food to get an A for my exam tomorrow," she laughed. "Yummy, Mummy," laughed Wendy. "But I have to dine and dash … off to work at Earls' tonight." Desmond sighed and tried to conceal the worry in his eyes. "I'll drive you. When you are done, call me, ok? I will pick you up." "You are a gem, Papa." Wendy was secretly relieved. She hated the ugliness of winter driving, and the winters in Calgary could be harsh and brutal. She was weary of them.

Desmond looked at his family and smiled. This was all they had in Calgary now—each other. Immigrants! He felt that life in Calgary was transient. He watched many of his friends come and go. Friendships interrupted by departures and goodbyes as people moved cities and countries for jobs as the downturn hit Calgary. He cut a piece of steak and shoved it in his mouth. Deep down in his heart, he longed for the fiery, spicy food of Singapore. Today, he was craving for chilli crabs and chilli *kangkong*. Hwee Ling often tried to prepare Singaporean food—satay, *hokkien mee*, chicken rice, *nasi lemak*, *mee rebus*—but it was never the same. Some special local ingredient was always missing. Always had to improvise. Some days, he just wanted to go to the open-air hawker centre everywhere and anywhere in Singapore and eat. Desmond reached for the Maggi chilli sauce he had bought from Chinatown and drowned his steak in it. Hwee Ling laughed at him, as usual. "Aiyoh ... you will suffer later." He shook his head. It was the closest he could get to authenticity. He finished his meal and reluctantly went to the driveway to warm up his Mercedes. It would take ten minutes for the engine to purr and the heat to even warm up. Desmond smiled as he thought about how he would never be able to afford the Mercedes in Singapore—it would be the price of a small apartment in Calgary! You win some and you lose some, he thought.

"Papa," said Wendy, breaking Desmond's thoughts. "I am tired of working at Earls'. You know, being a waitress is boring. I didn't get a degree to have old men ogle at me, Pa."

"I know, Wendy. It's been a year since you got your degree. Your mummy's job at the Rocky View Hospital is also in jeopardy. Nurses' jobs are on the chopping block. This government, ah, making so many cuts to everything."

Wendy shook her head and answered, "Papa, now with the downturn in Calgary, I am in trouble trying to get any jobs. I don't want to be a waitress all my life, Pa." Desmond hid his own worry. Even his job as an engineer in the oil patch was in jeopardy. Every day, Desmond expected bad news—when would that last day be?

"Papa," Wendy's cheery voice chirped. "I am excited about going to Singapore next week. Three weeks of sun, Pa. No snow. What the heck made you leave Singapore, Pa. I'll never understand." Desmond was spared from giving an answer as they reached in front of Earls' on 4th Street S.W. "See you at midnight, Pa. Thanks." Desmond tried to focus on the slippery ice but Wendy's question kept going through his mind. Why had they left Singapore? Become landed immigrants in Canada. Three long years of applications and waiting. Wendy and Weilin were only 12 and 13 then. In fact, it was because of them that Hwee Ling and Desmond had decided to leave.

Both girls were struggling in school. Weilin was barely making it, and she was only 9 years old. She would come back from school with so much homework. No time to play. Every day she had a meltdown. They took her to a psychologist, and Desmond remembered that horrid moment as he watched Weilin have a tantrum on the therapist's office floor, screaming that she did not want to go to school. Weilin barely passed any of her exams. Things just got worse. Wendy, on the other hand, was enjoying school and was in the gifted programme at school. But she had to spend every spare moment taking tuition classes to keep up. Pressure. Stress. Hwee Ling gave up her job to ferry them back and forth. They lived in a three-bedroom apartment in Toa Payoh. They had the smallest and cheapest car they could afford. Desmond had to work 12-hour days—expected if he wanted to keep his job. Turmoil. Desmond remembered how much stress everyone was under. Work. Succeed. Survive. Do or die. The Singapore formula. That one fateful Friday, he stopped by the Canadian Embassy and picked up all the forms. When he got back, he looked at Hwee Ling. "Let's get out of this pressure cooker before it kills us."

The irony was now that they were in Calgary, things were challenging. He thought about Wendy, a waitress with a business degree—now that would never happen in Singapore! He slowly glided into his garage. His huge, stylish two-storey house in Edgemont Estates, the same price as his three-bedroom apartment in Singapore. The Mercedes, one-third the price of the Toyota Corolla he had in Singapore. The joys of immigrating? Desmond realised that when they left Singapore, they only thought about the advantages of escaping Singapore. Little did they understand the challenges of being an immigrant— something they only learnt when they, actually, ended up in Calgary.

The day of their holidays, finally, arrived. Desmond felt the throbs of excitement in the pit of his stomach like little balls jumping up and down in eager anticipation as the plane took off on its long journey to Singapore. Home? He looked out the tiny postcard window at the icy white landscape of Calgary. Would he miss beautiful, peaceful Calgary? The welcoming peaks in the distance that lined the outskirts on sunny, clear days? He remembered that fateful day when they had all disembarked from the plane; Calgary—unknown, unheard, simply a place on the map. One of three Canadian cities to offer Desmond a job in Canada. Blind faith and hope. Over the years, they got accustomed to the relaxed, slow pace of Calgary. Cowboy town. Oil patch. Rich. The West. The stampede. His favourite time was fall, where he would admire the vibrant changing colours of the leaves from green to yellow to brown, eventually falling to the ground, crunching under his feet. The best part was seeing his children flower in school. Wendy came home crying one day—they were worried until she showed them why she was crying—her report card—all As. Life in Calgary had been intoxicating, challenging, and intriguing. So why was Desmond craving what he had left behind so willingly?

Finally, the plane landed! They stumbled out of the plane, half asleep and half awake. Singapore airport; ah, Desmond felt like a little boy all over again. His eyes popped at the beautiful airport. Huge. Exciting. Bright. Fresh. He felt his chest surge with pride—grateful he had never given up his Singapore citizenship. For some unspoken reason, he felt connected to Singapore. He fingered the red passport in his hand and proudly marched to the Singaporean line. Home. He was home. Outside the glass door of the arrival hall at the airport, excited relatives he could barely recognise were shouting out their names. It was wonderful. His and Hwee Ling's family members—some they had never even met—all pumped their hands and cried tears of joy. It took such a long time to greet everyone and thank them for their warm welcome to Singapore. This was what he missed in Calgary. No one. No family. He even missed all the annoying interference and family politics of the old days; some days, all that drama actually seemed engaging. Desmond's heart burst with joy just seeing brothers, sisters, cousins, uncles, aunts, nieces, and nephews ... what a clan!

The next morning, Desmond woke up at 4:00 a.m. Jet lagged. It had been a long and terrible journey from Calgary to Singapore. Twenty-four hours of taxis, planes, and waiting. In his father's semi-detached house on Haig Road, it was peaceful, except for a few stray cars that zoomed by. Hwee Ling was asleep, so Desmond crept out of the room and tiptoed down the stairs. Out the window, he saw the beautiful raintrees and angsana trees sway in the morning breeze laden with the smell of oncoming rain. He went into the kitchen to make a cup of coffee and jumped when he saw an ugly cockroach scurry across the kitchen floor. Those he did not miss! He boiled some water in a saucepan and opened the cupboards to look for the jar of NESCAFÉ. He made himself a steaming cup of instant coffee, unlocked the side door, and walked out to the strip of garden that bordered one length of the house. He thought of his sprawling yard in Calgary and the hours of fun he and Hwee Ling got from tending their beautiful Canadian flowers that bloomed in such vibrant colours every spring.

This morning, in the wee hours of Singapore, everything looked strange. His journey from the airport last night was in darkness. In the early hours of the morning, he looked as far as his eyes could see to savour his Singapore. Ten long years. He sucked in the smell of greenery around him. Different. Deep. Earthy. A few birds twittered a welcome ditty for him. He nodded his head in appreciation. No snow. No ice. No colours of fall. Just perpetual, lush green. He felt conflicted about loving two landscapes at the same time. Singapore. Calgary. Different. Breathtaking. Both deeply engraved and ingrained in his heart. The country of his birth and the country as an immigrant. Desmond reached down and picked up a handful of dirt—the Singapore soil flowed through his palm. It felt gritty. Lumpy. He gasped inwardly. Torn.

Desmond thought about how this Singapore soil had become precious over the years. Literally worth millions.

This island had sprung into a modern metropolis. More cherished land. More reclamation. And then there was Calgary with so much land, sometimes, stretching out for miles and miles as far as the eye could see. The majestic Rockies rising in the horizon as he drove from Calgary to Banff. Beautiful Alberta skies—the most memorable he had ever seen. Changing hues in such brilliance it took his breath away. He looked up at the Singapore sky and recognised the angry, black clouds of the monsoon. Soon, the heavens would pour and bring relief from the strange sensation of heat and humidity that Desmond was now unused to. He felt perplexed with all the conflicting emotions that this visit back to Singapore was evoking.

Desmond hardly saw Weilin and Wendy. They disappeared with cousins to explore the new Singapore landscape. In a way, he savoured his loneliness in reconciling with the land. So much had changed in ten years. Desmond could barely recognise some of the highways and the new buildings and shopping centres that had sprung up all over. The routes he used to take to work were different—snaking into newly built highways he could not place. He felt alienated: uncomfortable with so much change to his familiar. His visits to Orchard Road struck a chord in him. Nostalgic memories flooded back. He felt unexpected hot tears on his cheek. Homesick?

New shopping centres above ground and now, even underground. Brand name boutiques. People streaming in and out of these stores, laden with brand name bags. Rich?

For a brief moment, he missed the lazy pace of Calgary. Here in Singapore, people were rushing, pushing, shoving, in a hurry to get to unknown destinations. Four times the population of Calgary. When Desmond moved to Calgary, he was relieved at the nice blend of modern and easy going.

They had, purposely, avoided the big cities of Vancouver and Toronto. Too similar to Singapore. When Desmond and Hwee Ling blindly picked Calgary, they were delighted that their instincts were on target. Laid back, modern oil town! The best of both worlds. A little Singapore without the frenzy. He started laughing—was this the curse of the immigrant? Always back and forth and comparing and contrasting. Good. Bad. Bigger. Better.

Desmond felt hungry. Food! Every Singaporean's love. Starving for his Singaporean food. Open 24 hours, if you knew where to go. Not Denny's in Calgary, 24 hours of food that did not entice him. Desmond wished that Hwee Ling was with him today, but she was excited to catch up with her family, too emotional to even leave her mother's side. Desmond walked into the hotel—maybe, high tea? He could not believe the long queue that had already formed and was snaking around the hotel lobby. Forget it! He decided to take the bus home and try his luck at the never-ending option of hawker centres. Once he reached Katong Shopping Centre, the choices were endless. Inside the cool, air-conditioned mall or some of the stalls which were outside in the open air? Or keep walking down the street and pick one of the many shops and restaurants? No one would starve in Singapore, for sure. AC; too hot for him outside. He ordered chicken rice, *rojak*, *popiah*, and *ice-kacang*. He giggled when he saw the look of the vendors who delivered the food to his table, expecting more people.

Contented, he tucked in the hearty spread and felt a sense of belonging. A coming home. Belonging. His boyhood meals. The faces around him were all familiar. Malays, Tamils, Sikhs, Chinese, even Whites—more now than when he left many years ago. Their accents sounded reassuring, welcoming, comfortable. How easily had his tongue slipped into Singlish. He relished the sound of words pronounced in a lovely singsong fashion. Some of the words picked from all the languages of other races. A secret code. Some only Singaporeans would understand with the addition of the vernacular and slang. And "*lah*"—add "*lah*" at the end, like the Canadian "eh." The beautiful, musical "*lah*"—"Don't *lah*. Let's go *lah*. *Aiyoh*, why like that *lah*?" Not once in Singapore did he feel out of place or have to put on the right accent. His first few years in Calgary had been stressful as he struggled to lose his Singaporean accent. Sometimes, he noticed how the Calgarians scrunched up their faces as they struggled to comprehend his accent. Once or twice, he had let slip his "*lah*," much to the amusement of his Canadian friends. "You are a Canadian now. Switch to eh," they teased him.

Now, his children sounded Canadian. Their cousins in Singapore were mocking them. "Eh, you both sound like *angmo lah*." Wendy and Welin laughed at them as they tried to say "*lah*," but they sounded too Canadian. His stomach full, his heart bursting, and his soul at peace, Desmond strolled home to his family home a stone's throw away. Once he settled into the comfortable armchair in the living room, he eagerly picked up *The Straits Times* and hungrily devoured the news. He was out of touch with the home politics and the changing leaders of Singapore. He laughed when he realised he could have been a millionaire by now if he had wisely invested in property in Singapore. Who could afford the price of houses and cars in Singapore—Desmond gasped when he scanned the classified ads selling private properties and cars. "*Alamak*. How to afford," he grimaced at the price tag of $4 million for a private apartment nearby.

Desmond's father hobbled into the living room and sat with him. "How, Pa?" asked Desmond. His father looked frail. Old. Desmond felt a pang of guilt in his belly. Not a filial son, leaving his parents for Canada. He felt guilty for the extra work his siblings did for their parents.

"Papa, how? So expensive the private flats? Lucky we have HDB flats, right?" His father nodded and said, "You know, we call it the five Cs. Cash, career, condo, car, country club membership. That is the dream of some Singaporeans *lah*. More money. Work until they die. The S in Singapore is dollar sign." He guffawed and Desmond smiled. The Singapore dream.

But what about the Singapore dream? Desmond felt a surge of sadness. Or was it envy? He noticed some Singaporeans with their brand name cars, handbags, and clothes. Fancy cars. Million dollars' condos. What had happened? How had this small island become one of the most expensive places to live? Was this the pursuit of materialism? Could be quite the pressure cooker.

"Papa," Desmond countered. "What is the Singapore dream? Is it how much property and money you can accumulate before you die? I see people stressed, like zombies. No time to enjoy the arts or spend time with your family. Only work more and make more money, right. Monday to Friday. Even Saturday. Work till late night. Work till they die."

Desmond's 80-year-old father stared at Desmond for a long time, in silence. Finally, he took a deep breath and said, "My son, so easy for you to be critical. You left. You took off to Canada and disappeared from Singapore. If you wanted to make any change, you have to do so from here, what? You can't go to Canada and take the best. Come to Singapore and criticise the worst. How like that, son? Every place has its pluses and minuses. I am 80 years old. I started from nothing and worked myself to a good life. My family came from China—they gave up everything to make Singapore their home. My blood, sweat, and tears are in this Singapore soil. I started as an immigrant too. So, you how? First-generation Singaporean or be an immigrant in Canada? Must make a choice, right. Can't just complain *lah*."

Desmond was taken aback by his father's passion. True; he had never thought about the whole cycle of being an immigrant. His father had hit the nail on its head. Choose. Stay. Go. But you have to choose.

That night, Desmond looked at the faces of his family and friends around the dinner table. The restaurant was bustling, and steaming plates of chilli crabs, fried noodles, satay, and fried rice kept appearing, appeasing Desmond's inner hunger. He had barely spoken to his daughters and his wife as everyone had been caught up in the excitement of their vacation. Strangers in their own quests to belong. Sitting back, Desmond watched the intimate scene with a sadness he could not fathom. There was a high price to being Canadian immigrants. He looked at his mother's weathered face and realised how much he missed her. She caught his glance and she nodded as if agreeing. His father, next to him, put his arm around Desmond. "Eat, son, eat. Don't know when you can have authentic chilli crabs again." Desmond grasped his father's hand and felt the frailty of the years that built chasms between them. Phone calls and letters could never replicate just being there. What was Hwee Ling thinking? He did not want to burden her with his confusion. She looked like she was collecting memories and treasures to fill in those quiet, empty moments back in Calgary.

Desmond walked to his children and his wife. He sat down next to them, and he saw a look of hesitation cross their faces. "What is it?" he asked anxiously.

Wendy looked at her father and whispered, "Papa, Weilin and I have something to tell you. We are thinking of moving back to Singapore. We want to work, use our degrees, get some job experience. Singapore is booming, Papa. If you have a degree here in Singapore, your chances of getting a good job are high. Calgary is in trouble. Downturn. Oil bust. No jobs. We can't get jobs in our fields. We don't want to be waitresses." Desmond was floored. Stunned by the revelation.

Weilin cut in excitedly. "Have you seen the job section in *The Straits Times*, Pa? Jobs. Jobs. It's like an oasis. Grandpapa says we can stay with him. I can get a job as an engineer here, Papa. I am excited." She hugged her father, and he felt her exhilaration wash over him. Irony. He smiled at them and nodded. He glanced at Hwee Ling and saw the tears in her eyes. Absurdities. They had left Singapore ten years ago to give their children a new path in life. Here they were, back in Singapore, wanting to stay. Little did he know that the journey would take the full circle.

Goodbyes were poignant and painful that morning. Desmond and Hwee Ling could barely contain their pain and sorrow as they tore themselves away and jumped into the waiting taxi. Changi airport was throbbing with the crossings of many paths and destinies that morning. Desmond looked around at all the people on the go. Which Singaporeans were escaping, exploring, or on some mystical journey of life? Desmond and Hwee Ling sat in their seats on the plane, arm in arm. How strange it was now that they were leaving their children behind in the very place they had with them left ten years ago. Singapore had ensnared his adult children with its golden fingers and cast its magical allure over them.

Desmond looked at Hwee Ling. "Do you have any regrets about leaving Singapore?"

Hwee Ling wiped her tears. "I don't know. Life is a compromise, right. You have to choose."

Desmond gasped. There, the word "choose" again.

Hwee Ling continued, "You have to choose the best set of conditions that you can put up with and live them to your best."

Desmond shook his head and said, "What is the answer, Hwee Ling? Living the Singapore dream or rejecting it? We left Singapore to survive—for our children, for our sanity. Canada was our promised land. A land where we can live any dream we want. Now what? Choose, again?"

Hwee Ling pondered and slowly said, "Nothing is free. Especially not for the Singaporean dream. Not even for the Canadian dream. Not for any dream. Immigrants are forever conflicted … like we are. That is our unique burden to bear. No one tells you that leaving your country is not as easy as it appears. Leave your birthright, your land, your family, your food, your culture, your accent, your sense of comfort … until it is too late. Is there a turning back? Then, Canada is such a graceful, beautiful place for any immigrant!"

Desmond nodded and grasped Hwee Ling's hand. He looked out the window of the ascending plane into the disappearing landscape of the tiny island in the waters. It glistened and gleamed like a jewel bedazzling all those who held it in their hearts and soul.

Desmond stared at the shrinking landscape until it became only a speck in the horizon. His heart ached, and he wondered if it would ever stop.

In Towkay Lee's Mansion

Mak got a job in Towkay Lee's mansion. She refused to talk about Bapa, my father, in the Lee household as it made her sad. End of Bapa, end of story. It was only Mak and I here in Singapore. Mistress Lee agreed to accept me though she complained loudly; when she was mad with whoever and whatever, she screamed, "Employ one mother, two mouths come to eat!" Towkay Lee was kinder. He greeted Mak and me cheerfully, "Good morning, *selamat pagi*."

One morning he asked, "What's your name, little girl?"

"Rositawati."

"Your name is so *chantek*, so pretty, just like you. I call you Rosi, easier to say. Just like a rose, so pretty, so *wangi*, so nice smell like perfume." I was happy, now that I had a name in the house, not "Girl." I was a person with a name. I told Mak, but she was not impressed.

Mak spoke little, silently doing what was asked of her. I believed she was sad to leave Bapa and her parents back in Surabaya. Bapa worked in a lawyer's firm. Mak was a teacher at the Polytechnic. I was in school and Mak had applied for a one-year leave of absence from school for me. She had stated that I was to enrol with the British Council in Singapore for English classes. I was very excited to go to Singapore. I wanted to ride the cable car, go to Gardens by the Bay, Sentosa Universal Studios, and learn more English.

Soon, Towkay Lee patted me on the head, then on the cheek, then on the back. I was afraid to tell Mak that Towkay gave me $5 every time he patted me and said I was so *chantek*, so pretty. I kept the money between the pages of my book, in my school bag. It came in useful as the canteen food at British Council was expensive. I dismissed Mistress Lee's chatter as a matriarch who had a lot of unhappiness inside her. But I was careful not to upset anyone. Mak did the laundry and cleaned the house for them and taught Indonesian cuisine to Towkay's sister. Mistress Lee had a household of eight—Towkay Lee and her; young Master Lee, their only son; his wife, young Mistress Lee; their son's eight-year-old twin daughters, Agnes and Amy; and a baby, Adrian. There was also Towkay Lee's youngest sister, who was the cook and was single. She hardly spoke, moved silently catlike, that when she cleared her throat, I jumped. I wished she would meow when she moved. She slept in a room adjacent to the main lounge, while Towkay and family had their suites upstairs. I do not remember her going out of the house. She was Rapunzel trapped in the kitchen. No prince had come her way because she wore her hair very short.

Why, really why did Mak choose to work here? I did not understand why Mak had to come to Singapore to work as a housemaid and cook. She explained that Towkay Lee's sister wanted to learn Indonesian cuisine. Mak taught her all about Indonesian cuisine, while she taught Mak her Peranakan cuisine, a sort of kitchen cultural exchange. Towkay Lee had wanted an educated and reliable teacher for his sister. Mak explained everyone had to eat and to eat we had to work and when we worked, we had money to buy food to eat so we would be alive. She confused me. We did eat in Surabaya. We ate *bakso* (beef-balls in spicy soup), *penyet* (crispy fried chicken), and Bapa even took us to Japanese and Chinese restaurants sometimes. We had pizza and McDonald's and KFC too.

Mak's and my territorial space was the kitchen and the pantry where we slept. I was allowed to sit at the kitchen table after the day's work to do my homework. Mistress Lee's kitchen was large and handsome. It was adjacent to the dining room with its twelve-seated rosewood dining table. The first weekend, I discovered the table could be pulled along its breadth to turn it into an eighteen-seater table. The tablecloth and table runners were batik pieces. On one side of the kitchen, a wide door opened into the garden, where the gardener had planted herbs—pandan leaves, kaffir lime, curry leaves, chillies, *lengkuas, serai,* and in small planter boxes were *daun kesom* and *daun kemagi* for culinary needs. Beyond that were the rambutan tree, papaya plants, and banana plants. On the opposite wall were the stainless steel cabinets with several shelves. The Miele fridge, with tens of magnets from countries visited, and Miele dishwasher had their place beside the cabinets. The smaller Miele kitchen gadgets lived in the cabinets. The stainless steel worktable was an island in the middle of the kitchen. I was surprised that the table, like the dining table, could "unfold" to extend it. Under the worktable were open shelves for different small-sized bottles of salt, sugar, and pepper; different sizes of knives—long, short, big, and small; chopping boards; and washing-up liquid. At one end was a little DVD player for entertainment. Towkay's sister enjoyed keronchong and Mak had brought six sets of DVD for her. Her favourite was "Bengawan Solo," played repeatedly; I was suffocated and drowned in the River Solo. The Mieli hobs and hotplates had their own places on the third wall beside the triple washbasins. To soften the harshness of the stainless steel, the walls were painted a soft bronze. The pale yellow ceiling lights created a harmonised tone for the kitchen, which gave it a pleasant warmth. The loud air-ejecting fan noises, together with the pounding, cooking, and keronchong, formed an immense orchestra which transformed the kitchen into a lively Woodstock, a great contrast to the quiet living room. It was Towkay's sister's and Mak's turf, preparing every meal.

Our small kitchen in Surabaya was where Mak taught me the intricacies of the kitchen. We had a small TV hooked up on the wall. Mak's favourite chef was Gordon Ramsay. Our kitchen was a laboratory where Mak taught me the spices for *pepes*, *satay kambing*, and *sayur urap*. Scrambled eggs were my favourite breakfast. Mak was pleased it was Gordon Ramsay worthy. It would be nice if Gordon Ramsay said it.

Lying on the thin foam mattress in the pantry, my back rested against the sacks of Thai fragrant rice grade A, jasmine rice A, US long-grain rice, basmati rice A from India and Pakistan, brown rice, and organic rice. I didn't know there were so many varieties of rice. On the shelves above were rows of extra virgin, virgin oil, and cold press oils—olive, coconut, flaxseed, and almond among others. The stainless steel pots and skillets cooled Mak's back. Other electronic gadgets fought for space above. Soon I realised that gadgets were not the only things edging one another out. On the upper shelves were tins of infant formula, cereals, and milk. The cans of Australian abalone with the price label $105 a can and packs of Premium Birds Nest at $2800 for a 200 grams pack seemed to look with disdain at the cans of Yeo's Sardine in Tomato Sauce at $3.90, pickled cucumbers in small bottles at $1.40 among others on the lower shelves. There were enough beverages to float Datuk's (my grandfather's) sampan, a small fishing boat he had built himself. The pantry if had been slightly wider would look like a minimarket in my datuk's Kampong. Mak didn't mind the tight squeeze though and reminded me neither should I. That was my first experience sleeping uncomfortably on the floor but I felt wonderful in Mak's embrace. Now I understood why Mak and Bapa always slept together.

We had plenty of food, leftovers from the family meals. Most of the food Towkay's sister cooked we did not like. Some, Mak said we could not eat. We had Indonesian dishes most days as Mak "showed and taught" Towkay's sister the intricacies of our cuisine. Mak said she was a good student. She never knew her name, they addressed each other as "*kakak*." I thought it strange as *kakak* meant "elder sister." How could two women address each other "elder sister"? Mak brushed me off, "Never mind."

At night, Mak was busy writing in her notebooks. She had already filled one and was starting on a second. "What are you writing, Mak?"

"Some recipes, new kinds of food. Nenek and Datuk I'm sure will like these new dishes."

I wasn't sure my grandparents would like them. *Buah Keluak* comes from Indonesia. We cooked them in our favourite meat broth, Rowan. Mistress Lee cooked the black meat of the *keluak* nuts in spicy-sour gravy with chicken. Then there was *chap chye*, a stew of cabbage, carrots, and black fungus, which Mistress Lee called "rat's ears"—they did look like rat's ears, really; *itek tim*, a tart duck soup cooked with pickled, salted mustard leaves; *meesua*, strange fine hair noodles cooked with pig liver and kidney—yucks! Mak and I did not eat the *meesua*. As I didn't like these foods, I was very sure my grandparents would not like them either.

"That's our little secret and surprise for Datuk, Nenek, and Bapa. Don't tell anyone," Mak whispered. "Mistress might not like us copying her recipes."

One day I looked into Mak's notebooks. She had a lot more notes than recipes. She drew pictures of Mistress Lee's sarong and beautiful hip-length kebaya blouses enriched with colourful embroidery of birds, fish, flowers, and fruits. She had dozens of these kebaya and matching sarong skirts. She had several silver belts. She showed them to Mak. "Let me teach you about our clothes culture. I have seven chain-linked silver belts, all pure silver, and the clasp is 14-carat gold. This, three-inches-thick one is for important functions like New Year, weddings, and birthdays. This one is lighter and thinner for daily home wear, this for going out, the others whichever I choose to wear. See, the patterns of each link are different in each belt. This one is fish looking up, this one fish looking straight, these three flowers, and these two different birds." She then went on to show us her collection of *kasut manek,* beaded slippers with their loud giddy colours. She explained the significance of the different patterns and colours. She muttered that young people no longer appreciated their culture. They preferred jeans, pants, crop pants, T-shirts, tank tops, half-naked dresses, and flip flops as well as five-inch stilettoes. "Teach them a lesson. I'll sell all my antiques and jewellery. Nothing for them!"

That night I told Mak that Mistress Lee was so kind to tell us about her kebayas, belts, and slippers. Mak educated me on the sly ways of the matriarch. It was not to educate us, it was warning us she would know if we stole any of her valuables.

Nonetheless, Mak had her writer's "aha" night. She wrote all that Mistress Lee told her about the significance of each pattern on the kebaya, on the belts, and what colours were appropriate for which occasion. She checked with me the accuracy of what she had written. I conspired with Mak to listen carefully to what Mistress Lee said about her household and perhaps we could publish a story when we get home and earn lots of money.

Mak drew pictures of the colourful Peranakan chinaware with intricate patterns of dragons, phoenix, and chrysanthemums in different colours. She described the Thai rosewood "prayer table," another intricately carved sides and legs piece of furniture. On it were the daily offerings of joss sticks and fresh flowers and food offerings to the gods on "special days." That was young Mistress Lee's responsibility. Mak asked young Mistress Lee what the daily offerings meant and she was glad to chat with Mak when she had no lunch or tea appointments with friends. She preferred crops and cut out jeans and T-shirts: "More comfy." Mak wrote copious notes on each of her illustrations of chinaware that she had faithfully copied and coloured.

On Sundays, Towkay's siblings and their family came for lunch. It was the family tradition that the eldest son as head of the extended family ensured the ritual was kept. The kitchen was a beehive with mothers and daughters and daughters-in-law buzzing around, washing, cutting, pounding, cooking, and chatting. Queen bee Mistress Lee decided on the menu, buzzed instructions on how to slice onions, chop the meat, and how to cook each dish. She spewed stings to show her displeasure. At other times, she dribbled honey to show favour to another. And Mak wrote many stories of the domestic affairs, the hushed tones of gossip, illicit affairs, the single Miss Lee who was the cook—why she was single, or was she, and why was she the cook—the fights and the celebrations, and Towkay Lee's frequent business trips—what kind of business even his wife did not know about. I enriched Mak's writings with stories on Agnes and Amy, the twins.

I had responsibilities too. Three years older than the twins I was to be their shadow, to ensure they didn't hurt themselves, and to attend to their wishes. "They are still babies," young Mistress Lee reminded me. At eight years old in Surabaya, I was already boiling rice and cooking simple dinners for Mak and Bapa.

"I wish I could sleep in Mummy's arms like you and your mother, Rosi," Amy said sadly when she went to the pantry one afternoon. "We have to sleep in our own room. We can't even sleep together. Sometimes I see ghosts, but Mother said I was just being silly. No ghosts in our mansion. Only Father can sleep with Mother and Grandma with Grandpa."

Once, Amy suggested that they took turns sleeping with Mak while I slept in their bed. They would not tell anyone. Promise. "Please, *kakak,* just one night we sleep with you and you hold us in your arms, please." Mak would have nothing of it. Agnes and Amy made me sleep in their bed once, to empathise with their loneliness. Mak did not say anything so that meant I could. I sank into the mattress, the blanket smelt like the roses in the garden, the room was large, cold, and as I merged into the darkness, I felt abandoned. I saw ghosts too but was too afraid to scream and be discovered sleeping in Amy's room. I understood their need for their mother's warmth, why they felt sad. I was happy. Now in this grand mansion, I have something they didn't have. I no longer envied their rows of Barbie dolls and clothes. Mak said nothing when I told her how sad Agnes and Amy were. Mak did not say much when I told her about the twins. She wrote them in her notebooks.

"Rosi, you are so lucky. You can stay in the kitchen and help cook."

"Ya, we can't go into the kitchen, right Amy? Grandma said knives have a life. And if we drop them, they will come and sleep with us."

"Rosi, let's play *masak-masak*." But first, they had to change into their "play clothes." Their clothes were kept in separate closets—home clothes, play clothes, going-out clothes, special-functions clothes. Same with their shoes, all of which matched their clothes. It was tiring when I had to wait for them to change into their "right clothes for the right occasion" clothes. Why couldn't they be like Mak and me—one change into T-shirt and pants in the morning till we took our bath at night and changed into our pyjamas and went to bed?

Amy did the "marketing" for our *masak-masak*. She picked choice rose stalks, red, pink, white, and yellow roses. Not even the gardener missed them. Agnes enjoyed being the cook, she *masak-ed* sand into fragrant rice, roses and ferns magically turned into stir-fried vegetables, twigs into strips of meat, and water into soup. We had real dessert of fresh mangoes, rambutans, chikus, and jambu during the fruit season. Large palm leaves were dinner and serving plates. I was served. I stole some dishwashing liquid from the kitchen and they washed the dishes with the garden hose, after which the dishes and leftover "food" were thrown into the compost. They were happy, we were happy.

One weekend, with much fanfare, the grand piano eased itself to the alcove of the sitting room. Young Master

Lee proudly proclaimed, "Ivory and ebony, like the piano keys," as he placed an ivory miniature grand piano on the ebony piano. From then on, it was casually referred to as Ebony. Young Mistress Lee was pleased. Music and piano skills would display the twin's grace in good society. My task was to wipe and polish Ebony with the "piano cloth" till it mirrored me. In Surabaya, I wiped our piano with old T-shirts.

Teacher Pi An filled musical scores into the newly ordered ivory coloured bookshelf. "Mrs. Lee, I guarantee you, lovely Amy and beautiful Agnes will be the new-age Liberace, fingers fleeting across the blacks and whites (and in a lower tone) like mine. Within a year, another bookshelf for additional musical scores." Only the grandparents and parents were pleased.

"People say I'm the best piano teacher in Bishan, Clementi, and also Sembawang. What is a piano? Amy."

"Teacher Pi An, you are a piano teacher and you don't know what a piano is? That one, beside you."

"How many keys are there? Agnes."

"I don't know. Front door keys, room keys, kitchen keys, cupboard keys," she giggled.

"Agnes, piano keys!"

88–52 white keys and 36 black. I wiped them daily with the special "piano cloth." They were clustered in 8s. From middle C to end of left hand, the tone sounds lower and lower, while the right-hand keys go on to a higher pitch.

"People say I'm the best piano teacher in Bishan, Clementi, and also Sembawang. This is a clef, and this is a bass, symbols for right and left-hand keys. Listen carefully, I'll play this only once. What beat is this?"

"A drum?"

"My reputation is ruined! But I need to eat" and his "frustration" piece followed—"Pretend You're Happy When You're Blue." I didn't know that piece but I can play and sing "Supercalifragilisticexpialidocious" superfast. In Teacher Pi An's class, Adagios and Allegros intermarried; Forte edged Lento; Staccato and Legato were Best Friends Forever, Chromatic Scales confused Octave. Young Mistress Lee had insisted the lovely twins learn music theory immediately. Teacher Pi An in his agony had to oblige as he said, "he needs to eat," prepared basic worksheets. I needed another piggy bank for coins, a coin for each correct answer on theory worksheets.

"Mother, the 'theory' room is cold, noisy, and Teacher Pi An is the Wicked Witch of the East. He wouldn't let us go pee!" Ebony was abandoned, Teacher Pi An was ungraciously discharged and I still had to polish Ebony with the "piano cloth" daily. If only I was allowed to run my fingers on the keys, all 88 of them.

Agnes and Amy were excited. They had watched *Swan Lake on Ice* at the Esplanade Theatre. Agnes believed herself Princess Odette and that was when the fight started—who would Prince Siegfried choose, Agnes or Amy. Young Mistress Lee was pleased. Nothing like ballet for posture and grace in young ladies of good families. The chauffeur drove us to Belle's Ballet Studio. Young Mistress Lee had requested private lessons. "Ballet lessons are always taught in a class," Ms. Belle Lee snapped.

"I want the white tutu."

"Beginners, pink." Ms. Belle Lee was firm.

Our first ballet class, I packed their tutu, ballet shoes, hair net to bun their hair, and water to keep them hydrated during the strenuous exercises. We had to change in the public washroom that first time.

Ms. Belle Lee's studio proudly displayed dated life-size photos of her over the years teaching and winning awards. In her younger years, she had danced Coppelia, Cinderella, Giselle, Odette and several others I did not recognise. "Class, this is a slow exercise to test whether your posture is good, so make sure to keep your back nice and straight. Don't bend forward. And don't look down ever. Head and eye line nice and high."

The girls stood in line holding on the bar on the mirrored wall and mirrored Ms. Belle who held her posture and her breath for ten minutes. Ms. Belle was kind; she knew it took practice and more practice and patience to do what she had done for thirty-two years.

"Watch me carefully. I'll do this slowly. Practice at home, one hour a day." She did not explain how it was to be done. I told young Mistress Lee that to help practice balance and good posture, place an Oxford dictionary on their heads as crowns and for a start, sit on stools for ten minutes, gradually increasing to twenty minutes. Then walk around slowly, not dropping the Oxford.

"Mother, same, same, same. My toes ache, hands ache, tutu tickles. Our heads will shrink into our necks to our chest to our belly and pass out! Mother, do you want headless girls? Ms. Belle Lee is the Wicked Witch of the West!"

"Darlings, you want to be swan princesses, don't you? Rosi, put the Oxford on their heads, count to fifty. OK darlings. Love you both. Have to go for tea."

"Mother, how can we practise without any guide?" Two Apple laptops, one for each girl took their places in the large study room. The girls only had to login to YouTube and search for "Ballet for Beginners" for practice exercises. There were many.

"Mother, it's so boring. Why would I want to be a swan, ha?" Agnes, in tears, mourned.

"Ya, Mother, why would I want to be a swan?" Young Mistress Lee's unfulfilled dream as a child ballerina herself was shattered. She had to think of another sophisticated activity for her girls of a respectable family. Mistress Lee told her daughter-in-law not to pressure the girls, to let them take rest. Their genealogy already put them in good social standing. Mistress Lee's opinion always held.

The two Apples were stored in the storeroom together with the Bird's Nest. The iconic bite on the Apple had not had a byte on it.

Mak and I waited at the dinner table. At one dinner, Towkay Lee asked for extra virgin olive oil for his *sambal* pasta with lobsters and *petai*. I asked, "What is extra virgin?" As I served him, he smilingly looked at me straight in the eye replied, "You are extra virgin. And you are sooooo beautiful, Rosi." He fed me a little of the pasta with a dash of extra virgin olive oil and patted me on the cheek. It tasted yucky and I told him so. I was never present at the dinner table again.

Two months later, Mak told me that Towkay's sister had learnt all she wanted about Indonesian cuisine. We could go home to Bapa, Datuk, and Nenek. We had been away ten months. Agnes and Amy begged to go with us. I was sad to leave them. We had become close friends, a sort of sisterly bonding. I was also happy to go home to Bapa, Datuk, and Nenek. I was sad as I had to sleep in my own bed in my room, no Mak to embrace. I was happy to eat *bakso* again. Agnes and Amy gave me their laptops. Young Mistress Lee was nonchalant about them giving away both the Apples, one for me and one for Mak. It would help Mak in writing her notes.

Three months after we arrived home, Mak submitted her MA thesis on "Peranakan Culture: A Case Study in a Peranakan Household" to the University of Indonesia.

KAREN KWEK

Borungurup Man

Len has a feeling he can't quite explain. Not anger or sadness or anything like that. Not fear or dislike either. It's an odd sort of tingling at the back of his skull, steady and regular, like a warning signal. He connects it to the Airbnb place up by Devil's Slide. He thinks, maybe, it has something to do with the thing inside the house.

"A man like you might understand," Len says to Steve, the hired Airbnb cleaner who lives on the farm next door to him. Len looks around the homestead interior approvingly. Steve's furniture is plain and rustic. They are sitting at his hardwood dining table in the kitchen, drinking black coffee from ceramic mugs. "A man like you, Aussie born and bred, I mean. And you've been inside the place, you've seen it. Wasn't any of my business going up there, see, until Rosie busted her leash."

Len hunted everywhere for Rosie, asked at all the other properties up and down the mountains. None of her usual haunts has turned up anything. It's on account of Rosie that he went up to the house as a last resort. Not through the fields, not skulking and low-lying, quiet-like in the long grass, although he could've. No, he drove his ute, so that he could take the main entrance, like a proper visitor.

The driveway is off to one side of the sealed road. A passerby could easily miss it, but not any more. Now, on the property's open metal gate hangs a signboard that says SVARGA. That gives a man pause because "Svarga" isn't a word you come across often, at least not in Western Australia. The place names around here are about Noongar heritage. That's what the *-up* is, at the end—it means "place of." As in *Dwellingup*: place of mist and fog. *Nornaculup*: a deadly yellow-bellied snake moves through here. Closer to home, *Bolgarup*: haunt of an old ghost. And *Borungurup*, a mountain range so ancient that even the ancients can barely remember the aboriginal totem ceremony for which it was named. Not many can lay claim to being among the oldest ranges in the world, made when molten rock cooled into granite a billion years ago, fractured, exposed, and shaped by slow forces.

Of course, the land formations, estates, and farms also have other kinds of names—Castle Rock; The Sleeping Lady; Old Banksia Wines; Steve's Dairy Farm. Len likes that last one, he doesn't mind telling Steve. You know what you're getting with a name like that. But Svarga, see, that sounds neither here nor there. Turns out, it's Sanskrit for "paradise"—you can find out anything on Google—but Sanskrit, who could have guessed?

Steve admits it's not a name he'd have thought of himself. He moved to Borungurup only two years ago, from Kojonup, where the chippy is run by a nice Indian bloke, but Sanskrit? He doesn't know any foreign languages except a bit of Italian from his wife's side. What he does know is that Svarga goes for two-eighty a night. Living, dining, kitchen, and three bedrooms. Sleeps up to six persons. Dark wood floors, leather sofas, swoosh curtains— Steve moves his hands as if pulling on invisible track cords. Paradise has a great big potbelly stove, warms the house through winter, with firewood kept dry under the house. It has all the modern things you'd expect: TV, Wi-Fi, gas cooker, electric oven, electric kettle, microwave, toaster, sandwich-maker, a Weber barbie on the deck "—and you won't guess what, mate. They got a jacuzzi hot tub in the main bathroom—beauty. Hell to clean, with all the jets and sprays, but the guests go crazy for it."

Len hasn't seen the hot tub. Like he says, he isn't one to trespass. He'd taken the ute, so that the tenants would hear the engine and the gravel crunching on the driveway and not be caught without warning. He's a fair man, is Len.

He entered through the gate and drove along the steep, narrow dirt track until he reached the bend in the switchback driveway. To his right, the land dropped abruptly down and he could see his own trailer, a tiny red rectangle far below across the paddocks, and then more land, and then the rooftops of Albany, and then only the end of land and the Southern Ocean beyond.

As the highest property on the slope, Svarga commanded but didn't own this magnificence; the mountain trails were always open to the public, and Len has known some secret ones since he was a boy. They'd take you above Svarga, through a last line of karri thickets, and then you could climb the granite outcrops until you reached the summit. But the lookout they call Devil's Slide wasn't a proper mountain, of course. Like the other Borungurup peaks, it stood only 600 metres above sea level. Still—Len's chest expanded with pride—he'd never tired of the views. He turned the hairpin bend and the ute climbed steadily up the rest of the driveway.

A white Toyota was parked in the carport beneath the house. Three figures stood on the deck, staring down at him, and the aroma of barbecued meat made his stomach rumble as he got out of the truck. "G'day," he began, but the boys, for now he could see they were just teenagers, turned and hollered into the house, "Mum! Dad! Someone's here!"

A man and a woman stepped out into the golden evening light. Len couldn't gauge their ages, but their faces were youthful, their frames slim and slight. The woman's shoulder-length, straight dark hair was neatly streaked with white, and the man was grey around the temples. The boys came to stand beside their parents, a line-up of Orientals. The Weber sizzled and spat behind them. The woman said, "Yes, how can we help you?"

Len introduced himself. "Have you folks seen a dog this afternoon?"

They exchanged looks, shook heads. The boys, as if dismissed, returned to their responsibilities at the grill.

Len continued, "My dog, Rosie, she broke her leash and I can't find her anywhere."

"No, sorry," the man frowned. "I wish we could help."

The woman disappeared indoors and reemerged holding a notepad. "Maybe we could take your mobile number, give you a call if she turns up?"

"Oh, right, I'll just come up for a sec then." He skipped up the steps and wrote down his number. "You folks from Perth?"

"No," the man said. "Singapore."

Len nodded and made a mental note to Google that later. He saw they had a real spread on a side table by the Weber: sausages, a salad, a packet of marshmallows, ketchup, barbecue sauce, and several small trays of raw meat. He wasn't sure where in Asia they ate what kinds of meat. He swallowed and made his last appeal. "Rosie, she's a rottie—rottweiler, you know. Just a pup, really. Black, about yea high. A little skittish when she first meets you, but she wouldn't hurt a butterfly. She likes a good run, does Rosie. I thought she might've come through the fields up this way. No?"

They shook their heads again, with a touch more sympathy. "Wallabies came," the tallest of the boys offered, "but no dogs."

"We'll let you know if we see her." A pause. "You must be hungry. Here—" The two younger boys, instantly responding to their mother's prompt, moved two sausages and a chicken drumstick from the grill onto a paper plate, which the woman held out to Len.

"So I took the food and left them to their barbieecue," Len tells Steve. "I didn't want to intrude." From the deck he took a gander at the living room, but that's all. He's only been as far as the deck, and that by invitation, he hastens to add. He's never seen the hot tub.

Steve nods. "Well, it's quite something—the whole house. Dinkum Aussie, but … open-minded, if you know what I mean."

Now they are getting somewhere. Len leans in. "That's exactly what I came about, mate … That house … I mean, first of all, the artwork—paintings and wall hangings like in, what's that place—the island—Bali. Lotuses printed on canvas. And then that statue on the sideboard. Might be bronze or something. Looks like it would weigh a ton."

"The one sorta lying down, you mean."

"The Buddha, that's the one."

Steve shrugs. "I'm no expert but wasn't the Buddha"—
he rounded his shoulders and cradled his belly—"sat upright
and meditating? That one's always looked ... female to me.
You know, with the—" His hand moves vaguely over his
torso. "But, anyway, that's art for you. Gives the place an
international feel. And, of course, they've got that view up
there. From the hot tub even." Steve whistles. "Clear over
the paddocks and out to sea. No wonder folks come from
just about anywhere."

"Singapore, they said." Best airport in the world, or
one of them, according to Google. World's busiest port.
Tax-friendly, urbanised, multiracial, multi-religious, a
culinary melting pot. Place of wealth, thinks Len, place of
many gods, place where many fine things are consumed.

"Singapore, France, Puerto Rico ... In the guestbook,
it says all places."

Len scratches his head. "My brother moved up north
to Pilbara and been back just once these three years, and
that only to bury the old man. Five-hour drive, and he says
it's too long."

Steve jerks his chin in the direction of the Airbnb.
"The architect owner—he's a good bloke—he says to me,
people are in the market for something special nowadays.
He designed it fancy—that's right, you would've seen the
house come up from scratch—that deck going all the way
around, the split levels set into the slope, and solar panels
on the roof. Tucked away behind the house, there's a pond
collecting rainwater that gets piped to the taps. You don't
see too many houses like that in these parts. He says people
come for the experience." Steve's voice goes posh for a
moment. "Not just your standard wine-tasting package
tour to Margs. Eco-tourism, he says. Out here's like going

bush, only with all the conveniences, and the bottle-o and IGA just ten minutes' drive away."

So, not like going bush at all.

There's a pause, and then Len decides he may as well just say it. "I dunno that we should tolerate an idol, is all."

"Come again, mate?"

"The statue, I mean, it's not just art, is it? It's a different way of life: Svarga and hot tubs and all that. Time was, every family in Borungurup was known to every other, but these days it's hard to tell. You see my point?"

Steve isn't sure that he does, so Len goes back to the beginning. To be sure, twenty-first-century Borungurup is nothing like the backwater it was when Len was a boy. Why, forty years ago, Len's family had been one of only four on this side of Devil's Slide, to say nothing of the other hills that made up the range. That was before the Bolgarup Road was sealed and the lower trees cleared so the land could be parcelled up and sold. That blue gum in front of the Svarga house, Len wonders they didn't get rid of it too. He can see it from his trailer, a crooked, ill-boding finger— but it had been a proper Gum Giant in its day, trunk so wide your arms couldn't go round it, and the top rising clear above any other tree near it. Even now, the thing is quite a sight, half charred by countless strokes of lightning, the other half, pale and smooth, supple as naked skin. Is it dead or alive, familiar or strange? Neither? Both? Len can understand the Airbnb owner wanting to keep it, maybe, for old times' sake.

Ought to be more of that in the Borungurups, more respect for the old ways. Len is happy for people to come from as far away as Pilbara and even the Big Smokes out east, but he can't help wondering if going international is more than the place can handle. After all, it's always kept itself to itself. Does Steve know, for instance, that the karri trees here have been left alone so long that they are unlike any other karri forest and grow more hardy than anywhere else?

A thing is what it is, no need to go trying to be otherwise. For instance, Len's own land is only half the area of Steve's, but it suited his great-grandfather and his grandfather and his father just fine and now it suits him just fine. He has eleven sheep, forty-two chooks, and Rosie. Sheep and chooks are easy because they eat anything. Rosie is easy, too, docile as a lamb. She helps with the sheep and doesn't eat the chooks. There are things that fit, see, things that belong ...

But Steve is getting to his feet now. He says he's sure sorry about Rosie and the way things change, but he doesn't know what all that has to do with him. He's sorry if he's misunderstood—would Len set him right if he has—but he's just a caretaker who gets paid to do his job.

Len takes the hint. He sighs, gets up and takes his coffee mug to the sink. Steve's window faces the mountain slope and frames the moon hanging in the clear night sky, a lozenge in a glass. The lights of Svarga are going out, one by one, until up on the mountain the moonlight only reflects off the pale blue gum totem, a finger beckoning.

And then, all at once, the tingling at the back of Len's skull goes quiet, and he sees what it is he has to do.

They start out from the house just after dawn, following the well-marked trail through coarse-grassed heath and remnants of spring's wildflower bloom. Min documents them on her phone so that she can look up their names later: bursts of flame-peas, spindly wild orchids, crimson kangaroo paws.

They surprise and are surprised by a pair of wallabies, mother and baby, who retreat in rapid bounds, the older boys Nick and Caleb hotly pursuing. Tim, their youngest, opts to stay with Alec and Min. "Too slow," he says ruefully, showing them the blur of sunlight, shadow, and foliage captured on his phone, not a wallaby in sight.

Past the low-growing myrtle trees and banksia spikes standing upright like arrangements of pillar candles, the trail disappears into stands of marri, jarrah, and yate. Tim spots a shred of orange ribbon dangling from an overhead branch. The only other sign of the trail is where the dense understorey of tall grass, peppermint, wattle, and other shrubs looks trampled. "This way."

Snatches of colour flit about the treetops—blue wrens, parrots, cockatoos, and other birds too quick for the eye— half a dozen birdcalls. At the next orange ribbon, they catch up with Nick and Caleb. The wallabies are long gone, but Nick is excited to show them a slender creature before it burrows away. "It's a skink, guys. It'll make you believe that maybe snakes really once had legs."

About a mile in, the going gets steeper and the trees seem to press in. They are now stepping up a cascade of rocks like makeshift steps. Their eyes get used to spotting the orange ribbons, here beckoning from a branch, there tied to a stick driven down between rocks. The trail opens up onto a granite plateau. Min, stopping to catch her breath, turns to survey the treetops and plains below. Not for the first time, she considers giving up and going back to the house.

Nick saunters on easily. "Are you serious, Mum? Come on, we're already halfway up."

"This way, and don't step on the yellow stuff. It's moss or lichen or something—it's slippery," warns Caleb.

The next segment weaves through karri forest. The lean trees tower over them. Occasionally, they come across a trunk where someone has left their mark: *Simon ♡ Anna;* a smiley face; *Charles was here.* The trail is narrow but defined, a carpet of fallen leaves, shed bark, and dried seed pods on the dark red loam beneath their shoes. Beams of sunlight penetrate the canopy, and Min feels her knapsack damp from the sweat down her back.

But a wind is rising as the forest thins out into nothing. Here are domed boulders, for the most part easy to walk across. When they arrive at a rock face, they gratefully use whatever rope rails previous trail walkers have left behind. Alec, who has gone ahead to confirm the best route, doubles back triumphantly to announce that they are almost at the lookout. The three boys scramble past one another in a race to the summit.

The weather has changed since they left the forest. Clouds have moved in from nowhere, hanging low and grey, darkening the patchwork plain below. The karri forest, moments ago sun-dappled and inviting, looks now from above like a dull sea of army green, from which scrawny fingers of bare eucalypt branches protrude forlornly. The chilly wind bites. Min zips up her vest, trying to dismiss sudden unsettling thoughts. As a shiver runs through her, she makes herself face the mountain again and takes the hand Alec extends to pull her up the last ledge.

And then all five of them are standing on Devil's Slide.

They have only a few moments to savour the views. When the rain breaks, the wind disperses it in a mizzle so fine that they don't feel it through their hats and clothes. Only a sheen gradually appears on the rocks, making the descent a little slippery and slow. Later, in her celebratory mood at having scaled the peak and returned safely to the house, Min all but forgets her unease at the changeability of the mountains—until the boys announce that someone is coming.

A middle-aged Caucasian of average height, the stranger is heavyset, tousle-haired and bearded, wearing farmers' boots, cargo trousers, and a faded blue and white chequered shirt with the sleeves rolled up past his elbows. He is asking about his missing dog, but no one has seen her. On the notepad Min takes out, he writes down his name—Len— followed by his mobile number. They wait politely for him to leave but he remains standing on the deck, holding the paper plate of cooked food that the boys have given him.

"You folks seen much of the Borungurups yet?"

Alec nods, grinning. "Walked the trail up to Devil's Slide this morning."

"Oh, how'd you go? Alright?" His eyes scan the deck, then the hills beyond.

"Unbelievable views, just stunning."

"You know why it's called Devil's Slide, don't you?"

Tim puts down his tongs and scoots over. "No, but I bet you could tell us!"

"It's an old Noongar legend," the man begins slowly. "The Noongar, now they were the first people in this part of Australia. Folks say, one day the Devil got it in mind to claim a youth. He chased him all over the land and eventually this lad leads the Devil up to the highest point in the Borungurups. Just when the Devil thinks he's got him cornered on that smooth stone shelf, the lad slips past him and back down the mountain, and the Devil, on account of almost losing his footing up on that treacherous rock, has to let him go." His gaze, roving across the living room interior as he speaks, finally returns to rest on Tim. "How about that, eh?"

"Are *you* Noongar?"

"Me? No," says the man, smiling. "But my family's been in these parts long enough to know a thing or two. A hundred years, maybe more." A pause, a last look around and something like resignation in his voice. "Well, no Rosie then. Thank you, folks, for this, anyway," raising his plate slightly, "I'll be going now. Enjoy your barbie."

They watch the pickup as it rattles down the driveway, past the lone eucalyptus, and then out of sight. The setting sun colours the sky beyond in purple and orange streaks, making a striking silhouette of the giant leafless tree. Min, having already photographed the towering stump countless times, takes several more snapshots now. Caleb and Tim finish up at the grill, bantering as usual.

"Do you think it was the Devil-devil or a Noongar devil?"

"That was just a man, Tim!" Caleb jokes. "Nah, he must mean a Noongar evil spirit or something like that. They got tales to explain everything, like, how this river or that cave was created."

Nick laughs. "Mum's obsessed with that tree stump. Maybe they have a story about that too."

Min clicks her tongue impatiently. "Why aren't you guys eating yet? We said we were going to watch the stars tonight and it's already getting very chilly. Let's move the food inside …"

Alec had not intended to fall asleep, and when he opens his eyes, he becomes aware of a voice hissing in his ear, that he is being violently shaken, and that he is not in bed. None of them are. He can see three bundled shapes on the deck, and Nick's white face. "Dad, dad! Someone's coming!" All memories of stargazing flee, and Alec is only aware of the dark. No headlights, no purr of a vehicle engine, nothing but a soft footfall on loose gravel every now and then.

There are no fences in the Western Australian countryside. Well, there are bits of wire that mark property lines, and there are hedge boundaries, wooden posts, gates for paddocks, and so on, but the high brick walls, iron grilles, and automated gates ubiquitous at home are rare here. It's only common sense, really—and common dollars—it would cost too much to run a fence across miles and miles, when there is not much to protect except open space.

It's also common decency. There's no harm done if people pass through respectfully. A good host shows a kindness in facilitating the journey. Alec has always admired this largesse of Australian culture. Aren't we all just passing through, anyway? There are no true landowners, only stewards and custodians. A decade ago and in the smaller towns, people might have looked twice at the family, been surprised to see them at a church service on a Sunday, been wary about their background. Nowadays, however, people are likely to exchange friendly greetings with them, share local knowledge, or even invite them over for tea. No one means them harm—or do they?

The mild crunch of gravel has stopped. The visitor could be at the house now, at the bottom of the stairs. The five are all wide awake, still wrapped in their blankets, huddled against the side of the house in the shadows. Alec regrets turning off the motion-sensor lights that would have drowned out the stars. As it is, the night sky is aglow with heavenly bodies, but none to deter a trespasser. There is no time to cross the front deck, enter the house, and lock themselves in.

The floorboards creak lightly—someone is coming up the stairs. Alec waves the others around to the back of the house. He sees the weak beam of a flashlight sweep the front deck hastily and vanish. He hears the visitor fumble at the sliding glass door. They have left it unlocked, and soon the intruder is inside the house. Alec requires no further proof of ill will. His fingers reach into his vest pocket and find his phone. He presses the call button for Police Assistance.

Len is surprised to have made it this far. The living room is dark, but the nightlight outside the front toilet gives off enough of a glow that he can just about avoid bumping into anything. The place is silent except for the tick-ticking of a grandfather clock in the far corner. He heads straight past the sofas, skirting the carpet. He doesn't want to get dirt from his boots on the carpet—he's a fair man, is Len. He goes straight to the sideboard. The statue is at least three feet long, lying across the entire length of the cabinet. He feels for the head and curls his left arm around, cradling it. With his right hand, he grasps the figurine's feet and is somewhat surprised to find the toes so clearly defined.

The statue is smooth and icy to the touch, surely metallic, as he suspected. It comes off the sideboard with less of an effort than he expects—he must be more buzzed with adrenaline than he realises, or else perhaps it is hollow. He is glad to have left the sliding door open. Even so, it takes some deft sideways manoeuvring to get the statue out onto the deck, and he has to lean it against the wall outside in order to slide the door shut—it is a cold night and he is not a callous man.

Down the deck stairs he treads, hugging the statue almost upright, its hip supported against his, its head coming up to just under his chin. In the moonlight, he can see that the thing has a dark greenish sheen and a pointy hairstyle or headdress composed of tiny round bumps. Its brows are delicately arched, its heavy-lidded eyes closed. Its nose is straight and thin, the full lips upturned in a smile. One arm is bent, supporting the head. The other arm rests languidly along its side, the hand on its hip. Steve's comment about the figure's femininity discomfits Len. For a brief moment, standing on the driveway behind the parked Toyota, he has no idea what to do.

But the Gum Giant rises, foreboding, at the edge of his vision, bringing clarity and resolve. The slope is too steep to descend with the statue's weight. In any case, anyone fleeing across the paddocks would be plainly visible from the house. Len turns back and plunges into the long grass behind the house.

The pond is hidden from view by a small grove of banksia trees. Its surface is a calm, flat sheet of moon and stars that ripples and breaks up when Len lowers the statue, feet first, into the dark water. He gives it a good shove, sending it out of sight and away from the bank. He waits for the ripples to subside, but at the centre of the pond, the pointed tip of the head breaks the water's surface and the face bobs into view; the figure will not go under.

Len is about to wade into the pond when voices reach him from the house. Shouts are going up. Lights are coming on. Later, he will say in his statement that he has no regrets. A Borungurup man knows a thing or two and might be rewarded, after all, for his faith. He stands stock-still, listening. Against the mournful wail of police sirens, his heart swells to another sound. A frantic, familiar barking is descending from Devil's Slide. And in thanksgiving, Len raises his eyes to the hills that have gone about their business for millennia, from rock to tree to indigenous creature, inexorable.

MURALI KAMMA

The Route to Lucky Inn

He stared at the computer screen, trying to make sense of the terse unsigned email, which had a cryptic ending and the words "Is Jag really missing?" in the subject line.

"You write that Jag Reddy, who was living with his daughter, is missing," it read. "But if no foul play is suspected, as you put it, and he took only a few of his things, he could still be in town. Speaking confidentially, have you checked the Route 6 inn?"

For a moment that morning, before reality struck, the mundane task of scrolling through his inbox felt like the start of a B-grade spy thriller. Hari looked at the Gmail address again, but the word "Recog" was indecipherable— as if it were a code rather than, most likely, a jumble of initials and abbreviations of the sender's name. Adding a brief note, he forwarded the email to *Diaspora Weekly*'s editor, Rita, whom he could see through the open door of her office, where she was on the phone at her desk. After the call ended, she looked up from her computer and summoned him with a nod. Leaving his cubicle, Hari stepped over to her room.

"Who sent this email?" Rita said, removing her spectacles. Her dark wavy hair, cut short to just above her shoulders, had a couple of grey strands near her temple. She looked harried—or maybe tired—and he was embarrassed about mentioning what could be a trivial matter.

"No idea. It refers to a short news item about the man's disappearance in our last issue. Page 5. The inn came up when I searched online, but it's no longer in business."

Rita picked up a copy of *Diaspora Weekly* and, putting on her spectacles again, flipped through it. The tabloid-size paper's name was in big, bold letters at the top of the first page, and the tagline under it read, "A weekly dose of desi news and views."

"Oh, I didn't know the inn closed," she said, raising her head. "Maybe he's referring to some other motel. Lucky Inn, as far as I know, was the only inn on Route 6 within the city. Its owner—don't remember his name— built it after winning the state lottery. I wonder if he sold it. Anyway, we can't do anything at this point. Contacting Jag's family without additional details won't be helpful. How about getting more information?"

"Sure, I'll try to do that. Let's see if we get a response."

Getting busy with the new issue, after sending his email to Recog, Hari didn't think about it anymore—until he left the office that evening. Hired as a staff correspondent about a year ago, he found himself straddling two worlds at *Diaspora Weekly*. While Hari didn't mind the focus on community life, he sometimes wished the range could be broader and the pace a little slower, with more time and space for longer, more nuanced articles.

Switching on the headlights as he drove out of the parking lot, Hari felt no urgency to go home. His wife and son were in the Midwest, visiting her parents. On a whim, just as the remaining daylight leaked out of the sky, Hari got off the highway leading to his house and headed south towards Route 6. Within the city, it was often called IC—

short for International Corridor—because of all the ethnic restaurants and stores one saw along a mile-long stretch. In the evenings, and on weekends especially, diners and shoppers thronged this multicultural hub. But Route 6 didn't end there, and when Hari came to a quieter section, he realised that, according to the address, Lucky Inn was close by, although he couldn't see it or even a sign indicating its location. Had they torn it down?

Hari became conscious of the darkness and silence on this dead stretch before Route 6 exited the city. There were trees on either side of the road, and the traffic was unexpectedly sparse despite not being far from the humming IC. No wonder the inn didn't succeed. It was a bad location, and Hari wasn't surprised when no other motel came up on his GPS.

And then, just when he was looking for a place to turn around, Hari saw a side road with an illuminated lamp that revealed a painted-over signboard near the intersection. The name was gone, but the signboard remained, perhaps for a future owner. Could this be it? Turning quickly, Hari went down the bumpy road until he saw another signboard, behind which stood a dimly lit building. The sign read, in bold letters: PRIVATE PROPERTY. NO TRESPASSING.

While the side road continued, this property on the left had a narrow lane that led to another building in the rear. There was just one car in the front building's parking lot. No other signs were visible, and the place seemed deserted. This was Lucky Inn indeed, going by the GPS— but instead of lingering to explore more, Hari decided it would be wiser to leave.

The following morning, when Hari got to his office, Rita was not in. Then he remembered that she was at a day-long conference, which she'd mentioned at their last office meeting. Checking his inbox, he saw that Recog had responded.

Again, the email was brief, simply reading: "Meet me at Metro Café for more info. Not far from the Route 6 inn. How about four p.m. today?"

The mystery deepened, though not in a disagreeable way. Was there a good story here? Worth exploring, Hari thought, even if nothing came out of it. This man—who else could it be?—sounded intriguing enough to make a visit worthwhile. They would meet in a public place, after all, and if he turned out to be a bore—or worse—Hari would make an excuse and walk away. Without probing further, Hari replied that he would be at Metro Café by four.

At three o'clock, after pocketing his recorder and picking up his notepad, Hari left the office and drove in the smoothly flowing traffic. In an hour, the traffic would start building up—slowly at first, and then rapidly, turning the highway into a swollen river of vehicles. Taking the exit to Route 6, Hari kept going until he reached a commercial strip in a less conspicuous section of IC. Pulling into the parking lot, he saw that Metro Café shared space with a Tibetan restaurant, an insurance office, and a travel agency. From there, it would probably take fifteen minutes on foot to reach Lucky Inn. When Hari walked in, the café's only customers were a young couple, sitting close to each other, and an older man who was reading a Southeast or East Asian newspaper as he sipped his drink. Hari acknowledged the barista's greeting and found a corner table, away from the others and facing the door. Would this mysterious man show up?

He did, making his appearance from the side so unobtrusively that Hari, quietly watching the parking area, was caught off guard to see him enter the café and approach the table. His mostly snowy hair and a trim moustache, with spectacles perched on his nose, gave him a professorial look, although he would be a retired professor by now. He was a little breathless as if he'd done some unaccustomed walking—but he beamed at Hari and, before sitting down, mopped his flushed face with a handkerchief.

"I'm Jagan, also known as Jag," he said. "You must be Hari. Should I call you Harry?"

"No. Hari is fine." He smiled, eliciting a chuckle from Jagan as if they'd shared an inside joke. It didn't surprise Hari that Jagan was the man who got in touch with him. "What would you like to drink?" he asked. "I'm getting coffee."

When he brought their steaming cups from the counter, Jagan, with an imperceptible bow, murmured his thanks. For a moment they sipped their drinks in silence. Although he looked frail, maybe because of his age, Jagan didn't seem anxious—and he certainly didn't come across as a "missing person" without a home. Looking calm, and nattily dressed in tan corduroy slacks and a light-blue sweater, he could have been mistaken for a retiree who was spending a leisurely hour with his young relative at a café.

"Do you stay close by?" Hari asked casually. As far as he could tell, Jagan had walked to the café.

"Yes," Jagan said. "Took me over twenty minutes, but that's because I don't walk fast." Putting his cup down, he dabbed his lips with a napkin. "You might have seen the place. Used to be called Lucky Inn. Now it's not called anything."

Hari stared at him. "I didn't think anybody was staying there. It looked vacant."

"I know what you mean," Jagan said, dropping his voice and looking around, though the few customers in the café weren't paying attention to them. "For now, all the people are in the rear building, which you probably didn't see. And none of them have cars. Maybe I shouldn't be telling you this."

"Why … may I ask?"

"Oh, now is not the right time to talk about it. Perhaps we can meet again soon? I'm hoping you'll write an article in—"

"Well, that will depend on several factors," Hari said. "This is so mysterious. I need more information. Why did you leave your daughter's home without telling her? Does she know where you are staying?"

"No, but I told her not to worry. She got my message and knows that I want to be left alone for now. So I'm not a 'missing person,' as your paper put it."

"We rely on a syndicated news service—and according to them, you were considered missing at one point."

"Very true, Hari. That was because of my son-in-law. You see, we had problems. One day, after quarrelling with him, I just walked out. Couldn't take it anymore. I made the mistake of not informing my daughter right away that I was fine. She was anxious, but so was I."

"Why were you anxious?"

"Because I didn't want them to find me and make me go back to their house."

"Can I ask why you wanted this meeting? How will *Diaspora Weekly* help you?"

Pushing his cup aside, Jagan put his arms on the table and leaned forward. "You see, there was another reason for leaving my daughter's house. While the rift with my son-in-law was the main reason, I also wanted to join my friend's initiative. But it's controversial. That's why we need your help. We're not seeking publicity. We seek to educate people. That awareness will, I hope, lead to more empathy and engagement."

Hari looked at him in bafflement. Was he okay? Could this odd behaviour be the result of some age-related impairment? Or maybe he was just eccentric.

"I'm perfectly sane," he said, startling Hari. "But it's a little insane out there now."

Although there was a pause, Hari remained silent.

"We help people in need," Jagan continued. "Some folks like my son-in-law think the initiative is—how should I say it?—illegal. I disagree. You see, desperate times call for desperate measures."

"Could you elaborate? I'm still puzzled. Or do you want to talk somewhere else?"

"Sorry, Hari … I tend to ramble, I know. Please bear with me. Do you know how Lucky Inn got its name?"

"Yes. My editor said the person who built it had won the state lottery."

"Indeed. I knew him when we were growing up back home, though we weren't friends. Hari, I'm old enough to be your father, so please indulge me." Jagan smiled, his face crinkling. "Do you know what we crave most in life?" he asked.

"Excuse me?"

"What do people look for in life? What do they want? Is it riches?"

"How about happiness?" Hari said.

"Fair enough. But I'd argue that if we leave out our essential needs—sustenance, shelter, and security—what we crave most in life is recognition."

"Recognition?"

"Yes, recognition. It's as simple as that. We have problems and become unhappy when we're ignored. Whether it is love, appreciation, respect, admiration—or even the mere acknowledgement of our existence—it all comes down to recognition."

Now "Recog" made sense! "Interesting," Hari said, and realised the word was inadequate, sounding like a cliché. "We crave this recognition because we're not solitary creatures," he added. "Our lives are meaningless without other people."

"Exactly," Jagan said. "As small children, we're loved unconditionally. But that leaves a hole when we grow up— and for the rest of our lives, I believe, we're trying to fill that hole. That's our search for fulfilment."

"Fascinating. May I ask how *Diaspora Weekly* plays a role in this discussion?"

"When you write about people, aren't you recognising them? You acknowledge their achievements, you bring attention to causes, you create awareness among readers."

"And what cause would we be bringing attention to— if we write about your initiative?"

"Aha, this is where it gets tricky. But, Hari, perhaps we can go there in your car? It won't take long. It will be better if I show you."

"Certainly. We can leave now if you're ready."

Stepping out of the café, where only two other customers were sitting at a table, Hari saw a large group heading to the Tibetan restaurant. An enticing aroma greeted him when the restaurant door opened, and he had a sudden craving for momos. Maybe the owners of Metro Café were in the wrong business, Hari thought, as he started his car and backed out slowly. The drive to Lucky Inn was short, giving them no time for more conversation. When Hari got on the side road leading to the inn, he was again struck by the silence and absence of people. How strange this desolate stretch seemed, given its proximity to the buzzing restaurant, which would continue to draw diners for the next few hours.

Hari saw the NO TRESPASSING sign again, but even before he entered the parking area—which, as before, had only one car near the entrance—Jagan told him to continue to the rear. Hari found a spot between the buildings, close to the doors.

"This is where our guests stay," Jagan said, and Hari realised that this second building, barely visible from the side road, had a bunch of occupied rooms, judging by the light emanating from the curtained windows.

"How did you get here without a car?" Hari asked. "Did somebody bring you?"

"A bus brought me here. The stop is on Route 6; it's not a long walk from there. Lucky, as we call him, is out of town to raise funds. I'm keeping an eye on things. Let's go in."

Using his key, Jagan opened the door to the rear building and let Hari enter first. Walking into what seemed to be a lounge, Hari saw the startled face of a youngish man. He seemed fearful—but then, on seeing Jagan behind him, his expression changed. Looking relieved, he said hello, before returning to his chair. That's when Hari realised he was playing cards at a table with two other men. The room was functional, even drab, with two worn beige sofas, a flickering TV in one corner, two tables, upright chairs, and a threadbare carpet. Hari also spotted a small fridge and a microwave oven, along with a stack of empty plates and some cups on a counter.

Another door led to private rooms, presumably, and he could also partially see a flight of stairs ascending to the top floors.

"Let me introduce you to a few guests," Jagan said as the men, interrupting their game, looked up and smiled tentatively.

They seemed uncertain, if not nervous, perhaps wondering how they should view this newcomer. Was he a visitor, or was he going to join them as another guest? They seemed to be in their thirties, though one could have been older. They hadn't been in the country for long, but apart from that shared foreignness, they were very different from each other. The man Hari had first seen was Central American or Mexican; the older migrant was distinctly South Asian; and the third person appeared to be from the Middle East or maybe North Africa.

Following a few polite, stilted remarks in awkward English—touching mostly on the card game they were playing—Hari accompanied Jagan to another room on the same floor.

"We use this room as an office," Jagan said, pointing at a cherry-coloured wooden desk. A calendar displaying bright flowers adorned the otherwise bare white walls, while a stack of files and a laptop sat on the desk, which had a black swivel chair on either side. "If you can spare a little more time, I'll tell you what we do here," he continued, closing the door. "Please sit."

Pulling up a chair, Hari wondered if now was a good time to take the recorder out of his pocket. He decided to wait.

"It's nothing nefarious," Jagan said, a smile creasing his lips. "We help migrants ... migrants without documents. We give them a place to stay, provide simple meals, and often give other help until they're ready to move on and manage on their own. Because we don't have a lot of money, it's a limited, low-key operation. You may be wondering if this is legal."

"Is it?"

"Frankly, I don't care. My son-in-law, who's a decent guy in many ways, doesn't share my views. Look, I understand. I understand that people who disagree with me are not necessarily xenophobic or racist. It would be arrogant of me to think that. But they tend to be legalistic, and the world they live in has strict borders and a simplistic definition of fairness. I'm different. Think of the extraordinary challenges these migrants faced, and still face. I've heard harrowing stories. It's a wonder that some of them survived the journey. Anybody who has shown such determination and resilience should be an asset, not a burden."

"I completely agree," Hari said. "As an immigrant, I'm sympathetic. The route may be different, but our destination is the same."

"Exactly. Lucky is an immigrant as well, and he was a successful entrepreneur before he won the lottery. But instead of enjoying his success, he shut down the inn to do this. He's not afraid and feels it's the right thing to do in this toxic environment. In fact, it was the hostility towards migrants that drove him to take a stance. He's not really political. I feel the same way—that's why I was drawn to him." Jagan took a deep breath and sank back in his chair.

The revelation, while surprising, wasn't shocking. But the initiative seemed risky. While a few local officials were sympathetic, it wasn't enough to counter the fierce opposition to having a sanctuary city. The state government had a zero-tolerance policy—and at the federal level, the animosity towards undocumented migrants had reached alarming levels.

"Look, there are some religious institutions that are pretty conservative, even nationalistic," Jagan said. "But they don't care about politics when it comes to helping vulnerable people. Words like 'legal,' 'illegal,' 'documented,' and 'undocumented' become meaningless when people are in need. Don't you think?"

"Absolutely!" Clearing his throat, Hari continued: "I admire what you are doing … I do. It's important to speak up, take action. Staying on the sidelines, especially if you're an immigrant, cannot be an option these days."

"Yes, and I see that reflected in the opinion pages of *Diaspora Weekly*. You guys do a good job of keeping it on the front burner. I like that, and that's why I got in touch with you. But, are outrage and denunciation enough, no matter how cleverly expressed?"

"Oddly enough, we've been saying the same thing. I cannot take credit for the editorials, by the way. I'm a correspondent. At our last meeting, there was a vigorous debate about *Diaspora Weekly*'s future in the digital age. We have an online presence, but it's the print edition that brings in revenue. How can we keep it viable in a fast-changing media environment? As younger readers migrate online, how long can we hang on to our loyal print readers?"

"What about online revenue?" Jagan asked.

"That's very hard. The barriers to entry are low for online publications—and given the competition, we can't afford to have a paywall. That limits our options."

"So is there a solution? Do you have a strategy?"

"We're working on it," Hari said. "To be honest, my focus is on putting out the issue. That takes up my energy. But I can tell you one thing. Everybody agrees that we have to provide enough value to make people read *Diaspora Weekly* when they get it at home."

"And how do you define value?"

Hari grinned. "That's the big question, isn't it?"

"Indeed. Look, I know it's challenging. You have my good wishes. I'm not saying you have to write about this. That's obvious. In fact, publicity can be a double-edged sword! We want to build support for the initiative, not kill it. Editorials are good at the intellectual level, but we also need stories to humanise the issue … to make migrants relatable. Whatever path they choose, they're ultimately like any of us. They're trying to get ahead, take care of their families. I contacted *Diaspora Weekly* because I enjoy reading it."

"Thank you. We do want to publish more features that people can relate to. There's a definite interest in that. And speaking of value, our readers have asked for investigative articles as well. But we're not ready for that step. First, we have to strengthen our budget and our team. Is this the first time you're talking to us?"

"Well, I met your publisher several years ago," Jagan said. "I don't think he'll remember me. We only talked for a few minutes at an event, with people milling around us. Anyway, while you guys do a good job of highlighting the accomplishments of immigrants, have you given enough thought to writing about the most vulnerable people among us?"

An awkward pause followed. "Not enough," Hari finally said.

"Sorry, I didn't mean to put you on the spot. I know you're not the editor. I was just making a point. Creating awareness is my goal."

"No worries. I understand. One thing we do is profiles. Perhaps we could feature some undocumented migrants in an article … we can call it 'Lives in the Shadows' or something like that. It could even be a series. Names could be changed and, if needed, some details tweaked. I'll bring it up in our next editorial meeting."

"I like that," Jagan said, beaming. "I'd be eager to read it. And I'll be happy to provide leads, if needed. Your team has to decide what's appropriate. Shall we go?"

When they went back to the lounge, it was empty. Had the three men gone to their respective rooms—or were they all staying in one room? On the TV screen, a stand-up comedian was doing his routine, but to Hari, the laughter sounded eerie because the audience wasn't visible and he seemed to be performing in an empty room. Before they left, Jagan turned off the TV and the lights. Then he locked the door from the outside.

"I'm going to the other building, so let me say bye," he said, extending his hand. "Thanks for coming and listening to me. Let's meet again."

"Sure, it was enlightening," Hari said. "Can I ask you something? What will you do if they shut you down? I hope it doesn't happen … but it could, as you know."

Jagan stared at him for a moment, and in the pale-yellow glow of a single light bulb, his eyes flared. "That won't bother us … *me*," he said emphatically. "No matter what happens, the fight will continue. We won't stop."

Before parting, they agreed to meet there again in a week. Hari's wife and their son returned from the Midwest, and he fell back into his usual evening routine. When he told her about Jagan, she was intrigued and said they should make a contribution, even if it wasn't a big amount. Hari, agreeing, said he would mention it to Jagan. At the office meeting, the 'Lives in the Shadows' idea was well received, although Rita said they should start with one article and gauge the reaction. Hari was ambivalent about that approach, but rather than give up the opportunity, he said he'd gather enough material and work on the first article.

A week later, when Hari returned to Lucky Inn at the appointed time, it was already dark. Jagan had promised to introduce him to Lucky and talk more about their "guests" and the challenges they faced. Again, Hari was struck by how close this quiet, seemingly desolate spot was to the bustling stretch of Route 6. Without turning onto the inconspicuous side road, one would not even know the inn existed. Before it closed for business, there must have been a prominent billboard on Route 6 to alert motorists.

Approaching the NO TRESPASSING sign, Hari noticed a car coming from the other direction on the side road. Though unsettled by its abrupt appearance and blinding lights, he expected it to go past the inn towards Route 6. But when the car's flashing blue lights came on, to his horror, and it swerved to follow him, he experienced a sickening jolt as if he'd been struck by lightning. He stopped, and so did the police cruiser behind him, its lights still flashing.

Trembling, Hari remained in his seat for what seemed like a long time—was the cop doing a license plate check?—before he heard the opening and closing of the car door. Then came the crunch of gravel. Turning, Hari saw the beam of a flashlight slice through the air before resting on him. When his eyes adjusted, he saw the pale face of an officer as he leaned towards him. Where did he come from so suddenly? Was he patrolling the area?

"May I see your driver's license and registration?" The officer's voice sounded neutral, conversational, as if Hari had asked for directions. But there was a steely glint in his eyes.

"Yes, of course," Hari said, fumbling with his wallet. "I was just curious about the inn. Somebody told me about it, and I wanted to see if it was still open. I was passing by—"

When the officer, now examining the license, didn't say anything, Hari stopped talking. Though intimidated, he was struck by how young the officer looked, making him wonder if he was a rookie. His eyes, icy blue and still sombre in the glow of the flashlight, focused on Hari's face as he handed back the license and registration.

Hari exhaled and managed to smile. Was he going to let him go?

"What do you do?" the officer asked. "For a living, I mean."

Hari blanched, thrown off by this unexpected question. "I write for … I'm a reporter," he said. "But it's not a big publication."

"A reporter?" the officer said, his eyes narrowing. "What's the name of the publication?"

"*Diaspora Weekly.* It's a community publication based here. I have a business card."

"That's fine. You can go, but don't come back here. I'm sure you saw the NO TRESPASSING sign. The inn is permanently closed."

"Of course. Thank you, officer." Again, as a relieved Hari heard the crunch of gravel, a beam of light slashed the darkness in a sweeping arc. The cruiser's door opened and closed. The flashing lights were turned off—and then, to the accompaniment of sporadic jabber from the officer's radio, the cruiser spun around and quickly moved out of sight.

Cautiously, Hari turned around as well and got back on Route 6 to head home.

Had he been too obsequious, considering that he'd done nothing wrong? Before Hari was stopped, he hadn't even reached the NO TRESPASSING sign, let alone go past it. On the other hand, while he didn't have a gun, the officer did carry one—conspicuously, on his hip—and it would have been foolish, not to mention dangerous, to be anything other than polite and obedient in this quiet spot, where they were surrounded by darkness but not a single witness.

Feeling guilty that his dominant emotion was still relief, Hari wondered where Jagan was. And what happened to the people who were staying at Lucky Inn? Hope they were doing okay. Did somebody complain to the local authorities, making them shut down the place? Had Jagan been unable to contact Hari and inform him? Realising that he hadn't checked his phone in a while, Hari pulled into the well-lit parking lot of a closed bank. He took out his phone and looked, but there was no message from Jagan.

The next day, when Hari sent an email to Recog, he got a response—and again, it was unsigned. "Sorry, I neglected to inform you. It all happened quickly, and I forgot. Now the action has moved to the homes of concerned citizens." Jagan was being circumspect.

Earlier, as Hari was turning around to leave, he'd been surprised to see a lighted window in the front building of the inn. Was somebody staying there? The officer, strangely enough, didn't seem to notice it. The parking lot, though, was empty.

"Are you or Lucky staying at the inn?" Hari wrote. "I went by yesterday." Realising that, like Jagan, he should be circumspect, he said nothing about the officer.

"No comment, but I'll be in touch again," Jagan replied. "The fight continues!"

DARRYL WHETTER

Turquoise Water, White Liberal Guilt

It's no good getting old if you don't get cunning.
—Peter Carey

"Full point," Kat demanded, "for the ass hose." She crossed the Bangkok hotel room to Chris, who was stretched out there reading on the bed.

Chris Arnold was reading, in his phrase, "as a human, not as an editor," so he looked up. "As in Bangkok belly already or so smart to turn this toilet into a bidet or ... you kinda wanna date the plumber?"

Kathryn Beausoleil lay down beside him, rubbing her foot up and down his. "None of the first, mostly the second. For the third, you obviously haven't even turned it on. That's *hello* water pressure, not *Hell-OOOO* water pressure." She smiled as she curled into him. "Mostly, though, it's a good ol' dose of difference. We sho ain't in Kansas anymore, Toto."

Since they'd touched down two nights ago, every Thai toilet they'd met was the standard upright—no splash pads so far, blessedly—yet each also had what travel bloggers love to call the "bum gun" hose coiled patiently beside. These not-quite-worldly forty-something Torontonians had encountered toilet hoses with other, earlier partners in Spain (her) and Turkey (him) but hadn't anticipated them when planning their half-contentious trip to Thailand, their wager trip.

"Yeah, okay." He nodded mock-gravely. "Point yours."

A ludicrous bet, of course; so ludicrous they'd told only one friend each back in Toronto. Two crowded weeks in sweaty Thailand, at Christmas. When the trip had been an idea over a bottle of cab, not a sweaty, expensive reality, she'd said, "We can't live together until we've travelled together."

Kathryn was, almost all the time, a sous-chef at Toronto's busy Dish. Chefs—she only had to explain once to Chris—work insane hours. She described her chef's sun-starved December skin as "the colour of lard. Dish might as well be a fallout bunker for all I see the sun."

Two weeks together in Thailand would, he gambled, prove his theory that travel was overrated, a rip-off for not only bank account but soul. He knew how unpopular this was—might as well write *Kitten Strangler* on your profile—and he'd still brought it up on one of their early dates.

Normally, her restaurant hours and his career commitment to *the best words in their best order* gave them, to the half-surprise of their friends, early "dates" consisting of long, old-school telephone conversations while she chopped, shredded, and sautéed during prep. Kitchens are constant work but not—they can't be—constant sprinting. As sous, she was senior enough to keep her phone with her during the calm before the storm that was the morning or the prep decathlon that was the midafternoon lull. A full editor, if one foolishly still committed to fiction, not cross-platform celebrity bios, he'd earned the diminishing career privilege of having an actual office with a door he could shut. Let the assistants think he was coaching another doubting, deluded, or self-destructive writer. Just a few more minutes with this tough Kat at ten-thirty in the morning. Make up the manuscript time that night at home while she was five burners in.

"You know Christopher Hitchens? Yeah, no—he was more than just a professional atheist. Great writer. One of his thousand throwaway lines was about what's overrated in life. To him, it was lobster, champagne, picnics, and anal sex. He's wrong on three counts, but I admire the provocation."

With a knife in her hand, so, apparently, did she. "Totally. I mean … picnics. Lying on a blanket is no proper way to eat."

"The bugs," he added gratefully, closing his eyes and raising them ceiling-ward in unseen, telephonic relief. "For me, it's family, Christmas, travel, and marriage. Love, absolutely. Marriage—who needs the state, the church, and the cash register to celebrate their love?" In those early telephone dates, they already knew that neither had been married, suspected that each was consciously childfree. Blessedly, and ruinously, she locked horns over travel.

"Oh, dude: dig yourself out of this one. I live to travel."

Really, he'd been digging from the start. *Underwhelmed by travel* was one of the taglines in his Crush profile. A few women he'd never even contacted wrote him snarky messages to say how unromantic he was. "Maybe next time," he wondered, "I should just go ahead and list my career as *taxidermist.*"

"You weren't entirely suicidal. Wasn't quite *Hates going down and does it poorly.*"

"*Seeks a porn star who also cooks and cleans like Mom.*"

"*Financial parasite prone to overwhelming rage*," she tried, not yet confessing that was her stock summary of Blair, her ex.

All that just a few dates in. They were happy to brave all this so quickly, but she was just as brave to break out of the game. "And that's right, fella: my cooking is nothing like Mumsie's."

"Good," they were both glad to hear him say.

Like every Thai they saw, she worked with her body, whereas most of her friends rode desks. Her hands and arms were scarred from knife, boil, and oil. Like all chefs, she had a certainty, not a fear, of developing varicose veins. Not so surprising, to her, anyway, that someone who still made a living with her body had fallen for a book editor. Every night's dinner rush took her into a sustained, red-lining overdrive that was the very antithesis of polishing prose and air-lifting half-chapters. Yes, he had production deadlines. Yes, he had done sixteen-hour marathon edits far too close to the first squirt of printer's ink. Back when email was just part of his job, not, seemingly, its entirety, in those waning years of things still getting passed by hand, all those inked signatures for the bike couriers, he'd once paid two different motorcyclists to race Zip disks with identical files across the city to the printers. Drive between cars. Take different routes. Bonus for the guy who got there first. Two to six traffic violations in conservative Canada, but, they saw in the first minute of their cab in from the airport, standard driving practice in ludicrously congested Bangkok.

Perfectly sensible, to her at least, that every pause in the flow of honking trucks, cars, and three-wheeled *tuk tuks* found Thai scooter drivers of all ages slithering through traffic on every available inch of asphalt. One scooter after another, from civil servants to school kids to their grandmothers, wove around them in any available space. They didn't just drive between two lanes of cars or even three, but also on the side of the road. Throw a glance, then bump up onto the sidewalk for a stretch. The constant scooters cut across busy lanes, not just between them. "A crossword puzzle on wheels," he observed. "Down. Across. Down. Across."

Two schoolgirls wearing medical facemasks but not helmets half-circled their stranded taxi to travel three car-lengths in the wrong direction in the opposite lane before weaving back into theirs. "Just because you can survive something physically," she lamented, "doesn't mean you're not too young for it." Bangkok, Bangkok.

Not the time, he thought, to score the prostitution anti-travel point. But Kat handled knives and heat for a living, got paid to know how close she could work to danger. "Your point," she conceded. "All this suffering we see, what do we do about it? Look the other way."

"We pack bags," he agreed, "because only a bit of our stuff fits in them."

Although they'd flirted more by phrase than pic, they had still thought themselves no stranger to selfies and cell use. Then they arrived in Asia. "What is this," she asked on their first Bangkok afternoon, "the selfie Olympics?" Beside them in restaurants, young women would spontaneously pause midmeal to raise a phone and pan it through a three-foot arc to grab at least two dozen selfies. All canted jaw and mail-order bride eyes. "All the plate's a stage," she lamented.

"Excessive selfie narcissism," he intoned, "point my way."

"No update, no existence," she agreed.

Until now at least, probably still now, he claimed travel was almost never worth the money and rarely even the time. "I went to Helsinki for a conference once, blew off an afternoon for a boat ride along the coast and out to Suomenlinna, this fortress. I caught a little architectural wow, sure, an 'Isn't it great I'm not four foot eight and hoping to live 'til forty-six before I'm slaughtered with an axe?' but mostly I thought it looked like Georgian Bay. Mostly, truth be told, I read on the boat." He smiled. "Gorgeous place to read."

"I am happiest"—she shook her head down into an exasperated smile—"when I travel."

"Which I get, for other people." He hadn't forgotten everything she'd told him about a kitchen's succubus hours. "For most people, travel is a ritual to get away from work, a chance to be the person they'd be if they had money without a job. For me, unless a trip is Tuscan-villa, free-wine amazing, I'd usually rather be making books."

They'd fallen for each other's work as each thought they must. I love my career: if you want to love me, so should you. Where some of her female customers had personal shoppers for clothes, preschools, and wine, love earned her a personal shopper for books.

Julian Barnes?? she once texted him.

We can find better ways to get you spanked in the principal's office.

Atwood?

It takes a special kind of writer to make a double murder boring.

So love tumbled forward. The garnet comfort of it, this daily chat, this audience of one. Plus, of course, the body's other hunger. She'd succeeded, professionally if not personally, in large measure by how well she could handle meat. Both their careers (if not their souls) concentrated on how much you can, and should, change the essence of a thing. "No other animal cooks its food," she reminded both of them, "and no other animal has taken over the planet. We're heat." She once raised two slightly laden palms up in front of his collarbones. "Eat this," she said of the left, holding aloft a raw cashew. "And now this," with a roasted one.

Emotionally, of course, they'd both been burnt. Emotionally and financially. His avoiding the legalities of marriage also saw him, the self-cursed editor, avoiding a prenup for the default common-law into which the same legal-romantic machinery had dragged him whether he wanted to be or not. The neighbours in his small apartment building were all ten years younger, new teachers and never-single junior lawyers who wouldn't let the alimony vampire over the threshold. Still, he'd been the one to propose they get a place together.

"Call me twentieth-century, call me naive. To me, living together is more … together. The top of my foot pressing up into the arch of yours in bed. Spoons every night. Saturday pot of coffee us. Wine-cork us. You live together or you don't."

"Not," she insisted, "until we've travelled together."

"And been tested together," she'd added as Canadian autumn sank from the sun-dappled leaves and crisp-apple phase into the gloom of naked branches and deepening darkness. "Nothing easy for us like Paris or Berlin. No"—

this was coming on the fly but coming so right—"no English. Take us out of our comfort zone."

"No cruises. You're great but—"

"Not Flapper-Night great? Not Dentistry-School-Class-of-Ninety-Two great? Heartless monster."

His helpless grin.

Not Africa, with the bribes and the embezzled trillions, the bulldozed, count-the-ribs dead. India was too intense for a romantic test, with its weeping-sore beggars. Central America was too close and had—they were surprised to admit to each other, not just themselves—too many machine guns.

"If we're going to cross town to live together," she said, "let's cross the planet fist." As their Toronto searches became Thai plans, as two separate credit cards got keyed in, she added, "Time to admit who we are. The Asian mirror."

The Asian mirror of the West. On their first self-navigated trip on Bangkok's light rail system—modern, clean cars cutting through a hotter Dickensian smog—they overheard loud Americans bragging about how far their money went amongst all these servile Thais. *Yuk, yuk, yuk, 'massage.'* By the time they got down south to Phuket, the Daytona Beach of Asia, stars-and-stripes bikinis were a daily sighting. *Make America Great Again* hats were worn proudly, not far from the scarred Chinese fingers that had made them. As Canadians with disposable income, they were spoiled teenagers free to hate parents and neighbours alike. "Brexit and Trump are still idiotic here," he said after yet another restaurant meal beside loudmouths with globally famous accents, "but they're a little less shocking."

"Point, I believe, my way. Look at you: learning without a magazine."

He nodded and raised his glass.

At an elephant sanctuary up in hilly Chiang Mai, they laid all four of their hands across the swollen side of an enormously pregnant female. The longest gestation period of any mammal, they'd been told: nearly two years in the womb.

"Two years without wine," she sighed. The grey hide shifted its alien swell as the baby elephant swam beneath their thrilled hands. When it came time for the group of twenty tourists, all of them Caucasian, to bathe the elephants with mud then water, Kat and Chris wordlessly preferred the pregnant elephant and a playful young calf. They worked in muddy bathing suits in a dirty river beside fit English, American and German tourists all still living south of thirty.

"Point," she tried, scooping up two handfuls of dripping mud. "I'd never learn the smell of elephant pee in Canada."

"That," he said, stepping back for air, "is a half-point at best." He coughed with chin-puckering exaggeration in the ammonia cloud. His drawstring nostrils.

"Find your inner strength," she counselled, pretending to return to exfoliating an elephant. She flung mud straight back into his wet chest, certain he'd never throw some at her defenceless back.

The short flights north to hilly Chiang Mai and south to beachy Phuket also showed them the Asian mirror of the declining West. On a speedboat out to the Similan

Islands, at least half of the other island goers were Chinese. When they finally splashed ashore to beachy Similan, that paradise held hostage by tourism, the signs were written in Chinese, English, and Russian.

She nodded and half-gloated. "Geography lessons with warm sand beneath our feet."

"Warm sand full of plastic seals from water bottles," he contested.

Snorkelling, they'd both agreed, was mandatory for their "Thaitinerary." Even he was excited. "You either travel for art and architecture or landscape. We're not going to see a dozen Monets a day, so let's find a parrot fish."

"See," she'd taunted, "when's the last time you snorkelled in Canada?"

He raised affectionate eyebrows. "When my parents' TV had thirteen channels and only the Math Club knew what a modem was."

"It's not proper travel," she freely admitted, "if it's easy." On the ninety-minute speedboat crossing out to Similan, each had been wordlessly sympathetic that the Thai snorkelling guide spoke only broken English to a boat half-full of Chinese passengers. Come splash time, cultural sympathy got shoved aside by what they had to admit, and privately at first, might be their own racism. Twenty-five equally impatient, equally overpaying would-be snorkellers could only gear up and jump off the boat at two narrow corners of the stern (and just inches from gleaming, raised propeller blades). First, Kathryn, then Chris were purposefully pushed aside by Chinese tourists keen for coral. When they looked up in disbelief at this blatant, schoolyard predation, Chris tried a theatre joke. "At least they cross-cast." He nodded at the departing man who had shoved her and the four-foot, birdlike grandmother who had tried to send him into the hockey boards.

They swam in turquoise water and white liberal guilt.

Passionate theory and other delusions got jostled aside with them again in the warm, azure water. Even in the few minutes between their being startled by the shoving aboard the boat and jumping off its back corner, they'd each silently collapsed back into guilt. With a self-correcting shake of the head and their deepening romantic telepathy, he tried to say, *We don't even know if they're Chinese. Could be wealthy Laotians for all we know.*

You've obviously never been to Hua Long Market on Spadina, she replied, with stern eyebrows still visible through her mask.

Generalizing, and extending distrust or dislike from one onto all—this couldn't be them. Then they got shoved again in the water. "Starfish!" one of the barely-qualified teen guides called out, dripping snorkel briefly pulled aside from his mouth. To keep track of the bright red sea star or perhaps to avoid the piranha attack of snorkelling tourists he'd attracted too many times before, the guide dove back under. How Kathryn and Chris envied his enabling weight belt, its dutiful tug down and away. On the choppy surface, Kat was rammed in the ribs by another snorkeller's head. Chris's shin was raked by a fin. Snorkels and language barriers made apologies more difficult, but none was even attempted. Flabbergasted, they each shifted from swimming horizontally to treading vertical water. They looked around for their assailants but really only found each other. Slick, snorkelled heads of black hair retreated away from them, seals of angry determination.

He removed his snorkel to ask: "Point mine, or yours?"

"Whole new flavour of misanthropy," she claimed, displacing plenty of water with the long fins. "Can't wait for that communal picnic lunch."

Beneath their green polymer flippers, most of the coral was dead. It looked not so much bleached as ashen, some tumbleweed ghost town empty of even the wind.

They found a different kind of bustle back on the mainland when they tried to spend a few days in that fundamental travel quest: doing nothing on the beach. Yes, Phuket's Kata Beach was one long crescent of ecru sand. A nearby island broke up their view of the wrinkled blue horizon and invited all these visitors to think of things behind and beyond, out of sight if not out of reach. "Dark side of the moon," she said upon arrival, jutting her chin at an island too distant for paddle boards but the obvious run for the rented Sea Doos. Paddle boarders inched out at one end of the beach. At the other, Thai men in soaking shorts looked for tourists to take out in the narrow wooden arcs of their long-tailed boats, exposed diesel engines noisily coughing black smoke.

"Mmmm?" was all she had to ask when they first settled into rented beach mats in the shade of a frayed umbrella. Cans of cold beer were just metres away and a third of the price of a coffee back home. After their first beer, each taking turns half-reading or simply inhaling warmth with nearly all of their skin, he had to ask.

"So, well—here's something I still don't know." He nodded around them at a beach crowded with sand-playing kids. The body-proud had travelled from gym to swimwear store to beach. Plump, sunburnt men in banana hammocks flaunted or ignored their bikini wives. "We're quite a walk from a dirty public toilet where we'd have to pay—"

"Pay Canadian peanuts," she corrected, deflating his hopes a little.

"Sure but have to pay to pee, what, three times this afternoon? Yet we're also right beside an ocean ... already warm ... with its kajillion litres of sluice. Your vote on this?"

She kept her eyes closed but wagged a knee. "Tell me you're not really in doubt about whether I pee in the ocean. I eviscerate for a living."

"Of course."

She waited until he was just about to stand, angling weight he hadn't yet lifted. "So, how long have you been peeing in my shower?"

Just a nanosecond of sheepishness, then the sunny grin back at her. "How long have I been coming over?"

They spoke over each other deliciously.

"—Point," she argued. "The true us."

"—No point. I'd have told you in Toronto."

She wagged a sun-smeared finger. "But you didn't."

That, they knew, was couplehood. Everybody else saw another middle-aged white male with waxed shoulders risking a chest burn. She saw her beloved about to piss in the ocean.

Coupledom, they were also admitting again, gave more lift than drag, but it did have its drag. Your cut foot slows us both down. You pet one of those skinny street cats, we both get fleas.

Of course they'd been to beaches before, and almost no one goes on a beach vacation alone. Her and Marco in Spain: the tanning, the hash, the secretly flattering ogling. Chris and Meredith, *Meredith!*, in the fucking Lake District. They thought they knew beaches and beaching, but the fine Thai sand truly got everywhere. The hinges of his glasses. Inside her wallet. On their eyelids. Hotel sheets, towels, even their toothbrushes. Her own beach joy there in Phuket's opposite of a dark, cold Canadian December included eventually sitting in the water's edge to get doused by the incoming waves, that tame but unstoppable slosh. When they pulled her up to her feet, she continued the tug to slide wetly up against his hot, pink chest. "I literally," she whispered in his ear, "have sand in my hoo-hoo. We're not talking *bottom of my suit*. I don't mean *near* or *around*. We're talking *up went the grains*."

He smiled a very forty-something smile. "Let's get you back to the room and see if it turns into a pearl."

In the sunburnt morning, they finally caved and followed one of the countless *Laundry* signs down an alley. "No," she admitted, "I don't 'like' having all my damp and filthy clothes slowly making the less-filthy clothes in my luggage damp and filthy, but I do like taking two different routes to the same washer woman on two different days. Not great, I admit, that it's definitely a washer *woman*, but have you ever had your gitch weighed in a fruit scale before? Laundry by the kilo. Pick it up tomorrow. Me in flux is a great way to be me."

"I agree. Hence"—two hands, pinball flippers angling back towards himself—"a life of books. My flux."

"Books don't wear bikinis."

A nice claim, but they'd also now been in Thailand for ten days. They'd long been out of Bangkok, but Bangkok wasn't out of them. Late morning, they were both suddenly speed-walking back to their hotel bathroom, buttocks and other, more hidden, muscles clenched. "Who gets to go first?" isn't everyone's idea of romance, but it's certainly real.

"You, you," he claimed between shallow breaths. "Just another man trying to last over here." Bangkok belly and a warm toilet seat, that very definition of a mixed blessing.

At supper, he didn't go for the obvious. Almost all of the Thai food they'd had back in Toronto was better than the Thai food they'd had in five different Thai cities. Expensive restaurant or seemingly authentic roadside shack of cinderblocks and corrugated tin, everything was, in her withering words, "all so grab-bag. No cohesion. No sequence or vision. Just because an orchestra *can* all play at once doesn't mean it *should.*"

No, he thought, not the food. Time, surely now, for Mother Earth. "Recycling," he started as they, yes, tucked chairs under a table beside the moonlit beach. They did so before opening their fourth water bottle of the day. Or was it the fifth? Sixth? "Recycling you gotta give me. Sure, life outside the privileged West is cheaper, cuz, you know, it's—"

"Yeah, yeah: life outside the privileged West."

Tonight, as with every night in Thailand, they'd walked to a restaurant over half-ventilated concrete slabs covering what must have been raw sewage. Few are ever going to be attracted to *Disappointed by a lack of sidewalks* on a dating profile, but Chris disliked being unable to talk on half their date as they picked their way over a crowded series of poo bridges.

"I mean, Sweden is now basically zero waste. To travel is—"

"To waste. Sure is. To burn. Carbon. Water. Land."

He raised a palm, half in illustration but also, he thought, to grab a point. "You heard that Chicago couple the other night: Phi-Phi is a dying island killed by all the tourists going there for island paradise."

"All the tourists like us. Until four days ago, we didn't know Phi-Phi from Similan. And—do I even have to say it—the rest of the world sure as shit isn't choosing the Scandinavian way of life. The global vote is clear: Daytona Beach, yes; smart, healthy Finland, no. Are we any better? Whole lotta carbon and extraction getting us here against"—she saw that hand of his again—"your better judgment, yes. For now, the species plan is clear: buy shit and choke your grandchildren. Fight for a better deck chair on the *Titanic*. Most women have children. Some can't. Only a few of us choose not to."

He smiled at her, no hands in sight. "Fuck, do I love it when you're right. Medea with a cleaver."

She shrugged. "You gotta carve what you want out of life."

"So live with me," he said, dirty surf rolling audibly in a moonlight uncrowded by streetlights. "Contest be damned."

"The contest," she smiled, raising her wine glass, "was never really the contest."

"Winners(?)," he half-asked and half-proclaimed, also raising his.

"Winners," she agreed, mostly happy and clinking into his eyes.

ADELINE TAN

Babel

"*It's settled then,*" Meng Teck chirped in Mandarin. "*Now you'll always have a home. This home.*" He crushed his cigarette packet and pressed down on Meng Huat's shoulder, his knees cracking as he stood. Huat felt the linger of his brother's hand. Under the weak midnight moon, Teck didn't see Huat's bruised knuckles rise, dark as shadows, as he curled his fingers under his palm. "*The rain has stopped. Going to 7-Eleven; want anything?*"

Ten seconds was all it took for Huat to tip the display cabinet. The cheap trinkets glided smoothly down the top—like children on fast slides—hitting the floor first. For a while, time teetered on pencil legs, then lurched forward in a game of catch up. The glass doors cracked like sheets of thick ice. Huat brought his foot down on the back of the cabinet. The wood see-sawed and splintered into his flesh. Only the family photograph tipped backward and landed with a clatter. Three unsmiling generations hemmed in by a wooden frame. The wall clock resumed its loud, plastic beat.

*

"You're not selling the flat?"

"Teck says he'll pay for the upkeep. He's still teaching."

"That nobody'll live in?"

"It was my parents' flat," Mary said. "Teck and I would like to keep it. And Huat, you never know, he might need it."

"That bookie runner? The one who went to prison? Who's now in some temple!?"

Mary wished her husband would stop with all the questions. She gave her tiny crucifix pendant a habitual rub.

"Alan, I only have two brothers."

The buzz of the air-conditioning tickled Mary's ears.

"We'll discuss this when you're back."

Mary had forgotten how crowded Singapore could get, even at nine. From the hotel window, she watched the busy road—wet-slicked and neon-soaked from the annual Christmas lights display—teem with frantic last-minute shoppers and snaking cars. She missed driving. She missed work. She missed Alan. And Rachel. She'll miss the birth of her first grandchild. Will he have light brown hair and hazel eyes like Rachel? Or blonde and green like Tom?

The damp smell of the rain still clung to her, and a chill trickled down her spine. More than thirty years of living in Perth and still she couldn't get used to the cold. She pulled out a clean bathrobe from the closet and slid under the thick cotton cocoon. She would teach her grandson Mandarin. Road—*Ma lu*. Car—*Che*. Pedestrian … pedestrian … what's the word?

*

"Wah, long time no see! I almost didn't recognise you!"

Huat endured the friendly rub on his bald head by an acquaintance, a regular when he used to work here. He peered at the man's Thai amulet—pebble-sized and carved from ivory—ziplining back and forth on a thick gold chain. He felt accusation from the faceless Buddha. His throat was scratched from chain-smoked Dunhills, his head spinning from ten Carlsbergs, his dick throbbing from a Vietnamese hooker.

"*Come, come, come, place your bets!*"

Huat tried to pin down the dancing dice, a hand on his eleventh beer.

Big.

"*Two three three, small!*"

He slaps down another fifty dollar note. Big.

"*One two four, small!*"

Fifty. Big.

"*Small again!*"

Hundred. BIG.

"*SMALL!*"

Huat's fist went through the table; his body went out the door. He pulled his cellphone from his trouser pocket—two missed calls from Claire and six from Mary. Four text messages.

Claire: *Met Auntie Mary today. Call me?*

Teck: *Good news, come by the house!*

Mary: *I just called Teck. We'll keep the flat.*

Mary: *Love you.*

Huat raised his face to the drizzle and laughed maniacally. He punched three numbers on the keypad.

"Hello, police?"

He slipped out of the alley and headed for the main road.

"There's illegal gambling at Geylang. Lorong 24."

He pulled himself up a bus.

"To Ang Mo Kio?" he slurred.

*

Winged insects tapped at the fluorescent light. Teck chuckled. He remembered how he would raise a plastic basin of water with Huat, their feet tiptoeing on a flimsy platform of stacked stools, while they watched shadows of death dance on the ceiling. Huat was twelve years younger, barely fourteen then, but already the same height as him. They would pour the water away in the toilet and watch the wings and bodies float down the tiled floor and into the drain.

Teck flipped the switch. Evening washed over the living room—a soggy blue shroud over the rattan settee and the faded floral cushions, the display cabinet crammed full of trophies and medals, Father's photograph on the coffee table. His stomach was pawing from within, but he didn't want to risk leaving the flat. Mary might sneak back and chain the gate.

He returned Father to the ancestral altar, next to Mother. Both were smiling, like the happy couple they never were. The photographer had demanded their smiles. Teck curved his lips up and aligned his mouth with Father's, like how his bushy eyebrows, grey eyes, and folded jowls already did. Huat had his mother's button-hole eyes, fleshy nose, and tomato-smooth skin. He even had his mother's voice—soft as a lullaby. Mary sounded like neither of them; her tongue had become foreign.

Teck's cellphone rattled against the coffee table. Whether it was Mary, his wife, or his son, the answer was the same.

"*I told you. I'm not leaving the house.*"

*

"Pa said he didn't want anything to do with the flat," Claire said.

Mary fingered the tip of the metal spoon in the glass cup; the humidity smoothed her wrinkled hands and made her feel younger. She had insisted on meeting Claire and Janet at North Bridge Road. The *kopi gu you* reminded her of old days, tin cans of coffee on string. She eyed the two sisters—barely into their twenties, barely into work—sitting at the edges of their oily wooden seats. They had the same curated look about them: thin gold-rimmed glasses, fedora hat, terrazzo-printed top, wide-legged pants, jumpsuit. Both wore sneakers and hugged their tote bags close to their bodies, their arms avoiding the sticky marble table.

"You're sure? Huat doesn't want the money?"

"That's what he says now." Janet stared at the floating slab of butter greasing over the coffee. "You know that's … really not healthy, right?"

Mary liked Janet, feisty and full of opinions. She reminded her of Rachel. The daughter who had moved to Brisbane. She dug the metal spoon into the thick layer of condensed milk at the bottom of the cup and stirred. She wouldn't be able to eat dinner after this.

"How's your father? He doesn't pick up my calls."

"He won't, Auntie Mary. Unless it's an emergency."

Claire, always the explaining one. The forgiving one who wouldn't move to the other end of the country. Maybe she should've tried harder for a second. She had been too busy trying to love Alan, his loud guffaws and boisterous opinions had nipped at her desire for peace. But fate had been kind to her. He was a good man.

"And this is not? An emergency?"

Janet looked out at the stretched raindrops chasing each other down the awning, and Claire looked blankly at Mary.

"I'll try calling him later tonight."

*

Auntie Mary wants to meet us. What have you done again?

Janet's message troubled Huat like a ghost. He scratched angrily at his calves, where the stiff hem of his saffron robes filed his skin. He tried to fight back. *No, you don't understand. I didn't do anything!* Thunder rumbled and shook the metal bones of the temple office. His hands found his way to the desk where Auntie Wang sat in the afternoons, paying bills and issuing receipts. He slid the drawer open and there it was—a small black box, pregnant with donations.

He could pick the flimsy lock in a second. Easy money. Like the piggy banks he used to smash—Mary's always, never Teck's. He could smell the sour coins, the notes like old clothes. He lifted the metal box up and knew at once how much was in it; he knew the weight of money. It would be enough to get him back on track.

Huat walked out of the office, tightly clutching the box under his robes, against his pounding chest. Down the long corridor, he passed by classrooms filled with Pali chanting, so steadfast the rain seemed to bend to its rhythm.

"Phra Huat!"

Phra Raja. His fellow *bhikkhu*. His voice, so brotherly.

"What are you doing out here?"

Meng Huat's robes slapped angrily about him, the bright orange fabric thick and loud like a flag. He wanted Phra Raja's robes—muted and soft, billowing gently like steamed rice cakes rising with the magic of air.

"I have to return a call."

He had not spoken in days; his mother's voice startled him.

"You've been looking at your phone all day, Huat. Everything okay?"

Even Phra Raja's worry was soft around the edges. People here were so trusting, so full of belief.

"Yes, Raj. Everything's fine."

*

"*I won't leave this house!*"

The wind and Teck's voice sucked through the closing crack of the front door, chilling Mary's shoulders.

She heard the ding of the elevator and the shuffle of the locksmith's flip-flops. An empty chair greeted her when she turned around, and she placed the bicycle chain on the seat.

Teck was in the master bedroom, on the hospital bed where his father had died. He angled his body towards the window. Under his left arm was Father's photograph.

Mary talked to Father's face.

"I'm leaving soon. My plane's on Monday."

Teck talked to the window.

"*Of course, your time is more important than mine.*"

"What's there left to discuss? Father died intestate. The flat doesn't belong to you, so why can't we just sell it?"

"*You and your big words. I know what* intestate *means,*" Teck snapped.

They had always talked like this, a barter of language— Mandarin from him and English from her. Teck and Huat had studied in Chinese-medium schools; Mary went to an English-medium one. A role of the dice in their father's head, perhaps. She had been the gamble he was unafraid to lose.

"What do we need the flat for?"

"*Father said we have to keep the house. So there'll always be a place for the family to come together.*"

The flat howled like an empty shell, and rain rattled the windows like a lid over boiling water. Mary retreated to the living room. The air was tinged with the smell of burnt incense. She bent over and squinted into the dark of the display cabinet. Patina encrusted the trophies and medals. Behind the glass, she couldn't tell which ones were hers or Teck's. Her eyes wandered to the family photograph propped against the wall. It must have been taken during Lunar New Year—even Alan was present, wearing a shiny shirt with frog buttons. Mary had to hug Rachel close, to keep her from wriggling off her lap. Teck, his wife, and son. Huat, his ex-wife, and two baby daughters. Father. And Mother.

Mother had gone down on her knees and begged her to stay. *I have to go, Mother.* Mary's Cantonese was impeccable then; so was her Mandarin. She could scold little Teck and Huat into obedience, without lifting her eyes from her textbooks. Mother was always busy, selling curry puffs or washing the neighbours' clothes. When Father disappeared—sometimes for weeks—life would be easier. Mother could pretend the money she had earned was hers, and Mary's bruises had time to heal.

Then Mary met Alan, and she left. She vowed to learn how to love him because she didn't want her mother's life. They all left. Teck married immediately after university, then Huat—the child born between generations—who didn't leave so much as fade away. What was the point of keeping a flat no one would return to?

Teck took the fight to Mary. "*You can't possibly need the money. We should honour his last wish.*"

"Father's wish?" Bitterness soured Mary's voice. "Don't you remember how Father treated us?"

"*You weren't here. He changed.*"

*

Raindrops landed heavily at an angle on the living room window. Teck watched them strike and slide across the glass, till the opposite housing block blurred into a watery smudge. He returned to the dining chair that he had positioned facing the main door, and grunted as he fell back heavily onto the wooden seat. He could hear the frantic rattle of the gate and Mary's muffled pleas. She would've contacted Huat by now. Good. He glanced at the wall clock and estimated another half hour before the locksmith arrived.

Don't worry, I won't let Mary sell the house. Teck's eyes found Father on the ancestral altar. The photograph was the most recent he could find, a few copies tucked in a corner of his father's limp leather wallet. He had accompanied him to the photography studio, just two blocks away, and watched him smile for the first time. He didn't stop smiling in China either, or stopped talking, his lips constantly pulled wide to reveal his few blackened teeth. He jabbered to Teck as he showed him about the house, built with the money he had sent back to his hometown, as if he had lived in it all his life. Their relatives followed them like ducks in the rice fields, their questions overlapping with excitement; Teck could hardly understand them with their thickly accented Mandarin. *Would you like something to eat? How is life like in Singapore? Why have you never come back to visit us? Do you like the room we prepared for you? Is it true in Singapore you go to jail for chewing gum? Would you like something to eat?*

In the evening after dinner, they showed him a scratched photograph of the entire family clan. There were so many of them—a collection of blurred dots—smaller than the fingers that moved from face-to-face. Father's smile quivered as they picked out his parents and eight

elder brothers and sisters. At night, in the largest room of
the house, Teck watched his father sleep with a curl on his
lips and his body firmly splayed across the mattress.

*Did you have some happy memories when you were a
child?* Teck wondered as he replaced the joss sticks in the
incense pot. *Of your brother holding a basin to a light with
you, wobbling and giggling while watching winged insects
drown? Of your sister bringing home thick coffee with melted
butter, then using the tin cans to talk to each other, two voices
carried from room to room by string?*

Teck decided to confront Mary with Father's
photograph in his hands when she barged in. Let her avert
her unfilial eyes in shame.

*

A sudden gust whipped through Tampines Town Centre—
Huat heard the dull slams of doors from the flats above the
coffee shop and the crackle of dead leaves scudding across
the brick pavement.

From the corner of Huat's eye, Auntie Wang was
explaining to a passerby that monks cannot accept money,
only food that they will consume that day. Donations
should be directed to the temple.

"But that's so troublesome," the lady said. "I have to
lug packs of rice from the supermarket? Right behind us?"

Auntie Wang apologised. This was the rule of the
temple.

The lady hurried away, a cloud of perfume trailing after
her. It smelled familiar, like what his ex-wife would wear.
He closed his eyes and willed his body to feel the touch of

a woman. It had been three years, between prison and this. He felt his dick quiver and rise; warmth spread to the tips of his folded hands. Today was a difficult day to be patient.

Huat mulled over the text message he had received earlier this morning, at the shrine hall: *Come to AMK house ASAP. Teck going crazy again.* He watched his shadow, dark and defined by the sun only twenty minutes ago, fade on the grey bricks. Why weren't they contented? Father's funeral was more than three weeks ago. Teck and Mary could do whatever they want with the flat now. The final price should be substantial, the area being the Prime Minister's own constituency.

With the sale of the flat, they would all be gone, scattered. Father and Mother, who had married because their parents told them to. Who rode the churning wet of the ocean enduring the hollow of their stomachs for thirty days. Father, who carried gunny sacks of rice as a coolie for years at the Singapore River. Whose skin leathered from the burning sun. Whose teeth cracked from chasing dragons. Who could still, in his fifties, carry a discarded sink and walk for an hour. Who let him drink beer and laughed when he asked for more. Who gave him his first cigarette. Who whipped Mary when Mother had no money to hand over. Who turned his belt on him when he realised that Mary was smart enough to be a lawyer. Who didn't whip Teck because he was the eldest son.

And Mother, who had children because that was all she was good for. Who kneaded dough for curry puffs and scrubbed laundry for neighbours till her hands were free of fingerprints and palm lines. Who always gave the chicken leg to Teck because he's the eldest son. Who told him to respect his elders. Who let Father take her money. Who couldn't pick up more than a few words of Mandarin. Who crawled into their beds at night to sing them Cantonese lullabies, of rice fields and fishing nets. Who spent half her life on her knees begging Father to stop beating her children. Who begged Mary not to leave. And Teck not to leave. And him not to leave.

Another strong flurry of wind brought the earthy smell of rain. Huat began chanting the Pali saying over and over in his head as he watched a popsicle wrapper eddy around his bare, dusty feet.

The wise one who is rid of all desire is as calm as a pond unstirred by the wind.

JASMINE ADAMS

A Woman's Place

"Why are you smiling when your child is sick? Thinking of when you will meet your irresponsible friends for *Cherki*[1]?" Joo Neo pretended that she did not hear her mother-in-law's, Mrs. Tan Siew Gek's, shrill rebuke and went back into her bedroom to carry out the chamber pot.

Once again, Joo Neo's demeanour, nothing more than a morning greeting, irked and was deliberately misunderstood by the elder lady. The matriarch was still in her shiny, padded black silk jacket, the one with warm gold lining, specially tailored for her by Shanghainese tailors in Chinatown.

"Just because she is adopted does not mean you can disregard her, you know! What will other people say? What will the neighbours think! Already you do not want to give birth to your own. I said to you before and I will say to you again, your own child you can chop into four pieces and I will not scold you, but other people's child you need to treat better than a young empress dowager!" shrilled Siew Gek.

Joo Neo resigned to the fact that a long, difficult day, like other similar days, would have to be tolerated. Little Lilian was not, by any means, seriously ill. She had a dribbly nose which made her not-so-robust appetite

---

1 Cherki is a card game which was popular among illiterate Peranakan ladies. In lieu of numbers or letters, the oblong cards had black and white patterns with red overlay.

even less so. And Lilian, who loved her ballet lessons, would wail when told that Uncle Trishaw will not be coming today to bring her to the palatial ballet academy, a colourful ride away from their shophouse in Devonshire Road.

"Lilian did not have any fever last night, Mak. And she finished all the Horlicks. See, she peed a lot. She is just waking up. Will bring her downstairs in a little while." Joo Neo tried to placate her mother-in-law before her shrieks would arouse Gordon, her sleeping husband.

"What! You left her alone by herself? What if she falls off the bed!" Siew Gek shrieked in an even more irate voice as she wobbled away, as fast as her partially bound lotus flower feet could allow, towards the family servant. "Ah Luan, go now, go upstairs and see that small mistress is okay!" demanded the Lady Boss.

"Oh no, yet another disaster!" mumbled Joo Neo, knowing full well that Gordon did not like Ah Luan to go upstairs before he is ready to rouse from bed. "Wait, Ah Luan! Here, take; take and wash. Later, put outside on the landing. I bring into the room for young Tuan[2]," said Joo Neo hastily as she gingerly placed the chamber pot on the marble floor. Joo Neo rushed back upstairs, avoiding her mother-in-law's glares.

"Sayang[3]," she said as she stroked her daughter's face with a damp towel. "Later, you go down and eat a soft boiled egg. Mummy will put sweet soya sauce when Mama is not looking, okay?"

---

2   Tuan is a Malay word which means Master (of the house).
3   Sayang is a Malay word which means "my love," a term of endearment used to address loved ones and children.

"I don't want! I want *roti prata* with sugar. Like Daddy bring me to Ceylon Road coffee shop. And with one tablespoon of Daddy's thick-thick milky coffee," said Lilian petulantly.

"Daddy not yet wake up, Sayang. You eat the egg, first. Mama happy, happy, then we go out to walk, walk. Buy you new hairband," said Joo Neo soothingly to her daughter.

"I don't want. I don't want!" retorted Lilian, all ready to embark on a tantrum.

"Okay, okay. No need to eat," replied Joo Neo hastily as she thought out her next move.

"I tell Mama you want to eat pork porridge with juicy meatballs, okay?" reasoned Joo Neo as she brushed her daughter's fringe away from her eyes, tucking them behind Lilian's ears. "Lilian don't want, Lilian eat bread with butter. Must be sweet-sweet," said Lilian firmly.

"I want to go down now! I want to drink Milo[4]," Lilian yelled as she leapt off the mattress of the single four-poster bed. "At least she seems … energetic," mouthed Joo Neo in a silent prayer that her mother-in-law would return her silk coat back on its wooden hanger, signifying an end to this bout of "illness." Siew Gek wielded her Chinese origins when it suited her, even though it was way too hot and humid to wear such a jacket in the tropics.

"I get the shivers when any of my precious family members are ill, and so should you!" Siew Gek would point an accusing finger at Joo Neo when she said that. "We keep ourselves warm against the damp winds which bring on

---

4   Milo is a chocolate drink, popular among young children.

the colds. And it is your fault, letting your daughter run around in short-sleeved pyjamas."

Even though it had been many decades since her match-made marriage to a well-to-do local Peranakan[5] family in Singapore, Siew Gek chose to drag out comparisons with her early childhood in Southern China, when her father was still as wealthy as her father-in-law, the days before the turmoil and famines, which resulted in another round of mass migrations from China to Southeast Asia and beyond.

Joo Neo scurried down after Lilian in hope that breakfast would resolve itself.

"Good morning, Mama," chirped Lilian, while she skipped towards her grandmother.

"Oh my darling granddaughter, Lilian okay already? Head no more pain, pain?" expressed Siew Gek with concern. "Lilian hungry, Mama. Lilian drink Milo and Mummy make bread with butter for Lilian. What day is it today, Mummy?" her little words all rushing to come out in one breath.

"You see, Mak, Lilian okay already. I make her breakfast. Lilian, you go and help Mama water the plants

5 Peranakans refers to the descendants of Chinese, Indian, and other merchants who married local women. It means "locally born." Whilst Peranakans adopted some of the practices and religions of their forefathers, the influence of the womenfolk created many cultural practices, including food and a unique fusion subculture. These marriages or unions between locals and travelling merchants carried on for only a couple of generations. Marriages of subsequent generations were mainly matchmade, with bride/bridegrooms from other Peranakan families or from their home countries rather than the local Malays, many of whom had converted to Islam.

outside," uttered Joo Neo, rushing into the kitchen before her mother-in-law could protest. Joo Neo hoped her teaspoon of sugar could be disguised by the thick spread of butter and be securely enveloped between the springy soft slices of the simple sandwich, its brown edges carefully trimmed and sides tucked in.

Her mother-in-law showed the beginnings of a smile as she shouted to Ah Luan for a pail of water. I must remember to buy the small pink plastic watering can for Lilian when I head to town next week, Joo Neo reminded herself.

"Really? Was I that spoilt?" exclaimed Lilian as Joo Neo recounted that difficult day whilst fondly cradling her first grandchild in her arms.

"Of course! Mama loved you so, so much, just as I love sweet, sweet Kelly today. And Kong Kong[6] loved you even more. Even while he was dying of liver cancer and unsteady on his feet, he bought you the largest Steiff teddy bear from Robinsons."

"You know, Lilian," continued Joo Neo, "at that time, Robinsons was the most prestigious department store, not just in Singapore, but Malaya too! Only British colonials and other people shopped there. But Ah Kong was not afraid of going in and buying you a present that his bosses bought for their children. At that time, Ah Kong was still a big shot[7]. He dressed up every morning in a crisp white shirt, and Mama personally ironed the collars to make sure they were stiff and folded straight and sharp, like a paper aeroplane. Ah Kong spoke the Queen's English which he

---

6   Kong Kong, or Ah Kong, was the term used as a reference to one's grandfather.
7   Big shot is a colloquial term for a person with authority or status.

studied in the missionary school, so his English bosses, they considered him one of their kind. And they would always boast about their children's birthday parties and what they bought. So Ah Kong also went to buy a special present for you when you turned five years old."

"What a pity! We threw Brownie teddy out when I was eighteen. Even though Brownie disintegrated and was stuffed into a pillowcase, he may still be a collector's item today." They both laughed gleefully, remembering how Lilian clung on to the yellowing pillowcase, pleading for yet another reprieve on the grounds that a waft of that familiar scent was the perfume which would lull her to sleep.

"You know, Lilian, when your Mama first proposed that your Papa and I consider adoption after we lost your older brother, I refused. I could not bear the thought of her insisting on following superstitious beliefs such as swaddling babies to keep them from being too active. Norman would be crying all the time and have angry red patches. I always unwound the thick cloth and dusted him all over with baby powder. Mama suspected that I defied her wishes and would come into the room and berate the confinement lady, accusing her of disobeying instructions. Mama would not let me bathe Norman for one whole month, saying that he would catch 'wind'[8]. When he was finally allowed to have a bath after one whole month, it seemed as though his forehead felt too warm, and he became so listless shortly after. I cried so much when Norman succumbed to pneumonia that I had no more tears left. Everyone said that I was a lousy mother and only brought bad luck to the family." Joo Neo was sobbing as she recalled that dark period in her past.

---

8   Wind was a generic term for colic.

"I wanted to throw myself in the well after your brother died, but your Daddy said that it was not my fault. He assured me that the next time, he would not allow the old lady to have her way, and that I could do whatever I wanted to ignore her demands and commands. It was just too late. No matter how we tried, there was no baby."

"I was so surprised then, when Ah Kong got so involved with our household matters. It was one of the rare times when he interfered with what he always termed as 'women affairs.' Ah Kong asked around, and our neighbours who had eight boys said that their relative in Malaya was willing to exchange their youngest girl for our neighbour's youngest boy. He sent Mama there to negotiate and ask if the toddler could come to our family, since the patriarch had two wives and it would only be a matter of time before one of them would give birth to a girl.

I was still not ready, but Ah Kong's word was law. When the neighbours brought you in from Malaya, you were already walking, and Mama could not swaddle you.

"You reminded Mama of her sisters in China, so fair and eyes that were not brown or black, but were just sparkly and bright, and smooth, smooth hair. 'Not tanned and so unChinese like her daughter-in-law,' Mama would proclaim to anyone within earshot, when Ah Kong was at work. Mama was always disdainful of our Peranakan roots. 'I am pure Chinese, from the Middle Kingdom,' she would always proclaim whenever one of our relatives questioned her unconventional ways or looks. So Mama was proud that you looked just like her and not me! My Malay blood, injected so many generations ago, still runs strong and obvious in my features, just like your daddy and Ah Kong." Joo Neo glanced at her daughter and realised that Lilian looked utterly surprised! "Sayang, Mummy did not explain everything to you when you were young, but you knew, didn't you?"

"Oh, Mummy, the girls in school would tease me unmercifully about my looks all the time. They said that you and Daddy picked me up from the side of the road. And my cousins always laughed at the way I wore the sarong kebaya[9]. They said that I looked

macham sinkeh[10]. I always suspected that maybe you were not my natural parents, but you and Daddy, Ah Kong and Mama loved me so much, and I did not really care because I always got new things, while many times my friends complained that they got the hand-me-downs from their elder siblings. I just thought that they were jealous and told tales. Don't worry, Mummy, I was just fascinated to hear about the past. You always spoke in snippets! And I did not want to irritate you by prodding," Lilian said, with a smile in her voice.

"Sayang, you will always be our number one and our adorable Lilian!" Joo Neo exclaimed.

"Somehow, when you came to us, we were only concerned about your well-being all the time. Then, it seemed so unnatural and awkward for me and Daddy to talk to you in detail about this. But remember, you had to take the oath of citizenship. You were born in Malaya,

---

9 Sarong kebaya was a favoured outfit of Peranakan ladies, comprising a top garment made out of Swiss voile, lavishly embroidered and fastened with three brooches attached together with chains. It is paired with a sarong, held up by a thick belt made of hammered silver or gold segments.

10 Sinkeh comprises two Hokkien vernacular words, "sin" meaning new and "keh" meaning guests, referring to new arrives from mainland China, just off the boat.

before Singapore and Malaysia separated. I thought Daddy explained that to you then."

"Yes, he did. Kind of. But you know Daddy. He just said that we had to go to a special office and I had to read some words, and then we would all go out to Spring Court Restaurant for my favourite roast chicken! In those days, things were so much simpler and straightforward. Though I always got what I asked for, in comparison with my friends, even I instinctively understood that there was a limit to what I can say or do. Just by looking at the faces of the elders! Whether they be Mama or you or Daddy! Once there will be a frown creasing the forehead or a dark face, that is when I know it is time to shut up and not push my luck. Cross that line, and the *rotan*[11] will emerge from nowhere!"

"But with Kelly, it will be different, Mummy. James and I have decided that, even though Kelly looks a bit like you and Daddy, we will explain to her as soon as she can understand," Lilian said unreservedly.

"Yes, I think that is the best way. Like myself and Daddy, you and James tried so hard. For so long. Just because Kelly may not have your fair skin and have such big brown eyes, it does not change anything."

"I am sure, Mummy, just like you and me," said Lilian. "And you are the best Mummy in the world. Kelly will have a Mama who she can take after. Not so sure if we want her to be like us though!" Lilian said playfully.

"James calls it 'feistiness under a cloak of femininity' but he knew what he was getting into!

---

11 Rotan was a thin cane used to discipline errant children.

He thinks that there is nothing less attractive than silliness, so I am lucky that he is the opposite of chauvinistic!" Lilian chortled, knowing full well that she stood on equal ground with her engineer husband.

"Well, he has to be strong, considering how tenacious you can be, until you get what you want on your own terms," Joo Neo rebuked Lilian. The selfsame tenacity caused a fellow lawyer to brand Lilian a rottweiler, or Rocky for short. Lilian's litigation clients even once asked her to "show her balls" to the other party and their lawyers, before Lilian had to remind him that the only round things she had were above her navel!"

"We Tan women have our own ways of winning battles, and even the war, sometimes with our opponents without even realising it," Joo Neo said strongly. "Remember the time when Mama said that you had to stop your ballet lessons because you always looked tired and sweaty when you reached home? Mummy sneakily brought you to Doctor Goh, after which he called Daddy to say that exercise was the most important thing to help you strengthen your lungs and body. So Daddy insisted that you should continue ballet because you enjoyed it so much, and it was good for you. Mama had to give in, and till today, you and I have our special secret. We will never tell anyone where we went and that we instigated Dr. Goh to make the call to Daddy!" The pair giggled again, happily.

Joo Neo passed those difficult days stoically, always trying to balance all the demands of the individuals in the strong household, especially that of an imperative mother-in-law. However, as the years passed, the two women found an equilibrium which worked. Siew Gek grudgingly conceded that Joo Neo was a good match for her son.

Though Joo Neo observed how the dishes were prepared and cooked for daily meals and festive occasions, she left all the savoury, time-consuming dishes in the good hands of her mother-in-law and their Hainanese cook. Joo Neo found her forte in baking. Enticing aromas and pretty biscuits emerged from the Baby Belling oven, the last gift from her generous father-in-law, which vied for space on the cement countertop.

"My daughter-in-law made them herself, with the best Cold Storage butter. Takes a lot of time, you know. And must watch so carefully. One minute still yellow, and the next minute, burnt already," said Siew Gek with a hint of pride in her voice, when visitors praised the crispy, buttery icing sugar cookies and reached out for more during Chinese New Year visits.

Among the last things which Siew Gek did, before the morphine she took to overcome the racking pains of cancer and made her bedbound, was to beckon Joo Neo to her carved wardrobe. She told Joo Neo to feel below her piles of neatly folded batik sarongs and pull out her famous black silk jacket.

Though now matt and frayed with use, the padding was still thick and intact. Secreted in the lining were chunky gold belts embossed with intricate designs, dangling gold earrings, and thick linked chains. "This is all 22-carat gold, Joo Neo. When Ah Kong gave me extra for housekeeping or did something to make me angry, he would give me money to buy jewellery. And each time I saved enough money, I would buy only gold. Now I am old, but you can use it for Lilian. If she wants to go overseas, you can sell. Or keep for her, so she will always remember her mama and that she has a legacy from the Tan family," Siew Gek's last instructions to her daughter-in-law were still fresh in her mind as Joo Neo felt the touch of trembling taut skin clasping her fingers and knuckles.

"Little Kelly also has crossed oceans, to be part of our Tan clan. She may not look like you or James, but she will be so much like us in many ways," said Joo Neo, as mother and daughter gently caressed Kelly's creamy milk-coffee cheeks. Kelly's pink lips pursed a little, corners upturned as if in agreement to her initiation to the fold of the women in the Tan family.

SARAH SOH

Lingua Franca

"Will it hurt?"

"Of course not."

The ear pick couldn't look more harmless. I chose a bamboo one—a beginner's choice—for his virginal ear canals. It's just a few inches long, slender, with a tiny, shallow scoop nodding at one end. The other end is decorated with two wooden beads painted to look like a fat little man in a bright kimono—the sort of cutesy flourish nineteen-year-old Asian girls like me are supposed to love.

I prefer stainless steel myself.

It was, I'll admit, a tactical error. I'd thought cutesy kimono man would be disarming, maybe it just made the whole thing more alien to him.

"Don't bring an *angmo* home!" had been my mother's parting shot at the airport. I never understood why Singaporeans used the Hokkien word *angmo*—"red-haired"—to refer to Caucasians when redheads form such a small proportion of the population. Mum had called out the words to me as I was leaving Singapore to spend the next four years studying *angmo* words, eating *angmo* food, surrounded by *angmos,* in Scotland, the country with the largest percentage of natural redheads in the world—the epicentre of literal *angmo*-ness.

So statistically, the fact that the naked *angmo* in my bed actually has red hair isn't that big of a deal.

Confronted with the ear pick, Steve's face has that empty look people get when they don't understand my accent. It shouldn't frighten me, but it does. It makes me wonder what I've done to make the humanity go out of their eyes.

To be fair, he's one of the good ones. He's trying to figure out how to wriggle out of this ear pick business without offending me and denigrating the ancient civilisation of which I am the sole representative around these parts. Poor bastard's hemmed in on all sides: political correctness on the left flank, post-colonial guilt on the right, self-preservation at the rear ruling out a full surrender. I shouldn't be so hard on him. He could have told me to sod off, but it's 1999—almost the new millennium—and modern British boys embrace diversity and respect cultural differences. I'm probably taking advantage.

Still, I sit back and let him sweat.

I'm across the room but there is no escaping the sheer mass of him, a gigantic ginger teddy bear of a man sprawled across my single bed, head resting on Ralph Fiennes's arse, orange hair clashing mightily with the doomed desert sunset of *The English Patient* poster on my wall. There's nothing heroic about Steve's body—it's all rolling plains and mellow slopes, muscle and heat padded over by evenings of vinegar-sodden chips and cheap Student Union lager.

The goose pimples on my legs remind me I'm wearing nothing but Steve's T-shirt, just like the girls in the movies. It's snowing outside. The white powder will be grey slush by tomorrow. I saw snow for the first time last winter. That winter jacket I bought with Mum in Singapore was all wrong. It's big and plasticky, in a tired-salmon colour

Mum liked—I feel like a stupid foreigner every time I wear it. That first snow, though, I didn't care. I ran outside with another international student. It was crisp, quiet—we were the only ones left in the student halls at Christmas. She taught me how to make a snowman. I'd always thought that my first snowman would be jolly and fat, white—like in the books—but there wasn't enough snow and we ended up with a stunted, brown snow-pygmy, bruised with mud and grass.

I turn to look at the phone on my desk. No, it's too late in Singapore. Hospital visiting hours are over. They'll probably call tomorrow, hold the phone to Grandma's ear. Then I'll have to speak.

Something must have shown on my face.

"Get in here." He opens his great big teddy bear arms and in I go. "This ear-pick business … it's not some Freudian penis-envy bollocks, is it?"

"No, Steve, I'm not envious of your pe—just how do you manage to insert genitalia into every single conversation?"

I'm a little startled he mentioned Freud, but I should really stop underestimating him. Just because he studies engineering at the lesser school in the city doesn't mean he's stupid.

"What's going on then?"

"Nothing."

He looks around my bare, boxy room and finally sees what's missing—there are no stacks of books or paper, just a single dog-eared sheet on my desk.

"Don't you have an essay due, JT?"

"In two days."

"How much have you got done?" He's a conscientious student himself, lesser university or not. I respect that.

I say nothing.

"I thought ..." He looks unsure, a rare occurrence. "You said the scholarship people were already put out with you."

Put out. A mite miffed perhaps. Delicious understatement. What would the Brits say to impending Armageddon? *Well, chaps, looks like there's a spot of trouble ahead, but I daresay we've had a good innings.*

I suppose I could tell him that writing three thousand words on "Eighteenth-Century English Satire" makes no sense when I can't even muster up three Hokkien ones to say goodbye to my grandmother.

It's too warm in bed. I extricate myself and start plucking clothes off the floor.

"Where are you going?"

"For a walk."

"Well, don't go by The Mound, they've closed it. VIP visit."

"Who?"

"Our very own Prince William." The bed creaks as Steve leans his bulk forward. "Word is, His Royal Highness is thinking of parking his Royal Arse-ness at your uni for the next four years."

The future King of England in my school?

It chafes that people tell Steve these things and not me, and he doesn't even go here. Now he is up and by the sink, splashing his face, not a stitch on but entirely comfortable in his skin. People on my floor seem to accept his right to be here without question. I'd come back from class to find him in the common room, chatting to someone I'm barely on nodding terms with. He'd look up from his bag of crisps and the armchair where he's settled like a mountain, lift an orange-stubbled chin and go, "Alright?"

The mountain is frowning. "Your sink's not draining. I could have a go at unblocking it, if you'd like."

"It's alright, I'll just call Maintenance."

"You'll wait all day for that lot to show up. It's no trouble, I'll—"

"No! Really, thank you, Steve, but—"

His face falls. I've hurt him, but how do I explain that just because he's a plumber's son doesn't mean he has to stay a plumber's son?

I pull off his T-shirt and toss it at him. "Here. Put some clothes on before you scandalise the neighbours."

He's looking at me now, sink forgotten. Someone like me might be discounted on sight, condescended to, politely excluded, talked over, but a naked girl is a naked girl. I feel visible, having corporealised from ghost to objectified female. There is something quite reassuring about this—the equalising force, the democratising might, the all-transcending power bestowed by a pair of bare tits.

"Forget the ear pick." I start bundling up against the cold. The tired-salmon jacket makes swishy noises as I zip it up. "Let's go prince-stalking."

*

My grandmother used to pick my ears for me.

She lived in a sky-blue house on the edge of the rainforest. These villages don't exist in Singapore anymore, their rural occupants long evicted and moved to the newly built towns where people are stacked on top of each other in concrete boxes piled ten, twenty-high, towers so crowded with city heat and noise that the only way to breathe is to seal yourself behind darkened glass and inhale the coolant-scented air recycled by an air-conditioner.

Grandma brought up ten children in a wooden house that had four bedrooms, a double-bay outhouse, and an outdoor kitchen built for noisy, smelly stir-fries.

It didn't look like much. The tops of the thin walls were nothing but widely spaced grilles so that the air heated by so many bodies could rise and escape. The roof was rusty, corrugated metal. When the monsoon rain came down on it, the noise was tremendous, joyous, like the sky was having a great big piss after holding it in for too long.

The grounds felt huge and wild to city children. My cousins and I, freed from small apartments, ran barefoot everywhere, climbed trees, staged stick-sword fights, and generally behaved like little weekend savages.

When I was eight, my mother—who spoke Mandarin, Hokkien, and no English—gave me English storybooks to help improve my grades. The dolls, teddy bears, and golliwogs in them were always picnicking and picking berries in the English countryside, so I thought I would recreate a picnic scene on Grandma's lawn. I prepared jam sandwiches, chocolate biscuits, and tea. I didn't know what a "blackberry hedge" was, but Grandma had an old, knobbly rambutan tree, heavy with hairy, angry-red fruit. I plucked the reddest, roundest rambutans to join my bountiful picnic on the blue gingham cloth.

But this was Singapore, not England. The sun was hot, tea made me even hotter; ants came up from the grass, overran my gingham mat, and attacked my food when they weren't attacking me. Defeated, I retreated under the cool eaves of the house and tried to resume my picnic on the concrete porch.

I heard a noise and looked up—you could always hear Grandma before you saw her, the brisk *swish-swish* of a woman with ten children and even more grandchildren. She made a small, trim figure in her *samfoo* with its Mandarin-collared blouse and practical trousers, her hair neatly oiled and pinned back.

Have you eaten? she said in Hokkien. This was her usual greeting. In our Chinese household, there were no hugs or kisses, no I-love-yous. Food was love.

Usually, I would reply, Yes, I have eaten or No, not yet—that was the extent of my Hokkien. This time, I had no words to explain; I was about to continue my now-dishevelled picnic, so I waved mutely at the food.

Grandma sighed, lowered herself onto my mat, and regarded me with patient perplexity. She turned her gaze to the picnic where it lingered for a moment, then she pointed at the sandwich and said distinctly, "*Mi-pau.*"

Bread. She was trying to teach me Hokkien! This one was easy—it sounded like the Mandarin word. I repeated the sound.

She pointed at the tea. "*Teh.*" This one was easy too—just like the English word.

Rambutan was next. "*Ang-mo-tan.*" Harder, but still recognisable from the Mandarin word. "Red-haired-pellet"—exactly what the fruit looked like.

"Ma!" My mother was standing just outside the door to the porch. She said something to Grandma that made her hurry inside. Before I knew it, Mum had my chin in her hand. Her Mandarin was low and urgent. "The next time Grandma tries to teach you Hokkien, play dumb, okay?"

I didn't understand.

"There's no future in Hokkien. Save your clever little head for English, do you understand, Jia Ting?"

It occurred to me then that my parents had never spoken Hokkien in front of me, though I caught lashes of it sometimes, the pungent, nasal tones muffled by their closed bedroom door.

"Do you want to end up like Grandma? Look at this *dump!*"

I looked around, at the sky-blue house, at the tops of the walls where there was nothing but metal grille, at the underside of the rusty, corrugated roof. I still loved it, but she had torn a little hole in my love and doubt was seeping in.

By the time Grandma came back, the ants had found my picnic again and ruined it beyond repair. Only the rambutans survived. Grandma brushed the ants off one, twisted the shell open in a deft motion, and offered me the perfect white flesh. Cool sweetness flooded my mouth. "Come, don't be sad. I'll pick your ears for you," she said, or I thought she said.

Some nights, I still dream of it: my head on her lap; the sunlight misty through the purple mosquito net we sheltered under, the smell of rambutan on her hands; the spine-tingling tickle when the pick dipped into my ear, brushing past little hairs; the answering relief of the bamboo scrapping skin—loud, like rushing air.

*

It had stopped snowing by the time we got out of the Halls. This far up north, when you're lucky enough to see the sun at the right hour, the light is a warm and languid yellow, like golden syrup. The city is drenched in its sweetness— everything glows. I hold on to Steve's arm to keep from slipping on the cobbles. The snow is already melting, but it's covering the usual dog shit, club flyers, and cigarette butts on the pavement.

There's a more direct route, but we take the longer one which leads us down the main arterial road before opening left into the heart of the city and a spectacular view of the Castle.

The Castle is not a fairytale fantasy with slender towers and spindly spires but a fortress, a twelfth-century military complex sprawled atop a dark mass of craggy volcanic rock that seems to have erupted from the earth into the middle of a polite Georgian city. Below the Castle, a generous spread of gardens, now blanketed white, slopes up to meet the main shopping street of the city. Here, the locals go about their business, on foot and in trams, cars, and buses, oblivious to the hulking fortress behind them. There's a malty fullness in the air, especially strong when the wind blows west from the distillery a few miles away.

Something about the improbability of this scene, the sheer otherness of it, thrills me. We pause so I can drink it in. When I'm ready, I tug on Steve's arm and off we go up the street to our destination. The Castle may be here, but the prince we are seeking is elsewhere.

We join the small cluster of people waiting some distance from the entrance of New College. It's a group of mixed ages, surprising, given whom we are waiting to see. The mood is relaxed and non-committal, which suggests that most of the group had joined the cluster after chancing upon it. We don't speak to each other much, just stamp our feet and blow into our hands to ward off the cold, occasionally poking our heads over the police officers' shoulders, even though there is nothing new to see.

Something suddenly occurs to me.

"You don't think," I turn to Steve, "he could have gotten into my uni the usual way … with his grades I mean?"

"Probably not," Steve shrugs. "He doesn't need to. Put it this way—his gran's face is on the money."

I wallow in this for a while. I think about how hard I had to work to earn the grades and the scholarship, about everything I had given up to get here. I think about how I don't fit in here, how I don't fit in back home anymore and might never do again.

I look at the little group huddled here, waiting in the cold just to catch a glimpse of him, at the barricades and cones set up to seal off the road, at the policemen in hi-vis jackets scattered around, their faces professional and impassive. All this fuss, just for one person. Steve's cheeks have gone ruddy from the chill, giving him a healthy patina. His eyes are placid; I'm the only angry person here.

An elderly Asian couple, obviously tourists, approaches the junction near us. She is brisk in her movements, striding ahead of her husband while he lingers behind, raising a complicated-looking camera to snap a picture ever so often. When she finally doubles back for him, they confer over a map, seeming to disagree. Moments later, she is headed uphill towards us with the same quick stride, map in hand.

I stare as she nears. The similarities between her and my grandma are superficial but enough to give my heart a little squeeze. They are both small, tidy women with delicate features. This old lady too, has her hair pulled back tight against her scalp. What would Grandma think of Europe, I wonder? Would she hate the cold, or would she stick her tongue out to catch snowflakes when no one's looking?

The old lady ignores Steve and starts talking to me almost before she reaches me. The way she leans in and looks me full in the face tells me that she is relieved to have found me and expects me to understand and help her.

I can't. She speaks what sounds like a Chinese dialect, while I know only English and enough Mandarin to speak to my mother and pass the required school exams. I try to bridge the gap with my halting pidgin Mandarin and even some English, but she continues to pelt rapid-fire phrases at me, getting louder and louder, an expression of disbelief and betrayal dawning on her face. She's a stranger, but I feel like I've failed her. Steve looks like he badly wants to intervene.

Her husband catches up to us just as the Rolls Royce pulls up to New College. A tall man steps out and turns to wave at our group. It is not the blond, beautiful prince who takes after his glamorous late mother, but his much plainer father. In person, he is better looking than on film—his ears are less prominent, his nose less long. He beams at us, eyes crinkling like he is truly glad we are here.

"Prince Charles," the old lady says distinctly, waving at him.

"Prince Charles," I concur, waving as well, despite myself.

A few seconds, and he is gone, swallowed into the bowels of the building. The little group disperses quickly, while Steve and I try our best to give the old couple directions to where they want to go using the universal language of mime.

"My sources were wrong," Steve says. "Wrong prince. Where next?"

"I have to go back. There's a phone call I have to make."

*

I go over the piece of paper one last time before placing the international call.

My mother gets down to business almost immediately. "Grandma is awake but she's on a lot of painkillers, so she's not going to respond to you. Right now, we're just trying to keep her comfortable, do you understand?"

I manage a noise of assent.

"Alright, I'll hold the phone to her ear for a few minutes. But if she looks tired, I'll have to end the call."

"Of course, Ma."

I've been waiting days for this moment but when it comes, I feel caught off guard. The laboured breathing that has travelled thousands of miles to reach me sounds too clumsy to be my graceful Grandma. I smooth out the paper and begin to read. These are words deemed suitable to comfort a dying person, a respected elder, researched and written in my shaky, half-forgotten Mandarin, with the Hokkien pronunciation noted next to each character. I have no idea if the translation works that way, but it was the best I could do.

My mouth contorts itself into shapes that feel alien and wrong, and the sounds they mould lurch forth and stumble, malformed and ashamed of themselves. Still, I reach the bottom of the page too soon.

Outside, the damn snow is falling again, silent as usual.

The roar of rushing air through the receiver is loud and hollow.

So I try again, in the only language I have left.

I tell her it's cold here, so cold that five of the blankets we use back home wouldn't be enough.

But snow is beautiful. Tomorrow, I tell her, I will make her a snowman. Hasn't she seen snowmen on TV?

I tell her that Prince William might come study at my school. Wouldn't it be a funny thing to tell your neighbours that your granddaughter goes to the same school as the grandson of the Queen of England?

I tell her they feed me well here, too well, that the portions are huge, I'm getting fatter by the day, so she needn't worry about me, though I miss her spring rolls.

I tell her I miss her sky-blue house, that metal roof that made it sound like the sky was pissing when it rained.

I lie back on the bed, the receiver now warm against my ear, just listening to my grandmother breathe.

My mother picks up the receiver to tell me Grandma has fallen asleep. I thank her politely and hang up. It's easy to stay lying down.

I hear the door of my neighbour's room open, a familiar voice, then a knock on my door. Of course, it's Steve.

"You can pick my ears if you want."

I shake my head.

"Tea, then."

"Yes, please."

He doesn't make the tea right away. He puts his arms around me while we watch the snow cover the hilltops.

MOAZZAM SHEIKH

Sunshine

Dinner done, table cleaned, plates stacked away in the sink along with forks and knives; I anticipate Jojo's second wind before he finally agrees to be led to his bed. He's at the moment in the bathroom with his mother brushing his teeth as hurriedly as possible while she tries her best to reinforce the value of slowing down, self-discipline, and healthy gums. He has internalised flossing as something that's meant to create a rift between children and parents. In the meantime, I use that interregnum to check the news on my laptop, flitting from one website to another—celebrities dying, protests in Paris and elsewhere, politicians' promises and scandals, stock market plunging, rents rising, homelessness epidemic, opioid crisis, pedestrians getting hit by careless Uber drivers, drive-by shootings, Venice Film Festival winners, accusations of sexual harassment, swamis finding cure for a virus in cow urine, a temporary ceasefire, children in detention centres, young boys being blindfolded, a mass shooting in Texas. Feeling disheartened, depressed, even I move away. I am scared, startled.

"Turn off the lights, Dad!" he orders excitedly.

"Hey, hey, let mom settle down first," I say.

"Gotcha," he says as he exits the bathroom, looking all serious, like a miniature Toshiro Mifune acting the part of a samurai. Luna closes the door. Luna, that's not her real name, but when I met her, her friends called her Luna, so it has stuck. I pretend to look busy wiping the counter area around the sink and burners, putting salt and pepper shakers and other paraphernalia in their proper spots, so he'd give me an extra reprieve. Don't get me wrong. Of course I not only cherish the time spent with my boy—he's eight now—I love every minute of our nightly ritual even as I feel guilty; he should be getting into bed a bit on the earlier side. That's why I let him sleep late in the morning while Luna or I prepare his breakfast and school lunch. I know how to get him to school on time, which worries Luna because she believes I drive a bit recklessly. Perhaps, certainly faster than her, but it is more like I know which alternative streets to take if the usual ones are crowded. The issue of him getting to bed late remains a source of mild friction and lighthearted bickering between Luna and me. She concedes, a little grudgingly, when I proclaim how important this playtime, this bonding between father and son, is. But we are also trying to teach him forbearance, which he seems to value less and less since he's entered third grade. He was born with a backup supply of energy which he enjoys unleashing on Luna and me at whim. Luna is offended when I bring up my theory about children as being hyenas. Unless taught otherwise, they'll nibble on their parents' ankles till they buckle. It gets worse usually if one of the parents is too soft without being able to implement early discipline. The more the parents treat their children like a "*heina*," the more "heinous" they can become.

"Go change into your 'jamas,'" I remind him as I do almost every night.

"After we play," he tries to assert.

"Nope! You change first, then we play. Or it's bedtime now," I say with a mixture of authority and mirth.

Protesting, he goes to his room, but I can hear the sound in his head going *okay, okay, garbanzo bean!* I break into a smile. Luna's out of the bathroom, smiling too, shaking her head. I am done with the kitchen. Not spic-and-span, but good enough, good enough for Luna to lord it over her sister whose partner can barely boil water for tea.

He's changed. She's grabbed her book, Dostoyvsky's *The Idiot*, which she's restarted after a hiatus of a month. I close the door to our bedroom, so the noise of our horsing around won't bother her. Even then, she's bound to reprimand us a few times *hey guys keep it down, it's late, we have neighbours downstairs trying to sleep.* Jojo and I shrink ourselves, snigger or giggle when we hear Luna's admonishment. I notice that the tone of his skin colour changes. He stands, arms akimbo, in the doorframe daring me. I dare back. There's a smile lurking behind our sternness, like sunshine obscured by a passing cloud. I am not capable of keeping a straight face for long or appearing stolid à la Alain Delon like in *Le Samourai*. "Lights out!" I announce a clarion call. We flick the light switches off near us and the darkness descends.

The war begins. The entire area stretching from our kitchen, the short corridor from the entrance that brings you into the kitchen, and the long, combined dining and living room turns into a war zone, except for what little light sneaks in from outside despite the drawn curtains. Even real wars, I realise, never have total darkness. It takes time for the eyes to adjust. We are both good at hiding, with a bullet made of foam lodged in our respective nerf pistols. I summon a semblance of synchronicity between my mind and heart. In order to make our game convincing and fun, we pretend to hate the guts of our enemy. We take cover. I usually hide in the small corridor leaning against one of our bookshelves or squat by the closet facing the front door. I rarely go into the extra bathroom. Because if he comes pursuing me there, I am always nervous about him panicking and dashing into a sharp edge. He, on the other hand, likes to hide in the living room area because it gives him a sense of real-time action where he can hide behind a tree (sofa), a bush (table), or a bombed army truck (island counter). He crouches, lies down on the carpet, and crawls from the single sofa to the three seater; then from there, inching his way to zero in on his prize victim, to under the dining table. From there he rushes to his side of the island counter. I can hear his movements and by then I know exactly where he is at a given moment. I have a good "soldier sense," I commend myself, feeling embarrassed. I know he's going through similar realisations about his soldier sense but without any negative emotions, without any idea what real wars do to its victims and perpetrators. I imagine his grown-up face, muddied and intense as if he is on a movie set, somewhere out in a real location like the countryside of Morocco or the Arizona desert, along with his soldier buddies ready to charge the enemy. I shake my head, snapping out of my world of fear. I am grinning now, stifling my laugh, as I picture him, as if the room was awash with light, his endearing self led by a primaeval instinct for survival with a modern-day weapon of destruction, his cherished toy. Even though I resisted, I had to yield and get him his gun from Target for his friend's birthday party in the pristine Golden Gate Park.

Currently, he's obscured by a bookshelf that holds most of my fiction in translation collection, literary criticism, nothing too heavy that could hurt him if a book is to fall over, and if I were to come forward in order to cross over to the kitchen area—there's about six feet long path between the corridor wall and the isle counter—I will have exposed myself to his shot, though he misses often. I wonder if he's got a grin or a smirk on his face too? Earlier when we dared each other, I believed we both smiled, but sometimes I am not too sure about him. The thought that I can't be a good reader of my child's face saddens me. Sometimes, I suspect, there's no smile crouching behind his all-too-serious-for-a-combat look. Do I exaggerate? Maybe he does smile. When I summon an image of his, it resists stability, constantly metamorphosing, wobbling. Soldiers, or perhaps killers, don't smile, don't melt from the internal heat of hatred. They are supposed to be cold-blooded evil. But, on the screen at least, they smirk, cackle, guffaw, taunt, roar, right? It gives me a shudder. Admirably, he shows patience and, influenced by me, sits tight in one spot a long moment or two before skittering off to his next bunker or hideaway. Sometimes he retreats also, believing it to be a strategic move to lure me in, setting up a classic trap. It's easy for me to zone out when surrounded by silence and darkness. Two prerequisites to lure a nightmare when you sleepwalk.

Jojo's fascination with guns and shooting has taken me by surprise. It is all too sudden. Realising the power our national culture has on children, not to mention grown-ups who should know better, I made an early effort to introduce my son to the world of nonviolence or anti-violence, to the world of love and art. I exposed him to rock and roll, from Chuck Berry to John Lennon, to The Supremes to David Bowie to Annie Lennox. I told him that one of my girlfriends before I met his mother, was in love with Annie Lennox. I take him to local bookstores and public libraries, expose him to the world cinema with a child protagonist such as *Pathar Pancholi* and *400 Blows*. I think I regretted making him watch Tarkovsky's *Ivan's Childhood*, which left him disturbed, but he really loved De Sica's *The Bicycle Thieves*. He also loved some of the Iranian

films, with children lead nonactors. Sitting in a café with
him once, a middle-aged man's head turned towards us in
shock as Jojo unconsciously blurted out the opening riff
of *Satisfaction* as if his riff could bring the whole structure
down. Jojo kept humming unaware, the stranger's head
turned back, and I buried my head into my book gleefully.
I feel proud of the house I have been building for my boy. I
signal to my colleagues and other parents that it is possible
to build a different world. Not alone but with a little help
from others.

But the walls I build around him turn out to be, as
if, made of sand. For they cannot shield him from the
onslaught of rocks thrown at him which he brings home
after playdates, all from good families. Most kids his age
have been exposed to the world of violence and hatred via
various means of entertainment and electronic gadgets.
Despite the parents' denial and wringing of the hands, I
call it wilful complicity. Luna tries to knock some sense
into me. Says I have messed-up notions of how children
should be raised due to, perhaps—she makes an interesting
leap here—my own childhood trauma. She certainly has
a point regarding my convoluted convictions even if they
don't appear to me to be so convoluted. Why complain
about the world and the horror it unleashes on people if we
don't even want to change it? Talking about trauma, I want
to draw her attention to the possibility of why a trauma
cannot be from one's adult life instead? Why do we always
connect the two: childhood and trauma?

Others too tell me I worry unnecessarily, see the world
through bleak lenses. Instead of worrying and worrying
and fearing the world, they advise, enjoy the time spent
with your son. I know I can't change the world but it makes
me angry that even the smaller world around me is not in

my control, so I can't help but worry for my kid. That's why I love the time I spend with him playing games that make him happy, though I still believe in having some control over the smaller world around me and that's why I try my best to minimise the introduction of violence into his beautiful, still-forming mind. That's why, although I enjoy playing this game with him, I much more love wrestling with him afterwards. He relishes it when I throw a blanket on him, as if I am kidnapping him, and loves fighting back, punching and kicking, while I tell him to cool it since he can hurt me. I want to teach him the value to know that it is okay to hit back sometimes and when it is also okay to not hit back sometimes. When I am hurt and I choose to wince or go *ouch!* he stops and comes over to kiss the very spot he's caused pain to. It's never serious and I exaggerate. It's a sight to behold when he showers affection. Luna says that's his innate nature and it will remain intact despite the worldly influence. I like to believe it's my mentoring or at least partially.

The news of gun violence in America and elsewhere disturbs me, hurts my innards, so whenever I juxtapose him with guns or violence in general, I lose perspective. My projections run wild. I see him as a misogynist in the making and I start cursing under my breath at America's right of centre tilt, prayers in schools, and action movies. About school prayers, a close friend argues it's good for moral grounding. He, too, has a point. Kids these days take everything for granted. Children of affluence, a sociologist coined the term. They should learn to be thankful. And patient. I tell myself it's working, the patience part. The thankful part? I am not too sure. But I can't do it alone. Luna doesn't believe in my parenting philosophy. She doesn't believe in worrying. She believes in love though. Love alone is not enough, I say. She says it is. That's the only difference at the end, she says. Who lives to see the end?

Every once in a while, I catch myself running the most freakish scenario in my head: My son having grown up a loner, introverted, angry, unloved, unsexed, intoxicated with guns, normalising male angst, pimples and halitosis, obsessed with revenge, one of his exes, a redhead, blue-eyed trash from Modesto, cries on the phone with me harping on his callosity, his cleaning out her savings and absconding, and now all the major TV channels are flooded with the headlines of him walking into a middle school, spraying bullets everywhere, killing and hurting several students. Dizzy, I can't breathe, drop the phone; a tight knot forming in my stomach. I howl. I am yelling at my wife *Didn't I warn you, didn't I say something like this would happen?* I am startled by a phone ring. The police, a journalist, my brother from Austin, Texas, a friendly neighbour, lawyer. There's a knock on the door. My wife is screaming, banging her fists against a hard surface. I breathe in and out but only molten iron wafts. The sound is from inside the TV, the newscasters' office phones and fax machines and printers at work. There's chaos and police cars with flashing lights, cops running, taking cover. A unit of SWAT team. Helicopters. The announcer, full of mixed emotions, stares at the screen to announce, with gravity in his baritone voice, *The shooter goes missing!* I am relieved and hurt beyond words at the same time. I bang my head against the wall.

He's bumped into the dining table. My reverie evaporates. He hasn't *ouched*. I wait. If I talk, that'll get him mad because he'll know my hiding position. We'll have to start all over again. I try to contain the pain in my heart at the thought of my son in pain from bumping. I send a silent prayer his way. My wife and a few of my close friends tell me that I worry too much about losing him to the world once he's eighteen, once he's left the house for college. He'll be sold into the slavery of the modern corporate world. He'll end up selling his soul to Starbucks or Amazon. I, his Yaqoub, his Jacob, will miss him terribly, go blind from weeping and grieving incessantly. I breathe, exhale, thankful he hasn't winced in pain, a tough cookie that he is, he worries me because I think he has learnt to hold physical pain unless, of course, it's beyond what he can bite. Then he wants the world to weep for him instead. I don't like that. I tell him it's okay to weep or cry. Don't hold it in. Because that turns into aggression, unnecessary anger, which then can erupt in wrong places, unleashed on innocents, mostly women, caring people, people you actually love. *Be a pussy, don't be a dick* I want to elucidate. I will when he's a little older. I am still trying to mould him and I am hopeful, but when I look around the world, pessimism and fear take over. I decide to test his alertness or take advantage of his distraction caused by the bumping when I come out of the corridor to shelter behind the other side of the isle counter. His bullet whizzes past me missing my ear by an inch. I duck and I am safe. For the time being. I feel insulted and infuriated by the bullet. I see it not coming from him but the world. A teasing note about things to come. I block it out, the thought, the premonition.

"Did I get you?" he asks, revealing his location.

I hold my breath, signalling his bullet missed me. The battle is on. Now it's a matter of combat as we are both in the same room. From now on, we both peek out with the nerf gun, aimed, because the moment of locking the enemy in your imaginary reticule is too short. You must

fire on impulse. Reluctance will get you killed. Here's the
catch we both have to wrestle with. We're not supposed
to aim the face—that's our morality test in the midst of
an immoral game, though here it's based on the idea that
playing shouldn't end up in injury—but it's precisely the
face that's visible at first, so we lean towards hesitation,
conditioned to find the outline of our shoulders or arms.
We bob up and down like floating pieces of cork in water.
Bullets whiz by us. While I dunk, he moves swiftly to his
right without a rustle, and hiding behind a chair, he shoots
at my left shoulder when I arise looking for him where I
thought he'd still be.

"Did I get you this time?"

I fall and moan, "Yes, son, you did!"

"Yeah!" he ululates his victory.

"That's the exact opposite of the Rostam and Sohrab
story," I tease.

"What?"

"Just kidding."

Now the second part starts. Luna calls from the
bedroom excitedly, "You got dad?" but he doesn't listen
or doesn't care to reply, running to his bed. I read too
much into this. He's already devalued female participation,
feminist interruption as his subconscious mind sees it. Part
of me wants to tell him to answer his mother, but I remain
quiet. I feel complicit in fostering a misogynist behaviour.
I take too long to ponder. The moment has passed. I crawl
on my elbows and knees, injured, bleeding, fighting till the
last breath, chasing after my shooter, howling, "I'm coming.
Your bullets can't finish me off." I am not fighting for my

own vanity but the honour of motherland. I am inside his dark room. He's hiding against a wall. I sit scanning the room. He ambushes me from behind as I half-expected, his skinny but strong frame clinging to my back wrestling me to the ground. We take turns subduing each other. He's getting wilder and stronger day by day and I am worried I won't be able to tame his flailing and kicking limbs, afraid we won't be able to play this game one day. The thought makes me forlorn. He wiggles out of my grasp. Or I let him taste that power. I am not sure. I suspect it is both. He picks up a white pillow and hits me with it. I defend with my arms a few times, but he finally whacks me over the head; mildly astonished, I wonder how something as light as stuffed with feathers can hurt and shock one's senses. I look for another pillow and reach for one. I am already panting, unable to match his frenzy and excitement. Substituting his pillow with a blanket, our ritual enters its final phase. It's inevitable that I bring into play my natural advantage, my size as I stretch the blanket over him to make him cower, instinctively, a natural response from a child who's not sure how to handle a calamity descending upon his tiny self but is ready to assert, ballooning, like in TV cartoons from the 50s and 60s, deflecting the fatherly onslaught, flexing his inexperienced muscles. Separated by a thin wall, we can't see each other's expression as our eyes adjust to the lack of light. I wish I could read his mind then, the other side of the sunshine. While he thrashes about, a tiger caught in a snare, I cherish the time my fingers, my chest, my knees can feel the contours of his body, its energy, its alacrity, excitement, and terror. He's trying his best to escape the blanket and my hold, but due to his age and size, he's learning I am much bigger than him. I worry he'll suffocate. He knows his best weapon is persistence, knows he'll wear me down—that's the hope every victim has, but sometimes things don't work out that way. The aggressor wins, as he learns to slow down, he has more at his disposal, to do partnerships with the powerful, to break the spirit of the oppressed, he can lay and delay the siege, regroup to pounce again. To blame the victim for the violence. I do the same. I pant, I force a momentary truce, I dodge his blows. Then I come down with an exaggerated force to overwhelm him, remind him of his smallness so he'll surrender or back off, and then, in a moment of pure intoxication, I go all out. I have retreated into my childhood, or innocence, and I work myself into believing I have Jojo's body and energy. We are going at each other nonstop, muscle for muscle, bone for bone, blow for blow and I have lost track of time, not even aware of how long have I been doing this, but it seems like a long time has passed—days, months, years?— because not only do I feel spent, I feel I have aged, and when I attempt to pronounce his name, I don't recognise my voice, or his name ... *was it Jojo or Yoyo?* ... that's the voice of an old man; a man with a double chin, a potbelly, sagging leg muscles, stooped shoulders, which when I try to straighten makes me cry in pain, which elicits a concerned inquiry from Luna, who asks in her fatigued voice, "Are you okay?" though she knows what I am doing. It's her way to assert her will on me, remind me who's saner and who's gone bonkers; it's her way to tell me that's enough for today, but I am confused, lost for words, don't understand her behaviour, so lackadaisical, I can't explain what has transpired here while she was busy reading *One Hundred Years of Solitude*, the tragedy that has befallen us. I am stunned into silence and can't form a sentence to tell her why Jojo is not inside the blanket anymore. Even when she is in her room, she is here holding a small mirror to my face. I am not interested in another man's wrinkled face and unkempt hair. I am interested in my son. He was here, just a while ago. I can still smell his unique scent. Where did he go? When did he leave? Is he in the shower? He's nowhere near me, he's nowhere around the house; however, his traces linger, clues left behind on purpose to keep me hooked; has he melted into a memory? His childhood so fleeting has escaped my size, power, hold, and my love, my paranoia. It's just a nightmare, I console myself. I even run my hand over the holes in the blanket I have mended from time to time. There's no way. I don't know how to break that news to her. I can't find him inside the blanket, not even inside the patterns and colours. She'll kill me. I have looked everywhere even after having stayed inside the dark canopy for what seems like one hundred years. I fear that reality, its recognition, its admission, will break her heart, demolish her as it is breaking me into pieces, muscle by muscle, bone by bone, splitting one vein at a time ... even as I continue to collect myself. Or should I keep it a secret from her?

SUDEEP SEN

Gold Squares on Muslin

1

I admire her crisp off-white muslin—it is sheer and full
of well-worn elegance. It has—spread sparsely over its
cotton—scatters of delicate little squares of gold, zari
woven by hand, intricately, with care, two generations
ago.

These little pieces of gold spark narratives—revealing
intimate secrets of family, motherhood, and friendship—
stories hitherto hidden in a silo, secured steadfastly within
the hierarchy of starch, grace, and poise.

But this sari is also wrapped around someone whose
body is not quite there. Invisibly present and distracted,
she remarks to me—

"Look at the clock, it is so late."

2

The clock shows different times on the same dial—
reminiscing two separate moments on two separate
continents, simultaneously. The same time is two different
times for the two of us. And yet we are part of the same
story.

The slender hands move with mechanical precision,
not mapping the irregular heart and pulse beats that burn
constantly inside my body. The clock hands appear to move
fast, or not at all—and that is the fate of our histories.

3

Outside, I can hear the breeze gathering force over the waves as the tides prepare for the evening, their crests rising higher and higher. They make insistent surf noises, as each crown of white foam releases a strong scent of seaweed and salt. This is enough to make me intoxicated.

Inside, I sit on a white-cushioned cane sofa to catch my breath. On a side table next to me stands a large white porcelain lamp with a wide-brimmed off-white lampshade. On its perfectly convex belly are characters in bright red, painted and glazed in Oriental script.

So much is hidden in so little a space—a flourish of a Zen-like haiku, compressing more than it reveals, providing calm in such turbulence. The Japanese characters mean "happiness" in Kanji, and that quietly uplifts me more than my friend can ever imagine.

A clear low-watt bulb hidden behind the lampshade casts a circular spread of light on the heavy teak of the floor—the illuminated space and its fuzzy-edged circumference merge with the yellow of the light and dark brown of the hundred-and-fifty-year-old teak.

4

The sea breeze enters the apartment with its heady scent. The lemon-washed walls, the white ceiling, the books, the glass and granite bannisters, the surety of wood, and all the bric-a-brac from the world over provide the mise-en-scène of a film that has never been shot.

Yet all the characters in the cast are ready with their well-rehearsed lines, poised to trip off their lips in perfectly intoned delivery. I, too, am on the play's cast—a very minor character; a mute one—my tongue slashed for speaking of the heart's peculiarities.

And yet, I do not know any other way to live or to act—I just have to act the way my spinal split ends direct me. Only in this unmade film, the master puppeteer's many strings carefully hide the excruciating pain that I carry permanently on my bare back's nerve endings.

5

My friend tells me that we all have to mark our lives with tattoos of comradeship. Invisible tattoos they may be, but they have to be etched all the same, in spite of the pain that accompanies.

So, we summon the best tattooist in town. She is an artist with the slenderest of fingers and nails that reveal under them parallel striations of blood that give colour to the unpolished surfaces. She is a miniature painter and has the most exquisite hand for understated design. Her eyes have a sharp-honed focus that is so intense that it can, in a moment of instant combustion, split white light into its seven strands.

Amidst all this, I can only provide her with translucent white ink, one that she mixes with earthy natural hues. And the rest spontaneously draws itself out—exquisite, with an elaborate concentration of detail, minute and passionate.

6

I can hear voices, other people's voices—movements, shifting of paper.

"The demons constantly hover around in my mind," my friend said. "And now they are talking aloud, making themselves heard."

All this pain, a whisperingly silent pain, in my bloodstream—this shingle-sharp pain seems to reside permanently in me.

7

Next evening, on Mumbai's waterfront, I sit dangling my feet over the embankment with the sea below and Gateway of India behind me. I swallow the brackish air once again, taking in deep gulps. They provide brief toxic relief to my broken heart.

The brilliant evening light that, not too long ago illuminated the sandblasted ochre face of the monument and the white boats on the blue-grey seascape, has now faded. In the descending dark, the sea smell tries to induce a misplaced sense of romanticism in me. Selfishly, I try to grab on to any illusion of love that comes my way, but my heart can only gather the heavyweight of gloom.

8

I start making my way back to the friend's apartment that I now call home in this city. It is perched high on the city's skyline, watching over the electric night canvas of the streets and buildings below. I hope that upon my return, all that glitter and the sea scent will lift my spirits.

I, so dearly, look forward to those little gold squares on the muslin where I want to paint pictures. I want to talk to the little girl in my friend's small blue-and-yellow painting that has her fighting the winds to keep her umbrella in shape. I want to reread the poem that is inscribed below it.

But upon my return, I see that the muslin canvas I longed for has now vanished. It has been replaced with ordinary black linen, a colour I have dreaded facing, a colour I had donned myself last night.

9

"I hope we have at least gathered strength from our comradeship," I tell her upon my arrival.

"Our desire for love, for death, for rains, for chemical smells of paint, for Edith Piaf," I say, "is all meaningless, without our desire to breathe fully the air we create and are inherently blessed with."

"Let us go then, you and I / When the evening is spread out against the sky …"— *"Chool tar kobekar* andhokar Bidishar nisha … "*—Damn it, why do I only remember other people's poetry, poets whose work I admire, old lyrics, sad songs?—All this memory, there is too much latent memory.

But then, why not—you are an old companion— and I have been writing letters to you on onion-skin paper that I bought in your city. The paper has traces of lavender petals embedded in its pulp; its pages are bound in purple leather with Devanagari script printed on it in gold.

But this is not the gold I desire.

10

I still search for the off-white muslin to write and paint on. But it is too far now. I can see it in the distance—it is now a sail on a fishing boat fast receding into the horizon.

And the recent brilliantly orange-red sunset is stunning for the same reason as the level of toxins in my bloodstream.

"Wear that sari again," I ask my friend. But she can no longer find it.

AREEBA NASIR

Bench

Rukhsana watched the sun slowly drown in the stream of green mountains. Houses built in the terraced valley clung to the mountains like honeybees on the beehive. Rain was not rare but was uncommon during that time of the year. It had soaked her clothes and her cloth bag. Her umbrella was broken from one side. She held the partly broken umbrella over her daughter who was sitting beside quietly.

"I made *arhar ki dal* today, why don't you come home?" she asked.

No answer.

"I thought of getting some for you but I don't remember where I kept the tiffin box; do you have it?"

"It's kept in the cabinet above the fridge if no one has touched it," said her daughter, looking down at the weeds sprouting in between the rocks. The deluge of rain and the onset of darkness was making Rukhsana uncomfortable. She got up from the bench to look for somewhere they could take shelter for a while, but nothing could be seen, just the mountains, trees, and the bench with the umbrella. She turned around to ask her daughter if she would come home but she was gone.

"Why did she leave without saying goodbye again?" Rukhsana said, picking up her things from the bench.

"Where have you been in this weather?" Rukhsana's husband, Prakash, asked as she entered the house, soaked and shivering.

"Went to see Mimi, she doesn't want to come home; I told her I had made her favourite *arhar dal* but she left without saying goodbye."

Prakash had nothing to say. He took things from Rukhsana and handed her a towel.

Rukhsana and Prakash married twenty-five years ago. They both studied Political Science at Delhi University. Fell in love, got married, and had to move away from their respective families because their relationship met with a lot of resistance. When they moved to the mountains in Uttarkhand, they had to build their lives brick by brick. They had three children: two boys and a girl. Prakash worked as a lecturer in one of the colleges while Rukhsana worked as a homemaker.

"Rehan called up today, said he won't be able to come for the weekend because of the constant rain," Prakash informed Rukhsana as they sipped tea prepared by him.

"Tell him Amma will prepare *chawal ki kheer*, he will come home running," said Rukhsana.

Rehan, their eldest one, had to move to another town for work. He visited them over the weekends. Arjun, the youngest, was studying culinary arts and lived with them. Rukhsana and Prakash had built a cottage in a slightly secluded area located on a cliff, away from the hustle of the town. You could see the entire town from their yard. Even normal nights looked like Diwali evenings from up there. She had planted different coloured hydrangeas and bougainvillea at the front of the house while nature had planted conifers, pines, and fruit-bearing trees at the back of their house. White fence bordered the cottage, within it were the numerous memories and moments created by the family and sealed forever. An apple tree situated at the right corner of the fence had sustained a swing for more than a decade. Mimi had seen it at the public park and demanded installing one in her yard. Prakash built the swing out of wood and hung it with a thick, coarse rope, making sure it was sturdy enough. She grew up from a young girl to a woman swinging and painting her thoughts on the endless canvas above her head. Mimi had the intellect of her father and the wit of her mother. While Rehan looked exactly like Prakash and Arjun looked like Rukhsana, Mimi was a combination. She had taken best of both. She was enrolled in Bachelors of Architecture.

Prakash helped Rukhsana clean up the dining table post dinner while Arjun did the dishes. Rain hadn't stopped for three days. Arjun looked out of the kitchen window, it was dark out there; all he could hear were the raindrops splashing in the water that had started to accumulate.

"It hadn't rained that bad during this time in years," Arjun said from the kitchen.

"Yea, not sure what the poor farmers will do, this will destroy their crops," Prakash said, wiping the dining table with a damp cloth that used to be a T-shirt in its glorious days.

Rukhsana pulled out a packet of white chickpeas and drowned them in water to soak overnight.

"What are you planning to cook?" asked Arjun.

"I'll make *cholay*, Mimi likes them. She asked me to make them for her," she replied.

Arjun and Prakash looked at each other. Arjun scrubbed the sink and went back to his room without uttering a word.

"Do you want to have chai?" Prakash asked Arjun from outside his room's door after a while.

"No, I am good," Arjun replied from inside, without opening the door. There was a hint of disappointment in his tone.

"Ok," said Prakash and turned around, his eyes fell on Mimi's name written on a crochet cloth hanging on the opposite door. There lived an elderly woman alone in a cottage down the road who earned a living by stitching and crocheting. Mimi visited her often on her way back from college, she had gotten it done for her room. Unexpected downpour the night Rukhsana went into labour had forced them to stay home. The same old lady who crocheted delivered Mimi at home. Same night the Mayor of the town had passed away. In his memory, green coloured iron benches were installed on all scenic spots of the town. When Mimi started to walk, Arjun came into their lives. Rehan, Mimi, and Arjun. Rukhasana and Prakash had everything they had wished for. Prakash had discovered a spot where he would take his children every Sunday. It wasn't very far away but walking was not a good idea, thus a car was preferred. The three children waited eagerly for Sunday to spend time with their parents exploring nature.

"In loving memory of Shri. Satyanand Prasad" Mimi read the inscription on the bench.

"These were installed in his memory," Prakash told her.

As they grew up, the visits to the bench decreased. Rehan was busy in his studies and would often be out on

Sundays. Mimi and Arjun continued to visit with their parents but later on, Arjun was available less frequently. Soon everybody stopped visiting but Mimi. It had become her haven, the place where she could unleash her mind that was gradually being tamed by the society she was a part of. Trying to unlearn the rules of being a woman. Looking for her father's god and her mother's god to figure out which was the one to follow as there were two that she knew. The noises in her brain silenced when she was sitting on that bench watching the houses on the mountains turn into floating lanterns as the night overpowered the day. She was contriving her escape in those soundless surroundings.

After finishing the majority of her tasks, Rukhsana set out to meet her daughter who must be waiting on the bench. She packed the *cholay* in the tiffin box, it was there where Mimi had said. The road was slippery and muddy, the puddles made the walk to the bench challenging. She found Mimi sitting on the bench, wearing a green kurta and dark-wash denim.

"Am I late? The rain made it hard to reach here; look at me, I am all wet," Rukhsana said.

She placed her broken umbrella over Mimi and sat down on the wet bench. She replaced her cloth bag with the waterproof purse that had the box of *cholay*.

"Rehan will not be visiting us for the weekend because of the rain," she said.

"But you came here," said Mimi.

"Arjun and your papa haven't left the house since the rain started."

"I changed the sheets of your room, the grey one with yellow flowers, remember?"

"Yes, we got it from Manali."

"I made *cholay* for you today." She pulled out the box from the purse and kept it on the bench for Mimi.

"You found it." Both shared a smile.

An hour had passed already, the rain began pouring in torrents.

"Come home with me," she insisted again and again.

Mimi stared vacantly at dimming lights of the houses and the fat raindrops. She was unmoved by the ferocity of the rain. It was getting impossible for Rukhsana to sit unsheltered. She desperately wanted to get in the car but Mimi wouldn't move. She stood up and asked her to come in the car and accompany her home. The rain had lowered visibility drastically. Rukhsana squinted her eyes and unlocked the car with her keys to locate it from a distance. She turned around to ask Mimi to come with her but she had already left.

"Left again without saying goodbye." It seemed like Rukhsana was now used to her going away without informing. The box of *cholay* was on the bench, untouched. Somehow she managed to reach home driving in those awful and dangerous conditions.

"You shouldn't have left the house in this weather," Prakash said as she entered the house.

"My daughter was waiting for me, how could I not go," she said.

Prakash remained silent and went inside, disappointed and angry. He opened the door with the crochet hanging. Photo of Mimi welcomed him. Her room was the way she had left it except for the grey-and-yellow bedsheet that Rukhsana had changed. Prakash sat down glumly on her bed, eyes laden with tears. Memories of his daughter intruded relentlessly his exhausted mind. He looked at the reading glasses that she must have used before leaving the house that day, never to return. They were untouched. Six months had gone by since Mimi passed away. A fatal car accident was the reason for her death as informed by the police. The loss was ultimate. With the passing time, her family learnt to live with the pain inflicted upon them. It became a part of their existence. But Rukhsana was still stuck in that one moment. When they received the news of Mimi's untimely death, Rukhsana had fallen into denial. She couldn't accept her daughter's premature departure and lamented not being able to say a final goodbye. Her thoughts and mind were always occupied by the thoughts of her daughter. Trauma of child loss had weakened not only her limbs but also her mind that disregarded the present and favoured the past. She couldn't move for weeks. The variant petals of hydrangeas turned brown, the defunct bougainvillea and absence of care had transformed the front yard to a drab and grey piece of land.

Few months later, Rukhsana started hallucinating. It began when she had started to visit the bench to get back what was lost forever. She would see her in the same dress she died wearing. She would talk to her and according to her, she talked back too. Since then, not a single day passed when Rukhsana did not visit the bench. Prakash never stopped her. He was aware of Rukhsana's escapism but refrained from correcting it. Evading reality made her at least move out of the mental and physical confinement.

She had begun to take interest in her remaining family and her home. Prakash never tried to mention that he had buried their daughter a long time ago. Mimi would often jokingly tell her parents to bury her rather than cremate and that too during the day because she was scared of the dark. Who knew that they would one day have to make a choice.

"Mimi didn't take the *cholay*, she just left and I couldn't even say goodbye," she said, keeping back the plastic box on the table.

There was a loud thud outside, one of the trees in their backyard had come crashing down over the outhouse.

"Goodness, this is getting out of control. Let me go and check the damage."

"Leave it, Papa, we can see it in the morning," insisted Arjun.

They turned on the TV to get some updates on the weather. The state government had issued a flash flood warning in their region. People were advised to stay indoors.

"I don't want you to leave the house for a few days," Prakash said to Rukhsana sternly.

"I need to see Mimi," she insisted.

"Why don't you just tell her?" Arjun shouted at Prakash.

"Tell what? Don't you dare say a word," Rukhsana shouted at Arjun, fearing that she might just get to hear what she had been trying to deny.

The thunder and lightning outside had increased. But there was silence in the room now. Arjun went to his room, while Prakash sat there beside her resting his forehead on his left hand, torn between the circumstances and his wife's well-being.

"You need to understand, you go out you might just never come back, it's too dangerous," he tried to explain.

"But Mimi," she said as tears started rolling down her cheeks.

Prakash hugged her.

A deafening sound startled the sleeping family, all three of them woke up scared and shocked. The sound was followed by an earthquake. Three of them gathered in the living room, worried. They went outside to figure out what was happening. It was raining as hard as it could. The air was filled with horrific noises. There was water up to their ankles. It was already early morning. Looking down the fence, they witnessed the unimaginable. The whole town had been swept away. They saw the three-storey buildings, the huge statues, and houses crumbled by the force of water. The treacherous flood had wiped off their town. Cloudburst and landslides had caused severe flooding in the area. Their cottage being situated on a cliff was least affected by the destruction caused. Prakash took both of them indoors, frightened by what they had just seen, all of them looked at each other in silence. The sight was harrowing, they all were in a state of shock and not sure of what was to come in the days ahead. Another cloudburst could affect them too. Water uprooted the powerline poles and destroyed the power station; electricity was out. No grain went down their throats that day. Constant fear and remorse had engulfed their minds.

The rain had reduced to mere drizzle the next day. Aftermath of disaster is worse than the disaster itself, those who survive realise the extent of their loss and wish they too had perished. Memories of the blissful past haunt the present forever.

Flood hadn't lasted for more than five minutes but left behind a trail of death and destruction and a town buried in mud and rocks. All this while Rukhsana could think of no one but her daughter. She feared for something that had occurred long before. Prakash and Arjun had decided to go down to the main town and see if they could offer any help. Water had receded but the swamp made commuting nearly impossible. Desperate to see her daughter, Rukhsana also tried to leave the house but couldn't go much far, ultimately she had to return.

There were shrieks and cries everywhere, thousands of people had perished, and hundreds of houses had been reduced to rubble. Arjun saw a little girl sitting on a mount of mud, sobbing and looking around helplessly. While the army had been rescuing stranded people, this child had gone unnoticed. Arjun looked away but was intrigued. His eyes met hers again. Her stare was helpless. There were numerous such children who were desperate to see a face that was familiar.

"Where are your parents?" Prakash asked the child.

She didn't speak. They decided to take her to the relief camp nearby. None of them had encountered that side of humans. People fought for food like hungry hyenas fighting for their share of the antelope. That was certainly not the place anyone would want a child to be. Prakash registered his phone number and address and volunteered to take care of the child until her parents were found. They were certain someone would come for her, maybe relatives if not parents. They took the child home.

Few days passed. The little girl had fallen ill, no appetite and partly conscious just muttering the names of her family members. Rukhsana had not visited the bench since and now it had started making her sick. She was desperate to go but was too weak to drive or walk alone. Prakash and Arjun were tending to the two ladies trying their best to make them forget their losses. Rukhsana had seen the child once since then and she had confined herself to the room.

"Come with me," Prakash asked Rukhsana.

"Leave me alone, Prakash."

"Come with me, I will take you somewhere."

It was rare that Rukhsana had said no to anything that Prakash had asked for. She got up with his help and went along with him.

"Where are we going?" she questioned, sitting in the car.

"To meet Mimi." A smile occupied her face. She took a deep breath. On her way, she witnessed the destruction caused by the floods. Nothing was familiar.

They reached the place, both of them got out of the car. The mud was soggy and making it hard to walk without toppling. Rukhsana held Prakash's hand and walked carefully towards the bench that was nowhere to be seen. Just an empty spot. The green bench was gone. Desperate to see her daughter, Rukhsana looked around. She left Prakash's hand to look as far as she could but fell down in the mud. She saw her. She saw her standing on the edge of the mountain.

"Goodbye, Amma," she said and disappeared in the air.

"Mimi," Rukhsana called her out.

She was gone. The shrieks of Rukhsana echoed in the mountains. Prakash watched her cry from a distance.

Rukhsana goes to the swing in their yard the next morning. Swinging, humming, and smiling. Inside, Prakash finally hangs a garland around his daughter's picture. She comes back in, looks at the picture, and goes to her room. A little girl sleeps comfortably on the grey-and-yellow bedsheet.

DONNA TANG

How She Knew

"You are going to betray me," she is saying, but the words only make a small, futile fog on the glass. The airport doors will not open for her because she is not invited inside. She waves harder, both arms now, but her husband is walking away and does not see.

Leaning against the check-in counter is the woman her husband wants to leave her for. The woman her husband wants wears high heels with jeans. She leans and waits, bare-shouldered, one arm up, hand cupped around the back of her neck. Bracelets trickle down her wrists. When she sees him coming towards her, she flushes pink from her cleavage to her ears and reaches her fingers out to touch his cheek.

When the wife awakes from this dream, the traitor lies beside her. In the apartment upstairs, the neighbours' children are playing with marbles again. Their own home is always quiet—there are no family sounds, no small smudgy handprints or mini shoes. The marbles bounce on the hard floor, and each sharp sound goes through her clenched jaw.

Last week, she finally went one floor up and knocked on the neighbour's door. "Crazy ah, my children where got play marbles?" was what the culprits' mother said. "You don't like, you buy top-floor unit *lor*." She didn't even ask her name, just closed the door.

He coughs suddenly, chokes a little in his sleep. The Breathe-Rite strips don't work for his apnoea anymore.

Their doctor says it's just one of those things that sometimes comes with age, and there's no real cure. It's just something we have to live with, she'd said to him in a low, comforting tone after the consultation as they sat waiting to pay. But he disagreed. He was the one suffering and she didn't have to live with anything, and the way he'd said this made the clinic's pretty receptionist with the nose-stud glance up with a jolt, then look back down quickly, so as not to be staring.

She had gotten up then and walked to the toilet, and their doctor was there too, washing her hands at the sink. The doctor used to be her doctor but became their doctor after they got married—*sixteen* years ago, has it really been that long now? For this reason, she feels like the doctor knows them, but of course she does not. You can even live with a person for decades and not know them— she learnt this from her mother, who spoke of her cold and critical father as a good and caring man, even after he died. However the doctor does know quite a bit—such as about her putting her heels up on the wall after sex, about the sudden twinges later that stole her breath and all the colour in her face, about the bleeding afterwards, heavier than any period. About the years passing, about hope growing cautious, then weak, then still. But if the doctor was thinking about all this now too, she gave no sign of it, only put a damp, doctorly hand on her arm, smiled in the toilet mirror, and told her reflection she really should help her husband lose some weight now he was approaching fifty.

For nights after that, she lay awake. The constant gurgling sounds were one thing, but it was the sudden, urgent snores she couldn't prepare for. But also, she couldn't shake the idea that he might swallow his tongue and choke to death and it would be her fault. Imagine having to explain to the police—for surely the police would come—that she had slept right through it all, through him dying. Surely they wouldn't believe her! After all, a married couple should know, should they not—even separated by sleep or space or selves—if the other is in distress?

She reaches over now and strokes his chest, prods him half-awake so he'll turn on his side. He grunts and rubs his eyes. She will not tell him about her airport dream. "Booked taxi already?" is the first thing he wants to know. They leave for Batam at two—it's an hour away from Singapore by ferry, there will be no trip to the airport. He picks the destination for their yearly December holiday but does not like to do the planning. She has packed their matching bags with sun hats and insect repellent. It hasn't stopped raining in Batam for the past three days.

When they arrive, the grey sea and peeling wooden boats feel like the betrayal in her dream. Her husband takes a photo of the splintering jetty. He does not ask her to be in it. Later, they pick through puddles under separate umbrellas to a restaurant by the colourless beach, which serves value-for-money seafood. He mumbles when their table has no view of the ocean and their dinner comes on chipped plates, and it feels like he's talking about her. He thinks the way they do chilli crab back home is better and the fish does not taste fresh enough that it could possibly have been live as the waiter claimed. The cooks turn up the gas stoves with a sudden roar that scurries up the back of her neck like a shudder. He might wave the manager over and make a fuss, so she peels his prawns for him to cheer him up, sucking her fingers clean after she has placed the fat, pink morsels on his plate. Outside, it is still raining.

They are both quite wet when they get back to the hotel, and he is frowning because he might catch a chill, so she suggests he shower first and he does, even though she's shivering. While he's in the small bathroom, she looks around the room and thinks about how much better it looked online. Dusty, faded curtains. The cold tiled floor. Two single beds. She'd specifically left a note with her booking requesting a double, but she wasn't going to make things difficult for the young woman at the front desk. He has pushed the beds together, so hers is out of sync with its tacky, lacquered headboard mounted on the wall. When it's her turn to use the bathroom, she pulls an old T-shirt out of her bag, not the silk nightie packed at the bottom. The hot water runs out a third of the way through.

The air-con flails in the rain-drenched air, so she lies on top of the covers in the mugginess, and in the dark, she feels him edge towards her back. He is in the crack between their single beds, the heaviness of him threatening to split them apart. His hand is on her waist, then, his breath on the back of her neck. He only ever touches her when the lights are out now. Just the other morning, he told her there was an eyelash on her cheek but would not reach across and brush it off. Instead, she spent minutes moving her finger higher—lower—left a bit—no, right—until her inability to follow instructions frustrated him.

He shifts closer, widening the gap between the beds. She thinks about just letting him, turning her face aside, tolerating the intrusion until he finishes and rolls back over. But tonight she feels empty enough already, so she tries to be dirty clothes in a heap, breathing slow and keeping completely still. If the beds slid apart, he'd fall through onto the floor and be wedged there until she got up to help. Another sort of couple would laugh about it, but not them, not ever.

When he finally turns away, he doesn't even sigh. Once he's asleep, she tucks her body away under the covers. She looks for the airport departure hall again in her dreams, and the flights are all to romantic places.

The Seine is full of stars. Her husband is taking his lover on a night cruise. The Louvre and Notre Dame glow with magical light. She struggles as if for breath to name other buildings, but cannot, and she feels robbed.

His lover is tall and slim. Her hair is long and black and lifts gently in the night breeze. Paris is everything she has ever dreamed. She gazes into the sparkling water, rolls the pendant on her necklace between a finger and thumb, and whispers to herself, "If only it could be like this forever."

The wife watches from the other side of the river. "He loves her," she says, and she says this with wonder. In the morning, her husband and his lover sit side by side on rattan chairs outside the Café de Flore, and he caresses her hand beneath the seat. He orders both a croque-monsieur and an éclair and nobody nags him about his cholesterol. They sip espresso from tiny, thick cups for hours, and his eyes shine with laughter.

Back to Singapore. The same stubborn orangey grout stains in the bathroom, the relentless rain. The same wondering who she is and how she got here. The family upstairs stomps around loudly. It's clearly on purpose; rancour echoes through the thuds and taps. She goes to buy groceries and stares at all the women in case one of them is the one her husband loves—the one reading the organic rice-snack labels, the one with the sunglasses on her head, the one asking the cashier where the gluten-free pasta is.

Back in their own bed, they lie next to each other as stiff as sewing needles. She dreams that she is lost in a strange airport. One sign says Departures, another says Arrivals, and time is running out out out, but she doesn't know if she is coming or going. She wakes gasping. He turns away from her, taking more than his share of the blanket, sleeps hunched away at the edge, face pressed into the pillow, like he might disappear into it.

The days collapse into one another like dominoes. Doubt has infested her home like a case of mould she can't get rid of. They're just dreams, she tells herself, you're imagining things. But just when she thinks she's got it all, wiped it clean, it appears again the next day, patchy and persistent, infecting everything anew.

She goes with him to his annual office party, sips a Diet Coke and keeps to herself, trying not to interrogate the faces of the women who work with him to see if she's among them. But the sand fly bites she got in Batam won't stop itching, and she can't scratch them because her nails would rip the pantyhose she put on to hide them. The wife stands next to her husband, step-stepping from foot to foot while the itch rages like a hunger.

Then she can't bear it any longer. She rushes to the staff toilet, tugs her dress up over her hips, and peels her stockings off. She needs to scratch, desperately, but her hands are full of the damned nylons. She can't put them down anywhere because of germs, but they won't fit in the stupid little bag she brought—she stuffs and stuffs, but they just erupt back out like flesh-toned froth from a shaken can. Dress still half hiked-up, she forgets about

germs, slumps onto the clammy toilet seat with her bag
and the fistful of sheers in her lap, and rests her forehead on
the toilet-roll dispenser. Another sort of woman would just
throw them in the trash, but they're still good.

She'd had a crush on him for seven years before he
finally started liking her back. He wasn't interested at first
because she was sixteen and he was twenty-six, and she
was just his little sister's friend. When she was twenty, she
bought an orange halter-neck dress and told herself she'd
wear it on their first date. By the time he finally asked her
out, her dress was three years out of fashion, and too small,
but she wore it, anyway.

After that first dinner, he stopped at an Esso for gas.
While he queued to pay, she sat in his old car watching a
young man clean the windshield. He wielded the squeegee
with such gentle precision, the dance of the rubber blade
turning haze into brilliance, stroke by sure stroke. Only
glass separated her from his braided forearm muscles,
shining with sweat—only glass. As they drove out of the
gas station, she stared through her perfect window at the
boy and thought: I should be with him instead.

She stands up now, and staring down the throat of
the toilet, puts her pantyhose back on over the bites, very
slowly, one leg at a time. As she leaves the cubicle, some
woman tells her helpfully that there's a red mark on her
forehead. He doesn't ask where she was. On the drive
home, the Christmas lights along the streets drip and sag.

The next morning, after he leaves for work, the ceiling
screeches with dragged chairs. She hurries upstairs to catch
them in the act, but the neighbour just slams the door once
she sees it's her. She stands in the corridor ringing their
doorbell and breathing their house-smells—cooked onions

and sweet baby powder—but the neighbour just yells from inside, "Don't like is it? Move house *lah*! Don't come and disturb us!" and soon her kids are chanting it too: "Move house *lah*! Move house *lah*!"

When the other neighbours poke their heads out like snails, she slinks home. But someone upstairs is still at it, bang-bang-bang, bang-bang-bang, and anger blooms in her like a struck match. She grabs the longest thing she can find—a bamboo laundry pole—and uses it to hit the ceiling. The neighbours stamp and jump, and she swears and jabs wildly, not caring that she's outnumbered, not caring that she's leaving incomplete black circles on her white ceiling.

There are so many of them; but only her, alone. She knocks and cries until her arms are numb, then lets the pole drop, overcome with her own ridiculousness.

That night, as she lies squinting to make out the marks she left on the ceiling, she hears something outside their bedroom. She holds her breath, and there it is again, then again. Footsteps, in their living room. This used to happen when they first got married—she'd wake him in a panic, convinced there was someone in their new, unfamiliar house. He would sigh, heavily but indulgently, climb reluctantly out of bed turning on all the lights as he went, make a big show of checking every room, then come back to bed to ruffle her hair and fall back asleep, her head on his shoulder.

She knows what he would say if she woke him now. She was imagining things, the floors and walls of their apartment are thin and sounds filter through all the time. She would be a stupid woman for waking him when she knows he has to work in the morning. But she's quite sure she hears someone—and it must be the neighbour from upstairs, here to take revenge.

She wants to whisper, There's someone in the house, but her breath cowers. The neighbour could probably overpower her, and there's no way of getting a knife from the kitchen anymore. She can't take her down alone.

Another step. Soft, but undeniable. Loud blood beats in her ears. She sends her husband distress signals, pushes her fear wildly out in his direction, trying to cut through his consciousness and reach him in the tender centre of his sleep. She is holding her breath, pressing down as if constipated, and even through the haze of fear, she feels absurd. She should just reach over and wake him, but she's afraid he might make a sound when he wakes, he might say "What?" Or, "What *lah*, Jen." She doesn't want the neighbour to hear this, hear the irritation instead of concern. She doesn't want her to know her husband just calls her Jen, not babe, or darling. But the neighbour will know, anyway. The second the knife-tip presses into her neck, or the heavy vase is lifted over her head—the neighbour will see it in her eyes: *Please, I've never known true love.*

The intruder must be halfway to the bedroom by now, why has she stopped? She pictures her creeping along the walls, identical to those in her own house upstairs, her eyes sifting through the darkness. Her eyes are open too. Only her husband sleeps. He is so far away and always will be. She lies in the blue-black of aloneness, and the silence becomes longer and longer until she starts to doubt if anyone is there at all. She is still thinking about whether to get out of bed and confront their killer when she falls asleep from waiting to die.

When it rains in Paris, the gilded sculptures gleam more brightly in the wet. Couples walk bare-headed. They cannot stop touching each other and so, there are no hands for umbrellas. She sees him waiting for his lover at the foot of the Eiffel Tower—at the end of the path lined with trees and street artists which she has seen in movies—and she knows what she must do.

That is the last time she dreams about Paris. On Christmas morning, she wakes before he does. There are crusts around his sleeping eyes. The children upstairs are quiet for once.

When he wakes, he turns to wish her Merry Christmas, but she puts a hand on his chest to stop him. She tells him she knows there is someone else. She tells him she has noticed he hasn't unpacked his bags from Batam. He sits up in bed, looking surprised and hurt. "It's ok," she says. "I know you're in love."

He is silent, and then he tells her this is true and he doesn't know what to do and he wanted to tell her but he didn't know how. The bed lies open between them like a wound, and the air is very still. Then bewilderment overtakes guilt, and he has to ask. But how did she know?

She looks at him. She doesn't tell him about the boy who cleaned his windshield, and she doesn't tell him about the night they almost died. She doesn't tell him she has been standing by the Seine, watching and talking to him from the other side.

PHONG HUYNH

As Legal As We Are

Ajay takes a long puff. The white veils swirl in malleable waves in the bong, making a bubbling sound as the smoke rips through the water. He holds his breath. He can feel his neurons lit up like wildfire. His scalp seemingly shrinks and reels from the cold, tickling refreshing sensation. Then he lets it all out. The exhaled vapour eclipses his dilated pupils, which are staring vacantly at the ever-receding ceiling. He neatly puts the bong and what's left of the meth into an IKEA zip lock bag. He seals it and places it in the cistern in the bathroom. It's the wee hours on a Saturday morning. At other times, Ajay is a brown expat from Chennai in his thirties, one of the five partners at the law firm Bartleby, Lee & Tan in the heart of Singapore's Central Business District. He is also a gay man. Most people know this. But on Saturday mornings, only on Saturday mornings, he is also a junkie. No one has a clue.

*

Ajay cleans the lips of his wine glasses till they are free of any fingerprints. The gay society in Singapore is like the animal kingdom, and tonight the royalty is descending on Ajay's dinner party: beautiful, chiselled, six-packed, wealthy gay men, holding high-profile jobs in multinational corporations or being some sort of hipster yogi, barista, mixologist, watchmaker, or a policeman. Aiden is a policeman. Ajay is both fond and terrified of him, not sure which causes the other.

Ajay has stocked up ample wine, fifteen bottles of red and six bottles of white to be exact. The reds come with a vintage ominous label "19 Crimes." The whites are the opposite, carrying a modern tongue-in-cheek label "Quirky Birds." Ajay has curated the menu of alcohol to make sure everybody will be adequately intoxicated for conversations but not too drunk to last the night. That means no hard liquor. He gleams at the bottles of Monkey Shoulders on the shelf.

The abundant wine greases the conversations of a dozen gay men in the room: whether a banana taped on a wall is art, whether 377A will be repealed in their lifetime, whether the latest reincarnation of the keto diet is a farce, and so on. Eugene, an Instagram famous gay celebrity, is meanwhile dispensing skincare advice to Ajay on the sofa. Eugene is in his fifties though he looks like a twink with his bouncy, radiant skin, not unlike that of new-born babies. Ajay props his head up with his one hand while sipping the last of his 19 Crimes and savouring the panoramic sight of Singapore's gay royalty in his living room. He cannot bring himself to comprehend a ten-step skin care regimen any more than he can explain the elaborate arrangements in a Chinese funeral procession. Ajay thinks about the cistern.

"And that's the last step. Voila. Baby skin. Youth for eternity! Simple, right?" Eugene snaps his fingers.

"Excuse me, dear. I am going to get a refill. Tell me more about the toner when I am back!" Ajay leaves the sofa.

The living room in Ajay's condominium apartment is just spacious enough for a party of a dozen, but tonight, getting from one end to the other feels like a trek across the Himalayas. Each of these men is a treacherous mountain pass: boastful Luke, conspicuous Andrew, snobbish Ken, and nerdy Seng. All Ajay tries to do is get closer to Aiden. He is not sure if it is Aiden or the thrill of danger that is pulling him in. Aiden, a five feet tall, muscular born and bred Singaporean Chinese, has been in the police force for a month now. He met Ajay at Eugene's party last Christmas, and they have been hitting it off from the get-go, sharing the love of reading, bubble tea, and beautiful men.

"Aiden, are you enjoying yourself?" Ajay puts his arm across Aiden's shoulder, balancing the wine glass with the other.

"You have been reading Jonathan Safran Foer?" Aiden stares at the bookshelf.

"*Everything is Illuminated* is, well, illuminating!" Ajay leans further towards Aiden.

Aiden is whom one will describe as nerdy cute: a thirty-something wearing a pair of black-rimmed glasses and combed-back spiky hair. He doesn't speak much, but his reticence pulls people towards him. His big black eyes under the chandelier reflect the version of Ajay that he keenly wants Aiden to see beyond: a pudgy brown man that clambers but will never make it to the top of the gay kingdom.

"You want some more 19 Crimes?" Ajay chuckles.

"I actually need the bathroom."

Ajay thinks of the cistern.

*

Damn it, not now. Where are the pills? His heart rocks against his chest, sending the tremor through to his hands. *You will be such a pity piece if you break down into tears. Not now. Not in front of these queens. You gotta pull through.* Dollops of sweat from his palm smudge his half-empty wine glass.

His breath quickens. Ajay puts the glass down on the table and tumbles to the restroom, which feels like another trek across the Himalayas. There is an art to sneaking out and sneaking in that Ajay knows too well from his past moonlit trysts with boys in the vicinity. Right now, he is using that very skill to escape, unseen and unheard, tiptoeing on the edges that are his friends' lines of sight.

Closing the door behind, Ajay props himself up against the sink with his quivering hands. He sees his face in the wall-sized mirror melt into a muddle of iridescent fluid shapes, like the swirling rainbows on soap bubbles. *You loser! You can't go through a party without a big fuck-up like this? Who will date a social handicap like you?* The little voices bounce back and forth against the inside of his skull. He is all too familiar with them, the unforgiving ones. They told him off when his Data Science class result was "good" but not "meritorious." They told him off when his performance rating at work last year was "exceeds some, but not all, expectations." They told him off after the Singapore Qualitative Research Conference cocktail reception where he spoke to fewer than five people in the whole boozy evening. They told him off when Dayton did not give him a goodbye kiss after their dinner in a moving capsule on Singapore Flyer. They told him off when he failed to tell his mom how much he loved and hated her at the same time. They told him off all the time. The unforgiving voices slop around within the walls of his head, the recalcitrant neurons which refuse to stay down.

He lifts the lid of the cistern. The IKEA zip lock bag is still there the way he left it. Did Aiden see it? Probably not. Who the hell opens the cistern in someone else's bathroom? Nobody. Yet, the meth is still probably lingering in Ajay's blood and paranoia is just a natural side effect that he is all too familiar with. Ajay prides himself on being a high-functioning junkie. He will start each Friday night with a few puffs, then go on Grindr to find a sling, have sex all night to the beats of his favourite indie rock playlist trying all sorts of kinks, stay up all Saturday morning to hunt for the next bottom, play with the toy boy throughout the day, and then the cycle repeats. Through all that, he doesn't sleep. He doesn't eat. He only drinks water. And on Sunday evening, he will have his first meal and his first nap after he finally comes with the last boy. Through all that, he feels nothing, but desperately wants to feel something. Yet, in the end, to him, it just becomes a trance, a ritual, a routine. He will then drink lots of fruit juice because he has no appetite for any solid food. The next day, he will go to work, alert and seemingly normal, like anybody else. He has run through this routine for a year now. Nobody has noticed anything and he has never got caught. But tonight, the arrival of these A-gays is bringing him so much pressure that he broke his routine and started using too close to the party. And now the paranoia is eating him alive from the inside of his brain.

The cold sweat rolls down on his temples and his cheeks. A drop of his sweat stops on his upper lip. Ajay opens the medicine cabinet and reaches out for the Xanax blister pack on the top shelf. The doctor told him to take two tablets in an emergency. He never cared to elaborate on what would count as an emergency. Ajay never bothered to ask. *Emergency. This gotta be one.* What can be more unnerving than being arrested by the one you are crushing on? Ajay presses his finger against the transparent thermoformed plastic, breaking open the aluminium foil. The small blue tablet emerges, and then drops into the sink. Ajay picks it up and pops it into his mouth. The tablet slightly melts on his tongue, releasing a bitterness that resembles what he tastes every time he sees a happy gay couple on Instagram flashing off their happy life in happy places doing happy things. Ajay drinks from the cup of his hands and swallows the pill. He splashes water on his face and slaps his cheeks.

"Alright, who is ready for the beats on Neil Road?" Ajay emerges from the bathroom.

*

After a short cab ride from Ajay's condominium in Tiong Bahru through Singapore's uneventful late-night traffic, the herd of gay boys alight, descending onto Neil Road like untamed unicorns galloping out of captivity.

There is a winding queue outside Taboo, the favourite haunt for generations of gay boys in Singapore seeking a raucous night out. The neon sign above casts a violet glow on the half-lit faces of men staggering by the pavement, smoking cigarettes in their hands. Not too far away, a tall, toned brunette *angmo* in hip-hop swag is retching his guts out. His elfin local boyfriend is belting out in high pitch, "*Aiyo*, honey *ah*, *liddat* how to club. *Jialat*. We go home *lah*!" His one hand is rubbing the back of the *angmo* while his other holds an open silk fan.

"I forgot my wallet at your house." Ajay hears Aiden's whisper just right behind him.

"No worries. I will pay for you."

"Cover charge for two, please!"

The entrance into Taboo is a shadowy tunnel lit with strips of rainbow lights. Ajay and Aiden can sense the vibrations of a techno-mixed "I Knew You Were Trouble" by Taylor Swift in the theatrical fog that hisses around the dance floor. The ground is sticky with spilled alcohol.

"One gin and tonic, please! Aiden, what about you?"

"A whiskey sour for me. Thanks, Ajay." Aiden smiles, revealing his dimples. A strand of hair drops in front of his forehead.

"And a whiskey sour, please! Here are my drink coupons."

"Shall we go nearer to the DJ? The sound quality is more shiok there!"

"Yea."

Ajay takes Aiden's hand and pulls him through a pulsating crowd of gay men dancing to the anthem "I Will Survive." Aiden didn't let go. Ajay bops his head to the music and occasionally jumps up and down after the drop. Aiden, on the other hand, is quietly sipping his cocktail and occasionally sways. Sometimes Ajay wonders if Aiden is just observing the pack of animals on the dance floor like an illustrious zoologist running David Attenborough commentaries. Aiden's shy nature is what draws Ajay to him: an air of unassumingness that makes him feel safe, comforted, and calmed. The human Xanax that he needs. And then Aiden joined the police force.

Ajay reaches out, holds Aiden's hand, and turns him around. Aiden jerks backward, his feet scrambling for balance. "I can't dance. Sorry. I need to use the restroom."

"Oh. Okay. I wait for you here."

Ajay wonders if that was a stupid move. Taking a big gulp of his gin, he lets himself wash away in the fiery beats and blinding lights.

"There you are! We have been looking for you and Aiden." Eugene emerges through the fog.

"Yea. We lost you guys after the entrance. Aiden is in the restroom."

"Perfect that he is not here. Hey, I got something. Wanna try?" A little green pill embossed with an apple shape lies neatly in Eugene's palm.

"What is it?"

"Happy pill."

"You know it's not legal, right?"

"As legal as we are"

"Okay. Fuck it. Give it to me." Ajay grabs the pill and pops it in his mouth, not realising Aiden is just a few steps away at the bar witnessing the whole exchange.

After a few minutes, a hot rush runs all over through Ajay's veins. The musical vibrations in the air are now in his skin. His cells have finally awakened and joined in the party. But this is the thing; meth, Xanax, alcohol, and ecstasy are a damning foursome. After some crazy dance moves that look straight out of Picasso's contortions, Ajay feels his vision swirling, cold sweat covering his face despite the blasting air-con, and his heart slowing down. He drops down, his back against a pillar near the bar, his head in his hands.

"Ajay, are you okay?" Aiden approaches Ajay from behind the pillar.

"I am fine."

"You don't look fine."

Ajay stands up, puts his hands around Aiden's waists, and kisses him on the lips. Aiden pushes him back, half-startled and half-annoyed.

"What did you take?"

"Nothing."

"I saw you."

"Why the fuck do you care? You are not even my boyfriend."

"I saw what was in the cistern."

Ajay freezes. He feels a veil of doom wrapping around and strangling his throat.

"You …you did? Are you… are you going to arrest me?"

Aiden leans over and hugs Ajay, kissing him on the forehead.

"Ajay, I have liked you since the day we met. You being a junkie changes everything, except for how I feel about you."

"But you are in the force."

"I am off duty tonight. I can't see you again if I deport you."

Ajay does not know what to think anymore. His neurons are lit like wildfire again. His scalp shrinks and reels from the impossible situation.

"So, what now?"

"I am not sure. I just want you to be well."

"You have a duty to report me."

Aiden pauses for a moment. Becoming a policeman has always been his dream since he was ten years old. His father served in the force and so did his grandfather. Aiden got admitted to medical school and trained to be a doctor for years at the behest of his mother, the matriarch of the family. Yet, in the end, he dropped out and joined the police academy. There is a sense of justice that flows in the blood of his family, steadfast and unyielding, that tells him becoming anyone other than a law enforcer is against the order of nature. "You know being a policeman in Singapore is not like what you see in TVB police dramas, right?" his mom said to him when he told her that blue, not white, would be his uniform for life. They had a fight for weeks. Aiden's mom still cooked for him and cleaned his room immaculately. But not a word. Not a single word. That is how Asian moms say, "I love you no matter what," without ever using their tongue. Now Aiden finds himself holding his breath, stays perfectly still, looks out into the distance at the glitzy neon signs on Neil Road, seemingly in a trance, remembering how he fought with his mom to be in the force, remembering his childhood dreams, remembering his principles. He senses the blood of the law and order coursing through his veins, but he is overwhelmed by a current of warmth and compassion flowing through those same veins, for a lost, lonely expat gay man like Ajay, who has so much in common with him minus the respect for the law.

"Go to rehab ... for me. Here is the 24/7 hotline. Check yourself in tonight." Aiden grabs Ajay's phone and taps in a number.

"I have tried it before. I got better, and then I got lonely. Then I started using again. I do not think there is a way out for me."

"That was because you were without me. I am here now. I don't want you to get locked up or deported. I want to know you more. And for that, you need to try again, for me. Can you promise me?" Aiden gently rubs Ajay's back with his hand and pushes his head against his shoulder.

"I promise I will try ... for you."

"If you fail, I fail. Now, let me get you home."

*

Ajay slumps on the sofa. Empty wine bottles and half-eaten pizzas deck the living room. He takes out his phone and dials the number Aiden gave him.

"Good morning, this is Singapore Rehab Centre. How may I help you?"

Ajay stays quiet.

"Hello?"

He hangs up, goes to the bathroom, opens the cistern, takes a lighter, heats the bong, and draws a puff. He doesn't feel the need to open up Grindr. For the first time, he feels something stirring in his heart. For the first time, he feels something again. He does not know if it is the meth or if Aiden's care has finally revived his ice-covered heart. He takes another puff. He hears the echo of Aiden's voice, "If you fail, I fail." An intense sense of shame engulfs him. It feels chaotic and evil. The phone beeps. Someone messaged him on Grindr. It must be one of his regular fuck buddies. After all, it is Friday night.

He takes another puff. He sees Aiden's face through the swirling vapour. The ceiling recedes endlessly.

FARAH GUZNAVI

Saving Grace

It was *so* much worse than I had expected. And I'm used to expecting the worst because as the unlucky bastard in charge of Housekeeping, I invariably have to mop up the messes created by my incompetent subordinates.

A hotel that charges as much as The Regency does have to provide top-drawer service. So we do whatever it takes to convince our customers that we're the real deal in terms of luxury lifestyles. After all, as management likes to remind us, the hotel has a reputation to maintain—however painful the maintenance process may be.

I get that. I do. I just hate the fact that *I'm* always the one that has to pick up the slack. But let's face it, how can you expect efficiency from a cleaning crew when most of its members come from the dirtiest parts of the world? India, Bangladesh, Nepal, Sri Lanka, etc. To me, they're all the same, these Indians!

Some people might think I'm being racist, but to say that Indians have disgusting hygiene habits is just a statement of fact. I mean, most of them don't even know how to use toilet paper properly! The Philippines is completely different. That's why I resent it when people here—the Arabs, in particular—tar all migrant workers with the same brush.

Of course, there *are* instances when we have only ourselves to blame, hobnobbing too intimately with such people, as Grace is doing these days. I worry about that girl. I can't help it. She was the first to coax my guarded heart back to life after so many barren years.

Everyone regards me as Benny, a friendly guy from the Philippines, but the truth is I lost the ability to give a damn about anything a long time ago. Life is more comfortable with your feelings safely locked away. Emotions lead to mistakes. And the consequences can be deadly.

I'm aware that my coworkers consider me good-looking. My dark eyes, full head of hair, and toned body (I spend a lot of time working out—it helps to keep certain urges at bay) would guarantee me a steady supply of female company if I so desired. But that road leads straight to hell. The Bible is clear on the subject of original sin, and I know from experience that sex outside of marriage usually leads to trouble.

I was desperately lonely when I first arrived in Al-Nourain. There weren't many Filipinos here at that time. It was a Middle Eastern backwater. None of us knew then that it would one day rival Dubai, with its gleaming skyscrapers and the hordes of complacent European tourists frolicking on its beaches.

The city-state has benefitted enormously from the energy and foresight of young Sheikh Ahmed. He realised—after the suspiciously early death of his father brought him to power—that a nation without oil would need to find other ways of keeping up with its wealthy neighbours.

I was still young when I arrived here, at the tail end of my teens, and I was miserable to be so far away from my mother. She had always been my rock, providing unflinching support whenever I needed it. Mamma single-handedly raised me and my younger sister, Alice.

I don't like thinking about her, though. Alice, I mean, not my mother. She's the reason I had to leave Manila.

From the time of her birth, baby Alice was the light of my life. She gave me succour and strength. Despite being a skinny nerd, I was her hero. And when I was around her, I truly felt like one.

Papi left us shortly after my mother became pregnant with Alice. I was already the target of school bullies by then, considered a sissy and a mamma's boy. My father, the macho man, despised me for it. And it got a lot worse after he left—mostly *because* he left, actually.

He was a lazy bastard, anyway. Like so many men in the Philippines, good for nothing. Luckily, our women are strong. Look at my mother. Newly single, she took less than a week off work for Alice's birth. After that, she resumed her job with a Bangladeshi family, living in their mansion in Das Marinas.

The man, Mr. Rabbi, was a bigshot at the Asian Development Bank. It was laughable how he claimed to be doing development work to help the poor when neither he nor his spoilt wife and fat sons could pour a glass of water without ringing the bell for my mother! The Bangladeshis are such hypocrites.

But at least they aren't as perverted as some of the others. Al-Nourain is the kind of place that brings out strange things in people. For all the talk of "conservative values," there is a dark underbelly to cities like this. Forbidden activities aren't really forbidden, they just take place behind firmly locked doors. How else could they attract so many Western expatriates?

And it isn't just the Europeans who take advantage of the lifestyle here. Look at that girl, Amanthi, from Sri Lanka. You'd think that butter wouldn't melt in her mouth, so demure does she look. And yet she's a filthy degenerate, forever out drinking and partying, up to God alone knows what under the cover of the desert night. She's a corrupting influence on nice girls like Grace. "My" Grace as I like to think of her.

I tried to warn Grace about Amanthi. Grace is a Filipina, a Catholic like me, so I thought she would listen. But she smiled at me gently and brushed off my warnings. She says that Amanthi is like family to her, that she misses the many siblings she left behind in Cebu. And she insists that Amanthi carries her own, well-hidden sorrows, that her friend is simply misunderstood by people like me. I didn't let her see that her reaction had hurt me. She is so naive.

We are hardworking people, we Filipinos, but fools for love. Look at my mother. She worked so hard for so many years to raise me and Alice. But when that man Jaime Arroyo moved in next door, I soon realised that things were changing. I was fifteen and just beginning to recognise the evil that lurks in the world. But I hadn't yet realised that sin takes many forms. And it is all around us.

I didn't like Jaime Arroyo, though I couldn't quite put my finger on it. Mamma wouldn't listen to anything I said about him. Starved for attention, she was completely taken in by his greasy charm. She believed his honeyed promises of a better life for us. As if he cared about Alice and me!

Alice was so little then, only six, but that man made her behave strangely too. She threw temper tantrums and screamed for hours on end. She began acting completely unlike herself. I knew that something was wrong, but I was afraid to examine things too closely.

Somehow though, Jaime Arroyo managed to convince my mother that the problem lay with Alice, not him.

Travelling home late on a Sunday night, after a college-sponsored trip to the islands, I had a strange feeling of foreboding that I could not shake loose. Like a dog that senses the tick hidden away in its fur, gluttonously drawing strength from its blood.

I heard the wailing even before I entered the house, knew what had happened as soon as I saw the small figure lying beneath the white sheet.

My mother had allowed Arroyo to persuade her that Alice was troubled by some malicious spirit that needed to be exorcised. So he had taken my sister with him to get the job done—heading, ostensibly, to the church.

But when the priest brought Alice back, limp and broken, Arroyo was nowhere to be seen. Father Aquino said that he had found her body in the graveyard adjoining the church. There were finger marks clearly visible on her throat. And there was more. I will not speak of that. Ever.

God sees everything. Alice had paid for my mother's sins, for Mamma's foolishness in allowing the temptations of the flesh to overcome her better judgement. And the consequences had not stopped at the destruction of her own moral values. It had cost Alice her life.

At that moment, I could not forgive my mother for surrendering Alice to that man, even for a few hours. But that made two of us. Mamma would never forgive herself.

Over and over again, she said, "Benny, I failed Alice. I should have listened to you!"

I couldn't bring myself to reply as she babbled on. Was she trying to convince me or herself?

"Trust me one more time, for God's sake! I promise you, my son, I won't fail again. I won't fail *you*, Benny, I swear it ..."

But I was too far gone to hear her. I howled dementedly, like a man possessed. My hatred and horror poured out of me in surging, guttural sounds. Why had I left Alice unprotected? Why had I gone on that trip when I *knew* there was something wrong at home?

If I could have found Jaime Arroyo then, I would have proved wrong all the bullies at school who had tormented me for being weak. I would have killed him.

For months afterwards, I could think of nothing but revenge. Once an honour student, I lost all interest in academic achievements. In everything. To this day, I have almost no recollection of the months following Alice's death.

Two years passed and the madness showed no signs of abating. At her wits' end, my mother somehow scraped together enough money to send me to the Middle East, hoping that a change of environment would catalyse a miracle, that her once-devoted son would realise what she had sacrificed to save him.

Her gamble paid off. I came to Al-Nourain as a kitchen boy, clawing my way up to housekeeping, and eventually, to a managerial position. I had nothing but work to keep me occupied and distract me from unwelcome thoughts, anyway.

Years later, when Grace joined the cleaning staff, I felt an immediate connection with her. She reminded me of my sister. Grace was about the same age that Alice would have been had she lived. She had the same sweetness of disposition, coupled with a compassion that had not left her despite growing up the unwanted ninth child in her family.

Life in the slums of Northern Cebu was hard for everyone. From its frequent flooding and landslides to the chaos left in the aftermath of typhoons like Haiyan, the poor suffered the brunt of a changing climate.

Yet, despite all that, and being left to fend for herself too early in life as a result of it, there was a softness in Grace that you couldn't miss. She would help anyone, from a lost tourist to a battered street-whore, if she came across one. She even looked a little like Alice, with her large eyes and silky, jet-black hair.

But as with my mother, when it came to trusting those she loved, Grace's judgement failed her. That's what these toxic creatures, people like Arroyo and Amanthi, do. They break through your emotional barriers and release the creeping stain of their poison, leaving horror and destruction in their wake.

In biblical times, Amanthi would have been the serpent in the Garden of Eden. Even in the modern-day Sodom and Gomorrah that the world has turned into, her brazen nature and venality stand out.

There was something about her, something I had disliked from the very beginning. She had an insolent swagger—even then when she was a supplicant, desperate for a job. And she was dark as sin. So much so that her teeth and the whites of her eyes shone rudely against that bitter chocolate skin.

Her darkness was like the mark of Cain. It gave away what lay beneath that smooth surface. Yet I was the only one who saw it, just as I had with Jaime Arroyo all those years ago.

Soon, she and Grace had become inseparable. The hotel staff affectionately referred to them as "night and day," the contrasts evident not only in their colouring but also in their personalities.

Amanthi was popular enough, perhaps because she knew how to have a good time. That's an important quality in the booze-fuelled, party-driven lifestyle here, and something I have never been much good at. And she always seemed to have money to throw around, buying endless rounds of drinks for her friends.

I had never seen her with a steady boyfriend either, though there was no dearth of men amongst the company she kept—something she seemed quite happy to take advantage of. I even wondered for a time if she was getting paid for all her whoring around. After all, salaries at The Regency aren't *that* generous!

Anyway, I didn't want Amanthi on my team, but we were short-staffed at the time and I had no choice but to hire her. She turned out to be good at her job. Honest, too.

The rare instances of theft at the hotel are always carefully covered up, with guests being lavishly compensated, but none have ever taken place in the east wing, in the rooms where she works. Or if they have, we've never had any reported.

Usually, thefts involve missing jewellery. But most guests here are obscenely wealthy. They are unlikely to notice the loss of one diamond ring out of the dozen or so in their possession at any time!

Still, that girl gives me the creeps.

Since Grace wouldn't listen to me, I decided to keep a close eye on Amanthi myself. But I had never been able to pin anything on her. Until that day.

I was on my way to hand-deliver the two extra sets of Egyptian cotton towels that the guest in this room had requested. The ones that my moronic subordinate Joel forgot to bring up when the lady requested it over an hour ago. She had returned from the spa early and was in a hurry to shower.

Approaching the room from the opposite end of the corridor, I spotted that black bitch slipping out of there. Instinctively, I stepped back so that Amanthi wouldn't spot me. But I wondered why she was there.

It was hard to see what Amanthi could possibly be doing for that guest. There was no man staying in that room for her to "service," and it wasn't the scheduled time for room maintenance. Besides, she didn't work in this part of the hotel, anyway, though the cleaners did sometimes engage in unauthorised work swaps.

She was carrying something in her hand. I tried to make out what it was, but the distance made it difficult. It looked like a letter-opener. Each room had one. It was part of the stationery set in the desk drawer. But it couldn't have been that, surely.

I began wondering if she had stolen something from there. Perhaps the guest had gone out again, giving her an opportunity to do so. When nobody responded to my knock, I used the master key to enter. Something felt off about the room, but I couldn't quite figure out what it was.

I went into the bathroom to put the towels away, noting that the cleaner hadn't folded the edge of the toilet paper in use to display the downward-facing triangle that indicated recent servicing.

And then it caught my eye. A scarlet smear of blood— bright, freshly minted—on the underside of the toilet roll. Where had *that* come from?

Ever since the arrival of Jaime Arroyo and the consequent destruction of everything that was pure and beautiful in my life, I had learnt to listen to my intuition. I don't always understand the logic behind what I feel, but I know that when the time comes, it will be revealed to me.

Now, I started looking around the room. The bed was made up very neatly. For a brief moment, I considered the possibility that an extra clean-up, requested by the guest, explained Amanthi's presence in the room. Then I dismissed it, continuing my investigation. As I spotted the faint shadow, on a patch of brightly-coloured carpet near the bed, my stomach gave a warning lurch.

The marks were almost invisible. Someone had done a very thorough job of trying to remove them. Someone with plenty of experience in dispatching stains. Slowly, like walking through water, I dropped to my knees and bent to check under the bed.

She was lying very still, a pool of rapidly-congealing blood oozing from her torso. I knew before I looked at her face that she was dead. She wore an expression of shock, forever frozen on what had, in life, been an undeniably beautiful face.

Perhaps she had seen her attacker.

Perhaps she had not expected it to be a woman.

I struggled to understand how this had happened. I wondered, suddenly, if the guest had surprised Amanthi in the middle of taking something. This was, after all, the part of the hotel where the two jewellery thefts had been reported earlier. And the guest *should* still have been at the spa.

On a hunch, I checked the desk drawer. The antique letter-opener was indeed missing. As I pieced together what had happened, I began to feel sick.

And then it dawned on me: this was a godsend. A murder had been committed on the hotel premises, and *I* knew who had done it, though not her motive for it.

I suppose I should have been more shocked, but I had always known that Amanthi was capable of murder, even though I didn't expect her to be a murderer. Once you have met evil at close quarters, you learn to recognise it even from a distance.

It didn't matter why Amanthi had done it. All that mattered was that I had found a way to get rid of her.

I would threaten to reveal her murderous actions unless she agreed to disappear of her own accord. And she could never return to Al-Nourain once the authorities had pieced together the truth of what had happened.

Ever helpful, I would inform the police of a minor incident, one that I had almost forgotten: the time I saw

Amanthi coming out of that corridor in the west wing, with something in her hand. I had thought nothing of it at the time, but later realised that with all her service duties elsewhere, she had no reason to be there.

I would mention that she seemed to be holding a letter-opener. When they check the stab wound, surely they could determine whether it had been inflicted with something similar. Besides, her DNA would be all over the crime scene. Provided they knew whose DNA to look for, of course!

The Al-Nourain authorities took such crimes seriously. After all, they didn't want to risk frightening off Western visitors. Tourism was a vital artery in the economic lifeblood of this Middle Eastern nation, carefully safeguarded precisely because Al-Nourain had little in the way of natural resources.

It galled me that Amanthi would get away with what she'd done, but I knew it was better that way. If she was jailed, I would never be rid of her. I couldn't risk Grace pining for her friend, visiting the jail every weekend while she waited for Amanthi's release.

And I knew my Grace. She would either refuse to believe that Amanthi was responsible, or she'd find some way to excuse her actions: childhood poverty and abandonment by her mother. Something, *anything*, to avoid facing the truth. She had hinted once that Amanthi's promiscuous behaviour stemmed from sexual abuse at an early age. As if Alice would ever have grown up to be a tramp like her! If she had survived Arroyo's attack, I mean.

No, the best way for Grace to put her friendship with this piece of Sri Lankan garbage behind her was for Amanthi to make a swift exit from all our lives.

Grace would be safe from predators, and it would also get her away from other bad influences: the late nights, the alcohol, and the partying. Perhaps then, she would finally see what had been right in front of her all this time.

I marvelled at what a stroke of luck this was. It meant that I could make Amanthi go away, that she would be a fugitive for the rest of her life. And she would have to leave Grace alone forever.

God reveals his designs in strange ways, but it was clear to me that this was a message. One that He had sent just for me! I was being given a chance to make restitution, to redeem myself through His grace.

I set my jaw and prepared to do whatever was necessary. I *needed* to get this right.

I knew I had failed Alice. I would not fail Grace.

*

"You did *what*?!" Grace's voice, normally so melodious, climbed to a screech. I had never even heard my friend speak at that pitch, let alone shriek like that! I was already petrified, but her evident panic made it clear to me just how serious the situation was.

"I didn't mean to do it! I was just checking the desk drawer, and she appeared out of nowhere. You know she wasn't supposed to be in the room! I thought she'd still be at the spa, but she was in the shower. She came at me, and I had to do *something*! It all happened so fast ..." I said, dissolving into tears.

"Seriously?! I understand that you were startled, but you can't go around killing people, Amanthi!" Grace said, her face softening at my evident distress.

That's the thing about Grace, you see. She's such a kind soul. She can never stay upset with anyone for long.

The truth was, I worshipped Grace. She had given me back my dignity and added a sense of self-worth that I had never had before.

My mother abandoned me when I was a baby, leaving me with an uncle and aunt who didn't want me. Predictably, my aunt took out her frustrations on a child who had no parents to defend her. She hit me with whatever she could lay her hands on—shoes, wooden spoons, and once, an iron. That time she shattered the bones in my shoulder. It still aches from time to time, especially during spells of wet weather.

Still, what my uncle did to me as an adolescent was far, far worse. I ran away from their house as soon as I was old enough. It was never home to me.

I went through a lot before fate finally brought me to Al-Nourain. Along the way, there had been many men, a mix of good and bad. But no one had ever really shown me love before I met Grace. So I would have done anything for her.

I would willingly have died for her. But killing someone … that was never part of the plan!

It all started harmlessly enough. The wages we earned at The Regency were generous by the standards of our impoverished countries, but we also knew that returning home was never going to be an option for either of us. There was no security to be had amidst the typhoons and the terror attacks.

In both Sri Lanka and the Philippines, cleaners were at the bottom of the totem pole. It was a little different in

Al-Nourain, but even though we earned more, there wasn't much respect to be had. So we both needed a longer-term plan.

A more immediate problem was the fact that our boss had the hots for Grace. Seriously creepy the way that guy Benny was obsessed with Grace. Although she was too kind—and too cautious—to tell him to get lost, I knew that his fixation bothered her. So to cheer her up, I would joke about how we were going to earn a ton of money, retire early, and buy a beach hut in Thailand. Though the tsunami that hit Sri Lanka when I was a child had left me certain that I'd never be willing to live that close to the sea again, it was nice enough as pipe dreams go.

But things soon got worse. Benny had always hated me. He was jealous of my friendship with Grace, so he started using whatever power he had to try and separate us. For a start, he assigned us new roommates in the staff quarters. Then he made sure that we had to work in different parts of the hotel.

He never came out to party with any of the other staff members, and he also began badgering Grace not to join us on our evenings out. He never actually laid a hand on her, but I could see that Grace was beginning to feel increasingly trapped. Nothing else could account for the bizarre plan that she came up with to turn our fantasy retirement into reality.

I didn't like the idea, but Grace insisted that there was nothing wrong in what we were doing. The guests who came to The Regency were loaded; they would never miss the small trinkets we stole, she argued. I pointed out that a diamond ring, featuring a rock the size of my thumb, could hardly be considered a trinket. But Grace brushed off my protests.

We planned it carefully. She was the one who came up with the idea, and she was certainly the brains behind our operation, but Grace lacked the nerve to do the dirty work. I, on the other hand, had done little else for most of my existence.

So it became Grace's job to identify potential victims and case out their jewellery collections; after that, I would go in and pull off the actual thefts.

The advantage of this was that the pieces never disappeared from any of the rooms that I was responsible for cleaning. Just as well, because even if I *hadn't* done it, Benny would certainly have found a way of blaming me for the thefts! We both knew that he would never believe Grace capable of stealing anything, let alone planning an enterprise of this kind.

In truth, I don't think that she would have been if she hadn't been feeling so desperate. And this was the one area where Grace's otherwise strong moral sense could be persuaded to take a backseat.

"These people are so rich, anyway," she said to me. "It's not fair that they have so much, while the rest of us struggle to survive." Years of poverty in a crowded childhood home had left her with a keen sense of the injustices of the world when it came to money. Benny's unwanted attentions just provided the spark to light that particular fire.

We weren't greedy. We rarely took anything—perhaps once every few months, and only from those who had, as Grace put it, way too much. In most cases, the guests didn't even notice.

In the rare instances when jewellery was reported missing, the hotel authorities gave us a severe dressing-down and immediately compensated the complainant. But the truth was, even the management doubted the veracity of the few complaints that had been made. They assumed that it would not be in our interests to risk such lucrative jobs by stealing. And of course, under normal circumstances, they would have been right to think that.

This time, it all went horribly wrong. The lady in room 330 had informed Grace, when she arrived to clean the room that morning, that she should come back in the afternoon when the guest was visiting the spa.

Grace lost no time filling me in on the details of her latest plan. "The lady's spa appointment is at two o'clock, Amanthi. She's taking the full package, so she'll be busy there until at least 3:30 p.m. I want you to go into the room after 2:30 p.m., just in case she's running late. I've already slipped one of her rings into the desk drawer, next to the stationery. Find it as quickly as you can and get out of there."

"But what if she notices that the jewellery's missing after you've cleaned the room? Won't she suspect you of being the thief?" I asked.

"No," Grace replied, "I've already thought of that. I'm going to go there at four o'clock to clean the room after she's back. I'll tell her that I was delayed by an urgent call from another room, and I'll apologise profusely to pacify her. Then, I can either service the room immediately or come back later if she prefers. Either way, if she notices that the ring is missing, she won't connect it to me cleaning the room. So don't touch anything else while you're in there. When she comes back, it needs to look as if the room is just as she left it. Understand?"

I nodded.

When I let myself in with the master key, the room was empty. I could see that it hadn't been serviced, but it was really only the unmade bed which gave that away. This guest was unusually tidy for a rich person!

I had just opened the stationery drawer and found the ring when I heard the bathroom door open and turned to see the guest emerging in a cloud of steam. She was taken aback to see me standing there. After all, she didn't know me. She had only seen Grace—though, to most of these people, service-staff members all look alike.

"Who are you? What are you doing in here?" she asked, her eyes narrowing.

I couldn't think of what to say. I was so shocked by her sudden appearance. Then she saw the ring clutched in my left hand, and there was no need to say anything.

"Thief!" she spat. "How dare you touch my things!"

I can't remember if I managed to say anything in my defence. But then she lunged at me and instinct took over. The last time Aunt Mimi had beaten me really badly was when she used the iron as her weapon of choice. The broken bones and the burn on my left shoulder left me determined never to allow anyone to hurt me like that again. And perhaps Aunt Mimi herself realised that she had crossed a red line because subsequent punishments were limited to the occasional slap or kick.

Now, as the woman came at me, I was reminded of how helpless I had felt in the face of my aunt's repeated assaults. My fingers scrabbled in the drawer for something to fend her off with and closed around the antique letter-opener that was part of the hotel's stationery package. I brandished it at her, hoping to scare her, and her own forward momentum did the rest.

I must have stood there for minutes, paralysed in disbelief. Then, it was as if some survival mechanism automatically took over. I could almost hear Grace's voice in my head calming me down and telling me what to do.

There wasn't much blood, surprisingly—except when I had to take out the letter-opener, which I did after bundling her body under the bed. Then I scanned the room, trying to figure out what to do next.

There was a small bloodstain on the carpet near the bed from when I had dragged her body there. I ran out into the corridor and found the cleaning cart, which Grace had left in anticipation of servicing the room later that day. It had everything I needed.

After I had finished, there was a wet patch on the carpet but no stain. I washed my hands and remembered to dry them using toilet paper, so that I could leave the remaining towels undisturbed.

And even though I knew it was against the instructions that Grace had given me, I tidied the bed before I left the room. If anyone came in, they would assume that the room had been cleaned in the morning.

I knew from programmes like CSI that they had ways of finding out how long someone had been dead. I had never been more grateful that Grace's cleaning shift for this part of the hotel was around 10:00 a.m. each morning, several hours before the woman had died.

Already, I was having trouble facing the truth. The woman hadn't "died." I had killed her.

But the important thing was that neither the theft of the ring—which no one would hear about now—nor the woman's murder, could be connected to Grace's servicing of the room, given the time frames involved.

I slipped the ring into my pocket, but the letter-opener wouldn't fit. So I tried to carry it unobtrusively in my hand. And as I walked down the deserted corridor, I thanked my lucky stars that most guests were, at this time of day, either enjoying a late lunch or sleeping off a heavy meal from one of the hotel's five-star eateries.

Now, as I looked into Grace's familiar face, distorted by the worry lines that appeared on her forehead and bracketed both sides of her mouth, I knew we were in real trouble.

"If they decide to take swabs from all the hotel staff, they're going to find my DNA in that room! I don't even have any jobs in the west wing!" I said, with a fresh sense of panic.

"That doesn't matter," Grace said firmly. "I'll just say I asked you for help with the clean-up service that morning because I was running behind schedule."

But despite her reassurance, we were both aware that things could get very ugly indeed. Even if we fled Al-Nourain, they were bound to come after us. We'd always be hiding, living in constant fear of getting caught.

Perhaps it was best just to try and brazen things out. But it was hard not to feel torn about what to do.

I didn't say anything because there was no point in scaring Grace, but I wasn't at all sure that we could pull this off. In fact, I had no idea how we were going to get out of this mess.

But there was one thing I did know. That idiot Benny Octavio deserved to pay for what he had driven us to!

And then, it came to me. The idea was so simple that I couldn't understand why I hadn't thought of it before.

The beauty of it was, Benny's hang-ups about women were common knowledge. Who could guess the depths to which that might drive him?

"Grace, I still have the letter-opener. What if I wiped off the handle and slipped it into the back of Benny's desk drawer?"

Her lovely eyes lit up in relief.

I had no doubt myself that Benny would guess who was responsible for framing him. But any counter-accusation he made, any attempt to pin it on me, would lack credibility. After all, everyone knew he'd been out to get me for ages ...

JON GRESHAM

Dog at the End of the World

My mistress's eyes are red. The silver trail of her tears runs down her cheeks. She smells of vanilla and crushed lavender. I stick my tongue out, lick the air to make her laugh. To cheer her up, I race around the condominium. Scampering claws, skittish on the marble tiles. I chase my tail.

Woof.

"I love you, boy," she says, kneeling down to ruffle the hair on my head. She hugs me and I wiggle my butt. I used to be a wagger on the street of love. Now I'm a wagger in the condo of isolation.

She smiles. I'm her buoy. Someone to hang onto. Someone to save her. She is the only one and I'm keeping her afloat.

"Only a couple of weeks," she says. "The two of us together while this whole thing blows over. Just you and me."

She looks at me with her big grey eyes and flutters her eyelashes. She's trying to comfort herself by reassuring me. I try to slurp her face. Cover her in slobber. If only I could lick her all over to leave a thin layer of saliva on her skin. This alone would shield her from the world's end. It's the least I can do. Make her wet. Hang my tongue out, ready to ink her with the old black nose. I leave a little saliva on her earlobe. Rub against her. Mark her with snot and dribble.

Woof.

My mistress weeps at the end of the world. Her eyes are nothing like the sun, but she is mine. And that's all that matters.

I'm not worried. About anything. Nothing will change between us. In fact, I'm hopeful. Looking forward to being together, nesting in our tidy pad. Smelling her close.

The cats know something's up. Mittens next door left two days ago when the news first came through the inter-tubes. Shook her head and told me no more moggies in Clementi. Not so much as a purr on the way out. Slinked away into the night, left with a harsh meow. "Time to hit the road, Boy," she said. "The end of the world ain't no place for felines. Ain't no place for anything on four legs."

Frigging Mittens. I recall an argument with her before everything went pear-shaped.

"Man does not live by dog alone," she said.

"Rubbish. There is no stronger bond," I barked back. "Humans live to be friends with dogs. Look at what we do. Guard the family, dig the rubble, sniff for kidnapped kids, fetch dead birds, sit beside bombs. We're responsible. Not like you frigging cats. Humans love us."

"Get real," she said. "Haven't you been on social media? There are at least twice as many photos of cats as there are of dogs."

I was without a woof.

"Cat used to get devotion even though does nothing," she hissed. "Now I'm leaving because my human is sick in bed, frothing at the mouth. Time to go."

"But … but they love us …" my voice wavered. "And we love them. We stay. We're their people."

Mittens strutted away, tail in the air, her pink sphincter clenched in a toot towards me.

Our helper, Siti—who smelt of bleach, peppermint, and ABC Sambal Extra Pedas—ran away too. Went to Best Denki. Then caught the last boat to Batam with a brand-new rice cooker and an Xbox. She messaged my mistress from the ferry, "Ma'am. Are you OK? I escape with husband. Yes, the engineer. We go back Pekalongan. Dorms not safe. We're alright, but what about you? You've got the dog. That's OK. Bye."

The bees die. The parrots are mute. The canaries keel over. Should I leave too? Inconceivable. I ain't no cat. Cats are tamarind and kimchi. I am cinnamon and orange peel. My place at the end of the world is beside my mistress. People must stay together.

Woof.

My mistress, she used to work in IT. When the plague hit, she was asked to code from home. I never understand that crap. Mostly because I can't read. Frick, I'm a Labrador retriever. Coding's beyond my pay grade. I don't have opposable thumbs. How am I supposed to pick up a book or click on a mouse?

I tried to headbutt the TV once. Singed the eyebrows. The golden locks stood on end. The electricity made me smell like a burnt newspaper. I'm sorry. I thought it was a portal, a time machine to take us somewhere else. Like a kennel. Boy, did that hurt. It was just frigging glass. Look, I'm loved for my loyalty. They don't pay me for my brains.

At night, we dogs talk. I really enjoy the midnight howl. Woofing about the world with my canine mates. Billy, the cocker spaniel, says these are the end times and crosses his chest with a single paw. The Alaskan husky in the condo on the other side of the road says there's insufficient toilet paper. Hairy McLairy, the border collie, says it's all the monkeys' fault. Hanuman at McRitchie gone "berko." Upending wheelie bins, stealing bananas from wet markets. It must be true because his master says so. Ralph, the miniature schnauzer, begs to differ. His boss told him that a scientist at Biopolis spilt a test tube and this is why we are where we are. We all bark together. As though it's happening somewhere else. Woofing at the world as it collapses.

These are days of miracles and wonders. The plague sweeps the Island. The monkeys are revolting. Deer prance along the CTE, stand in the traffic, defiant and resolute, willing cars and trucks to strike them. Antlers fly. Wild boar race down concrete canals from Bugis to the East Coast. I smell cordite, burning plastic, and the produce of evacuated bowels. I see rats burrow out of the green slopes of Mount Faber and snakes slither along culverts. The beasts of the earth flee from the centre of the island making their way to the sea. I take this all in from the third-storey balcony of my mistress's place: a cookie-cutter, smaller than advertised, executive condominium. It's really quite tidy for the two of us with its pastel-hued soft furnishings and generic teak minimalist furniture. We're safe here? There's a cactus and bougainvillea on the balcony. Dog stays in place.

Pop, my old man, asked me once what I was doing with my life? He insinuated that chewing sneakers all day was a waste of time. He wanted me to be a drug sniffer. Fat chance. I'd be happier being a blind dog. At least I'd get to wear sunglasses. Didn't happen. But I haven't let Pop down, have I? What I'm doing now with my mistress is the best thing ever.

They say the plague exiles us from others. Truth is I've never felt happier being at home with my mistress. Lying on the couch. Food is delivered. Whoever said a quiet, safe life is a form of death never had a dog to love and be loved by. My mistress passes the time by untangling my blonde locks with a steel comb. So relaxing. She watches old box sets—The Sopranos and Friends—and plays Skyrim. She dances to Dua Lipa and records her moves on TikTok. Then she chills with Kingdom on Netflix.

Woof.

Do dogs get masks? If not, why not? I wish to get high on my own breath. What will happen to us if we get it? "Don't worry," my mistress says. "We'll be safe up here on the third floor, above the palm trees and the street."

Where will we go once this is all over and we can go out again? I remember what it was like before all of this. Hanging my head out a car window. Feeling the wind smarting my eyes and cooling my face. The scent of chicory and carbon monoxide in the nostrils. Why do humans love big metal boxes on wheels? Why do I chase those boxes? Why does my mistress tickle me under the chin? Does she remember our ancient days of wandering? Up Bukit Timah Hill around MacRitchie. Are those days really gone?

How I love being here with her. Just the two of us. The joy of sniffing her rose-petal butt after a bath. The texture of her coriander legs. The elixir of her armpits. It's okay. We have each other. I make her laugh. Tongue lolls idiotically out the side of the mouth. My mistress loves me.

My mistress gives me something hard. But it isn't a bone. It's a wireless speaker.

"Sorry, boy, there's no more bones. Goodbye, Alexa," she says as I chew. Black plastic shards splinter across the carpet. It tastes okay. I have my mistress and she has me. "Keep on loving me," she says. "Keep on loving me."

Woof.

She used to arrive home from work, pour herself a gin and tonic, then flop down on the sofa. I used to then lick her. She smelt of cigarettes, staplers, and Chanel No 5. Why do humans use fake smells? Why don't they make do with the scents they've got? I lick the back of her hand. Her skin is soft like moss. I lick her on the forearms. Her hair sends tingles along my tongue. She pats me on the head. She caresses her shiny stone with the tips of her fingers. She talks to it. Watches videos and scrolls. Scroll. Scroll. A cat picture. Grrrrr.

My mistress knocked and rang the bell next door to see how Mitten's boss was. Nobody answered. Mittens must have left with her human.

Since the plague, our lives are simple. Extraneous features stripped away—no more washing or socialising. So why don't humans use this as a chance to get rid of their clothes? Reduce themselves to the bare elements? Live unadorned, like dogs. Remove all ornamentation. Pare back to the functional. Get naked. Shit, eat, sleep, make love?

We have our simple joys. Hang out together on the balcony. I show her how to lick the rain. I do some housework: lick the dust off the spines on books. In her apartment, there are no surfaces I haven't tongued. Well, maybe there are some.

Everyone on their balconies sings Home. Except for me. The stench of platitudes is in the air like forgotten, defrosted prawns. How am I supposed to clap? I've just got paws for frick's sake. I hang my tongue out and lick the air.

Mistress shuts her bedroom door but I know what she's up to. She touches herself out of boredom and desire. When she finishes, the door opens. And she gives me a biscuit. As though this is adequate compensation. Thanks for leaving me alone. Thanks for giving me the snip. I'm the last dog in my family, so all I've got is her. The least she could do is involve me.

She spends most of her time tapping the shiny stone. She burns the back of her eyes. In bed at night, she isn't sleeping. Just gazing at the shiny and scrolling. I try to get attention by licking her armpit. I send her dog thoughts: "Look into my eyes. Look into my eyes. Now imagine the world anew. All I want is you." She swats me away, cuffs me behind the ear, and keeps scrolling.

She throws my steel comb at a pigeon on the cactus. The comb flies over the balcony railing and clatters on the concrete below. The pigeon shits on me. My hair is a mess. We've run out of shampoo. She calls me Rasta and compliments me on my dreadlocks. How embarrassing.

She can talk. My mistress's hair is growing. She looks like a dog now. "Look at you with your floppy velvet ears," I tell her. If only the whole world were so soft.

I don't understand why she can't be happy with just the two of us. My job is to sleep at the end of the bed, snuggle up, consume leftovers, fetch sticks, and protect her from night terrors and door-to-door evangelists. Oh boy, I love her. Isn't that enough?

She is depressed. Before she smelt of butter and velvet, now she smells of bloodied cut toenails with the flesh taken at the clip. And after she goes to the toilet, she smells like a cow. I don't like cows. I know we don't have much water, so the least she could do is lick herself clean.

"Will we die?" she asks me. "Are we doomed?"

Woof.

We don't know that.

Woof.

Question is not what happens next but how we're going to live now. I keep woofing this at her but she doesn't get it and taps her shiny instead.

Things are getting worse. She fills buckets on the balcony with rainwater. Tekong water. The electricity keeps going off. Her shiny stone beeps. "Fuck, Gerald, don't come over. You idiot," she says.

Woof, I agree. Gerald is her ex-boyfriend. I never liked his smell.

She practises her golf swing on the balcony. I hate golf. A hideous sport that smells of fertiliser and isotonic drinks. Golf eats land. I frolicked once at Royal Orchid, transgressed across its wide-open spaces. That's where she met Gerald.

"I didn't expect a dog. I thought you'd be a cat person," he told her after she teed off. I ran down the fairway chasing her ball. She got mad at me for bringing it back. That's the game, isn't it? No? The ball has to go as far as possible. Okay then.

Now, at the end of the world, she makes a mini-putting green in the apartment. Practises her strokes until I sniff her balls and bounce them over the balcony with my nose. She isn't speaking to me.

Her shiny stone loses its signal. It beeps for the last time. She pushes me away. She stares at the black, lifeless shiny and weeps.

At night the howling stops and instead, there are screeches like the squeals of squashed otters followed by the dull sound of cleavers through flesh and bone. Where did all the dogs go?

Nobody bothers to clean the streets. Garbage piles up beside rotting carcasses. Our food is running out. No more Grab. I live on her old sneakers. That pair she used for muddy walks in Sungei Wetlands are delicious. They last a week.

One day, outside our front door, we hear a wail like a cat shagging a bagpipe. My mistress looks through the peephole and jumps back with a shriek. There's scraping on our door. Next thing I know, my mistress has emptied the bookshelf and has started to hammer nails into the front door barricading us in. We're trapped. But that's okay; the thing in the corridor can't get in.

There is no exit, is there? This lockdown is now our natural state. Electricity gone. Shiny dead. Water no more. Door nailed shut. Funnel on the balcony. Catching raindrops with a thread and plastic bag. Anaemic turds curled in an ice cream container ready to fertilise tomatoes

and bean sprouts. Wet wipe showers. She should play with
me. But she doesn't. She just sits on the floor tearing up
books and eating pages.

I would die for her. If only I can get down from this
balcony. I'd prowl the neighbourhood and find stuff to
eat. Mynah birds. Rats. Old tubes of toothpaste. There are
plenty of slippers on racks in HDB corridors.

"Hey, there's no need to cry. I'm here," I say as I nuzzle
against her. Remember the good times. Remember when
she first saw me at the pound? Dopey eyes. The slight tilt
of the head. A wide whacky smile. Gleaming teeth. Pink
tongue lolling. A little whimper and the gentlest flex of an
eyebrow. Got her there. Woof. She took me home. That
was a long time ago.

We eat toilet paper dipped in condensed milk.

I shit in the ceramic Chinese plant pot on the balcony.
Bits of shoelace and sole. The bougainvillea—hardy,
gnarled, and dry—loves taking my poo and turning it into
beautiful pink and purple flowers that trail down from the
balcony across the palm leaf fronds below.

I see two people dance naked in the rain on the road.
Tearing off their masks and kissing in the downpour. Socks
on their zakars. They attempt a bark!? Humans impersonate
dogs? Whatever will they think of next? The sheer dumb
joy of it. The larrikin spirit. Who are they to believe that
the rules don't apply? The nutters. Don't they realise there's
a plague going on? My mistress joins me on the balcony.
She smiles for the first time in a long time.

Almost as though our hope kills them, they splutter
and cough and fall to the ground. Pink froth at the mouth.
Writhing beside the bones of the other dead dogs in the

street. They lay on the grass and sleep. They never wake. Me on the balcony, tail still. Wag gone. Mistress stops smiling. We'll never go out again, will we?

A few days later, I spy another fool in the streets below. He wanders towards us, wrapped in transparent plastic overalls and a full-face mask. Some hunch-backed creature slouches towards our balcony. What rough beast is this?

"Rapunzel. Rapunzel, let down your hair." A voice cries out from halfway up the palm tree beneath our apartment. My mistress snoozing on the couch perks up.

A grappling hook zips over the balcony and snares around the bougainvillea pot. The rope goes taut. I do my bit and bite the fibre. Grimy hands in fingerless gym gloves grasp the edge of the railing. I am about to consume a finger when my mistress yells, "Gerald?"

"At your service, mistress."

He struggles to haul himself onto our balcony.

"I've come to save you," he says as she helps him over.

A bloke in rags with a scraggly misshapen beard and an overladen rucksack on his back emerges from within his PPE. He stinks like a bombed-out Italian delicatessen. Bits of dried tomato, tagliatelle, and fennel are tangled in his messy, unkempt facial hair. I would eat that for days but his squinting, beady emerald eyes put me right off.

"I knew you were alone, so I hiked over."

She's not alone, I growl.

"From Novena? Gerald," she smiles, "I'm impressed, but there's just no need."

What on earth does she see in him? Flabbergasted, I try to bite.

"Woah there, matey."

I'm not your mate, pal.

"Down, boy," my mistress cries. I heed her command and flare my nostrils in his direction. I smell him.

"Look, I think we can ride this out together," he says. "I know we haven't always been good for each other." That's an understatement. Last time they saw each other, she threw him out after he sneered at her weight and ridiculed her chicken and broccoli lasagna. I can't for the life of me understand what she sees in Gerald. He doesn't get you, I bark.

"Let's make a new start. Just the two of us."

Two? I'm here. I count. Don't forget about me.

"I've got three rolls of toilet paper, a month's supply of instant noodles, and ten cans of baked beans," he says as he pats his backpack.

She licks her lips, and in that moment, I know he is staying.

"Quarantine has been good to me," Gerald says. "I managed to get a bulk deal on loo roll. I sold it online by the piece. Made a hell of a profit until the power went down. We have to work together. People have to work together."

What about dogs? Are we not people too? Why are dogs not counted? I can understand why cats aren't people. But for the life of me, I never considered that I was not people.

He tries to pat me on the head.

Don't you try and be friends with me, pal. I'll have a piece of you, I snap. He reaches into his rucksack and offers me three Scooby snacks from the palm of his hand. I'm still not your mate, but I'll have those, thank you very much.

For a brief moment, we make eye contact. Then his eyes dart away. I smell his envy and slimy mind.

"I guess there's more meat on a dog," he laughs.

Did he just say that? Why is she laughing? Have they no decency? We don't crack gags about eating each other where I come from.

She looks at me and shrugs. She turns back to Gerald. She takes him by the hand and leads him to her bedroom. Before he shuts the door, I see her scented candles and incense sticks. I can't stand their canoodling. Makes me want to puke. I can't frigging compete, can I? Not with a bloke.

Hours later, when they emerge, they stink of snails. A stench that lasts because nobody's showering. Not even with wet-wipes.

He stays. He tries to grow tomatoes on the balcony with a packet of seeds he looted from NTUC Fairprice. A week later, a little emerald shoot emerges. He is ecstatic until I pee in the pot and eliminate his growth.

She takes his side and hits me with a sandal. I am bereft. She has long since stopped tickling me under the chin. I guess it happened as I got fat on her soles and heels. She had more shoes than Imelda. Purple Charles & Keith ones. Red-soled Pradas. Louboutins. Jimmy Choos. I grew stronger, while she and Gerald weakened on their paper and bougainvillea leaf diet. Where does my love go if my mistress doesn't want it? I am inconsolable. What am I supposed to do? That night I take my revenge and chew up her Birkenstocks.

After a month, we are eating cardboard seasoned with curry powder. Gerald keeps looking at me and licking his lips.

"Look, I think you have to face it," Gerald says as they sprawl across the floor. "We're going to die," he furrows his brow in fake sympathy. "Unless we eat the dog."

I would die for her. But there is no way I am dying for Gerald.

"Never," she says. "He's my boy." And I see her tear up, but she won't meet my eye.

Can I ever regain her loyalty? She stares at me strangely. Frick. My mistress is not there anymore. Her soul has gone and she's left her skin behind. I know I'm in trouble when she pinches my flanks, feeling for a different form of tenderness. Is this the end of everything I've spent my life living for?

I stay awake all night. No one is going to consume me in the small hours. Unfortunately, I fall asleep and have nightmares of verdant fields, daffodils, and cows. I am not afraid of snakes or spiders. It's cows that freak me out. Their brown eyes as big as frigging ping-pong balls. They smell of shit. I have a nightmare that they paraglide into the apartment and stand on my paws.

I wake to find Gerald trying to zip-tie my hind legs. Bastard. I bite. He loses a little forearm. It tastes remarkably similar to the soles of her Converse gym shoes.

The two of them look at me, licking their lips. All gaunt, thin shadows under sagging eyes. What we had ... it must count for something? Blood drips from Gerald's arm. If push comes to shove, would I bite her too? How do I escape this apartment? Oh yes, I remember: no thumbs. I can't climb down a rope with frigging paws. Where the Frick are Paw Patrol when you need them?

Gerald comes at me. I scramble to the balcony. Gerald lunges. She yells, "Watch out ..." It's too late. Gerald trips on a trailing branch of Bougainvillea. He screams and topples over the balcony. I dare not cast my eyes below. Expecting a splat, I hear a dull thud. A sack of pumpkins on concrete.

The mistress groans and collapses in exhaustion to the floor.

With an outstretched hand, she reaches to stroke my mottled and matted hair. My mistress's eyes are gunmetal. The trail of her tears runs red down her haggard cheeks.

"Boy. Don't worry. It's me."

I offer her a paw. Chew on this if needs be, my mistress. Chew on this. She holds my paw in her hands, feels the firmness of my pads. She shakes her head and holds me tight. She crawls to the bedroom and grabs a sheet. She ties a big sling and beckons.

"Go find food," she says.

She wraps me up and with her last remaining strength, she lowers me over the balcony. She runs out of bedsheet when I am at least two storeys above the ground. I hang there swaying slightly in midair.

"Oh boy, I love you."

I have to do what I have to do. I jump. Bump. Ouch. Howl. Yelp.

I break my fall on palm tree fronds and a pile of splattered, pink flesh that once was Gerald. Nothing is broken except the bond between dog and people.

I look up through the gnarled, tangle of Bougainvillea trailing from her balcony. The mistress wails and waves a thin, fragile arm.

Oh boy.

I turn and run.

And I run. I run so far away.

CONTRIBUTORS' BIOGRAPHIES

Adeline Tan

Born and raised in Singapore, Adeline Tan is passionate about stories in all their varied forms. She has been working as a video editor for the past sixteen years; she builds images into compelling visual narratives, one shot at a time. Surprising family and friends (and herself), she decided to try her hand at writing by enrolling in the MA Creative Writing programme at LaSalle College of the Arts in 2019. She is now fascinated with constructing stories that depict the frustrations of modern-day living, one word at a time. *Babel* is her first short-story submission and publication.

Babel by ADELINE TAN ©2020, ADELINE TAN

Areeba Nasir

Areeba Nasir is an Indian author whose debut novel *No Exit* was published in 2012. She holds a master's degree in English Literature from Delhi University, India. She has also studied creative writing at British Council, India.

Areeba's short stories have appeared in *Indian Review* and *The Brown Orient*. Her stories revolve around sociopolitical conditions of India. The debut novel highlights militarisation of Kashmir. She mainly writes fiction that is close to reality.

Areeba currently resides in Canada and is working on her second novel. She considers herself a feminist writer who constantly raises her voice against patriarchy and traditions.

Bench by AREEBA NASIR ©2020, AREEBA NASIR

Darryl Whetter

Professor Darryl Whetter was the inaugural director of the first taught creative writing master's degree in Singapore and Southeast Asia, in a degree conferred by Goldsmiths, University of London. He is the author of four books of fiction and two poetry collections. His most recent book is the 2020 climate-crisis novel Our Sands, published by Penguin Random House. His essays on literature and creative writing pedagogy have been published by Routledge, the National Poetry Foundation (US), and Presses Sorbonne Nouvelle, etc. He is currently editing an anthology of essays under contract with Routledge. www.darrylwhetter.ca

Turquoise Water, White Liberal Guilt by DARRYL WHETTER ©2020, DARRYL WHETTER

Donna Tang

Donna Tang is a former lifestyle journalist and editor. She lives in Singapore, where she is pursuing an MA in Creative Writing. Her articles have been published in over twenty magazines and newspapers (SPH, Mediacorp, and indie publishers) since 2002. Her poetry and prose have been featured in anthologies such as *Love Gathers All* (Ethos Books), *SingPoWriMo 2017: The Anthology* (Math Paper Press), *Meridian: The Asia Pacific Writers and Translators Drunken Boat Anthology of New Writing*, and shortlisted for *The Masters Review* Flash Fiction Contest 2020. She is interested in memory and identity-construction and is working on her first novel.

How She Knew by DONNA TANG ©2020, DONNA TANG

Farah Ghuznavi

FARAH GHUZNAVI is a writer, translator, newspaper columnist and development worker, who tells stories because they refuse to leave her in peace until she does so. Her work has been widely anthologized in the UK, US, France, Canada, Germany, Singapore, India, Nigeria, Nepal and her native Bangladesh. Farah's rst short story collection is *Fragments of Riversong* (Daily Star Books, 2013). She has also edited the *Lifelines* anthology (Zubaan Books, 2012). Writer in Residence with Commonwealth Writers in 2013, her award-winning stories include *Getting ere* and *Judgement Day*.

Saving Grace by FARAH GUZNAVI ©2020, FARAH GUZNAVI

Jasmine Adams

After practising law for more than 20 years, Jasmine ran a design practice until quite recently. Currently, she is a licensed tourist guide with the Singapore Tourism Board. Jasmine has a master's degree in South East Asian Studies from National University of Singapore and is a passionate collector of culinary artefacts. Although writing has always been incorporated in her various careers as well as her part-time job as a copywriter for design ranges from furniture to scarves to jewellery, writing short stories is a hobby which she has taken up only recently, enjoying the process of capturing memories into stories. Jasmine has attended various courses on writing and her stories have been read to the public at libraries as part of the Silver Arts Festival.

A Woman's Place by JASMINE ADAMS ©2020, JASMINE ADAMS

Jon Gresham

Jon Gresham is the author of the short story collection *We Rose Up Slowly* (Math Paper Press, 2015, 2nd edition) and co-editor with Elizabeth Tan of *In This Desert There Were Seeds* (Ethos Books and Margaret River Press, 2019).

His writing has appeared in various anthologies and literary journals including *Best Singaporean Short Stories 1* (Epigram Books 2020). One of his stories was shortlisted for the 2020 Short Fiction/Essex University Prize.

He currently runs the Asia Creative Writing Programme, a partnership between the Singapore National Arts Council and Nanyang Technological University. He is a co-founder of Sing Lit Station, a literary community and charity.

Dog at the End of the World by JON GRESHAM ©2020, JON GRESHAM

Karen Kwek

Karen Kwek has worked in publishing and as a freelance writer and editor. She lives in Singapore with her husband, three teenage sons and their dog. She enjoys a good cup of tea and is thankful whenever the fullness of life overflows into a story. Her short fiction has appeared in various anthologies, including *The Epigram Books Collection of Best New Singaporean Short Stories* (Volumes I and II, 2013 and 2015) and *Hook and Eye: Stories from the Margins* (Ethos Books, 2018), a recommended 'O'-Level literature text in Singapore. "The Dispossessed" won the 2011 Golden Point Award for English short story, and "Night Fishing" was shortlisted for the 2018 Commonwealth Short Story Prize.

Borungurup Man by KAREN KWEK ©2020, KAREN KWEK

Kelly Kaur

Kelly's poems and works have been published in Sanscrit, West Coast, Singa, CBC, Mothering Anthology, New Asian Short Stories 2015, Short Story Dispenser (Central Library), online YYC Portraits of People, Time of the Poet

Republic, Canada, and Word City Monthly. She is a 2019 Borderlines Writers' Circle participant through Writers' Guild Alberta and Alexandra Writers' Centre in Calgary. She has also completed the first draft of her novel *Letters to Singapore.* Kelly teaches at Mount Royal University.

The Singapore Dream by KELLY KAUR ©2020, KELLY KAUR

Moazzam Sheikh

Born and raised in Lahore, Moazzam studied Cinema and Library Science in the US. Librarian by profession, he has translated fiction in Urdu, Punjabi, and English. He is the author of *Idol* Lovers and Other Stories and *Cafe Le Whore and Other Stories.* He guest-edited a special issue of Chicago Quarterly Review on South Asian American Writers (2017). His fiction has been anthologised and published in several literary magazines. He lives in San Francisco with his wife and two sons.

Sunshine by MOAZZAM SHEIKH ©2020, MOAZZAM SHEIKH

Murali Kamma

Murali Kamma's debut book *Not Native: Short Stories of Immigrant Life in an In-Between World*, published last year by Wising Up Press, won the 2020 Bronze Independent Publisher Book Award (IPPY) for multicultural fiction.

Born and raised in India, Kamma now lives in Atlanta. While he did dabble in fiction as a youth, it was his life as an immigrant straddling two cultures—and his work as an editor—that inspired him to pursue it more seriously. His short stories have appeared in numerous journals, including *Rosebud, South Asian Review,* and *Cooweescoowee.* Nineteen of the twenty stories in his collection were previously published. One of his stories won second place in the Strands International Flash Fiction Contest.

Currently the managing editor of *Khabar* magazine, he has enjoyed interviewing Salman Rushdie, Anita Desai, William Dalrymple, Chitra Banerjee Divakaruni, and Pankaj Mishra, among other authors. His columns have appeared in *The Atlanta Journal-Constitution* and *India Abroad*, and he received a Gamma Gold Award from the Magazine Association of the Southeast (MAGS). He earned degrees from Loyola College, India, and SUNY at Buffalo.

The Route to Lucky Inn by MURALI KAMMA ©2020, MURALI KAMMA

Phong Huynh

Phong Huynh is a Vietnamese spoken word poet and writer based in Singapore, currently pursuing Master of Arts in Creative Writing at LaSalle College of the Arts. His works deal with the themes of individual identity, LGBTQ+ rights, mental well-being, family relationships, and social mores. He has performed spoken word poetry at various local platforms such as Spoke & Birds, Singapore Poetry Slam, and Destination Ink. He recently published his debut poetry anthology *AIR,* centering around his experiences as a gay man and his relationship with his parents. His short story "The Canyon" was published in the June 2020 *LGBTQ+ anthology* of the Beyond Words International Literary Magazine based in Berlin.

As Legal As We Are by PHONG HUYNH ©2020, PHONG HUYNH

Sarah Soh

Sarah Soh was born in Singapore and has previously lived in the United Kingdom, Ireland, and the United States.

She is currently a student in the Creative Writing Masters programme at LaSalle College of the Arts.

Lingua Franca by SARAH SOH ©2020, SARAH SOH

Scott Platt-Salcedo

Scott has been selected for several writing fellowships and national writing workshops in the Philippines. His works have appeared in Salt Hill Journal and The Chaffin, both of which nominated him for the 2020 Pushcart Prize. His other works of fiction have been published in SAND Journal, K'in Literary Journal and *The Best Asian Short Stories 2019* anthology by Kitaab among others. He lives and writes in the Philippines.

Mud-bound Country by SCOTT P. SALCEDO ©2020, SCOTT P. SALCEDO

Seema Punwani

Born in Spain and raised in Mumbai, Seema Punwani has now lived in Singapore longer than India. A "local-expat," she straddles the insider-outsider boundary when it comes to her writing about Singapore. Her debut novel *Cross Connection* was launched at the Pune International Literary Festival in India in 2018. She has read at the Singapore Writers Festival, the George Town Literary Festival (Malaysia), and the Australasia Association of Writing (Australia). Her short fiction was anthologised in *The Best Asian Short Stories 2019* by Kitaab, her poetry has been a finalist at the Poetry Festival Singapore 2019, and her play will be staged at the Dastak Theatre Festival in Singapore in 2021. Seema is a single mother who works as a marketing consultant and is in the final year of her MA in Creative Writing offered by Goldsmith, UK, and LaSalle College of the Arts, Singapore.

Spin by SEEMA PUNWANI ©2020, SEEMA PUNWANI

Sudeep Sen

Sudeep Sen [www.sudeepsen.org] is widely recognised as a major new generation voice in world literature and "one of the finest younger English-language poets in the international literary scene" (BBC Radio). His prize-winning books include: *Postmarked India: New & Selected Poems* (HarperCollins); *Distracted Geographies*, *Rain, Aria* (A. K. Ramanujan Translation Award); *The HarperCollins Book of English Poetry* (editor); *Fractals: New & Selected Poems|Translations 1980-2015* (London Magazine Editions); *EroText* (Vintage: Penguin Random House); and *Kaifi Azmi: Poems | Nazms* (Bloomsbury). *Blue Nude* (Jorge Zalamea International Poetry Prize) and *The Whispering Anklets* are forthcoming. He is the editorial director of aark arts and the editor of *Atlas*. Sen is the first Asian honoured to read his poetry and deliver the Derek Walcott Lecture at the Nobel Laureate Festival. The Government of India's Ministry of Culture has awarded him the senior fellowship for "outstanding persons in the field of culture/literature."

Gold Squares on Muslin by SUDEEP SEN ©2020, SUDEEP SEN

Yap Swi Neo

Yap Swi Neo is a retired educator having taught for over 40 years in secondary schools, polytechnic and as adjunct lecturer at all the universities in Singapore. She holds a MA Applied Linguistics (NUS), a Teaching Certificate, Diploma TESOL (Distinction), RELC Singapore, and Life Skills Facilitation (Canada).

She has facilitated Life Skills Funshop for middle management staff of various organisations. She co-authored two academic books on the teaching of English and one on Life Skills.

She has a memoir titled "Is the Soup Done?" in the collection *My Life My Story* 2015, published by National Library Board.

She writes short stories as a hobby since her retirement. A happy Peranakkan grandmother, she enjoys reading, writing, the kitchen, sambal belachan, and finds cooking therapeutic. Her exercise routine is long, wandering walks along the Park Connectors, then a sumptuous lunch at the Food Courts.

In Towkay Lee's Mansion by YAP SWI NEO ©2020, YAP SWI NEO

EDITOR'S BIOGRAPHY

Zafar Anjum (Series Editor) is a Singapore-based writer, publisher and filmmaker. He is the author of *The Resurgence of Satyam, Startup Capitals: Discovering the Global Hotspots of Innovation,* and *Iqbal: The Life of a Poet, Philosopher and Politician.* His short story collections include *The Singapore Decalogue* and *Kafka in Ayodhya and Other Stories.* He is also the founder of Kitaab and Filmwallas.

THE B·E·S·T ASIAN SERIES

THE BEST ASIAN SHORT STORIES 2017

Monideepa Sahu, Guest Editor • Zafar Anjum, Series Editor

32 writers. 11 countries. One anthology of its kind in Asia.

The stories in this anthology by Asia's best known and well-respected contemporary writers and promising new voices, offer fresh insights into the experience of being Asian. They transcend borders and social and political divisions within which they arise. While drawing us into the lives of people and the places where they come from, they raise uneasy questions and probe ambiguities.

Explore Asia through these tales of the profound, the absurd, the chilling, and of moments of epiphany or catharsis. Women probe their own identities through gaps between social blinkers and shackles. A young Syrian mother flees from war-ravaged Aleppo into a more fearsome hell. The cataclysmic Partition of India and its aftershocks; life and death in a no-man's land between two countries; ethnic groups forced into exile; are all part of the wider Asian experience.

Life flows on in the pauses between cataclysms, bringing hope. Fragile dreams spread rainbow wings through the struggle to succeed socially, earn a living, produce an heir, and try to grasp at fleeting joys and love. These symphonies of style and emotions sweep across Asia – from Jordan and Syria to Pakistan, India, Bangladesh, Singapore, Malaysia, the Philippines, Thailand, Japan and Korea. Crafted with love, they continue to resonate after the last page.

THE BEST ASIAN SHORT STORIES 2018

Debotri Dhar, Guest Editor • Zafar Anjum, Series Editor

This is the second volume in the series which contains well-crafted stories with innovative characters, gripping plots, diverse voices from 24 writers in 13 countries.

While Rakhshanda Jalil is a seasoned writer known to many in South Asia, Aditi Mehrotra is an aspiring Indian writer whose story delightfully juxtaposed textual passages and news clippings on women's empowerment with everyday life vignettes of domesticity from small-town India. Martin Bradley's story highlighted the intersecting themes of travel, historical memory, and communication across differences. Today, when latitudes shift, cultures collide, and we are all travellers in one form or another, in ways perhaps unprecedented, these stories must be told.

THE BEST ASIAN SHORT STORIES 2019

Hisham Bustani, Guest Editor • Zafar Anjum, Series Editor

War, loss, love, compassion, nightmares, dreams, hopes and catastrophes; this is literary Asia at its best. From a wide range of geographies spanning from Palestine to Japan, from Kazakhstan to the Malaysia, mobilizing a wide array of innovative narrative styles and writing techniques, the short stories of this anthology, carefully curated by one of Asia's prominent and daring writers, will take you on a power trip of deep exploration of local (yet global) pains and hopes, a celebration (and contemplation) of humanity and its impact, as explored by 24 writers and 6 translators, many of whom identify with many homes, giving Asia what it truly represents across (and beyond) its vast territory, expansive history, and many traditions and languages. This book is an open celebration of multi-faceted creativity and plurality.

THE BEST ASIAN SPECULATIVE FICTION 2018

Rajat Chaudhuri, Guest Editor • Zafar Anjum, Series Editor

Between singing asteroid stations with a secret, and chilling visions of dystopia, between mad sorcerers with an agenda and time-travelling phantoms perplexed by the rules of afterlife, this volume of stories offers a unique sampling of flavours from the infinite breadth of the Asian imagination. If science fiction, horror, and fantasy are the genres you swear by, but miss Asian voices and settings, then this anthology is your oyster. Call these stories speculative, sff, or by any other name, they are really tales well told, and they always take off at a tangent from the big, blustering 'real'. Here the imaginative spirit is aflame, casting a rich lovely light. Tales from sixteen countries of Asia plus the diasporas. Freshly minted, told by seasoned writers and new talent—a smörgåsbord of Asia's finest speculative imagination.

This volume features stories from 34 stories from 16 countries.

THE BEST ASIAN CRIME STORIES 2020

Richard Lord, Guest Editor • Zafar Anjum, Series Editor

Fittingly for a crime collection, this debut anthology offers thirteen stories, stretching from India to Japan, with key stops along the way in Singapore, Malaysia and the Philippines. Some of the authors whose work is being showcased in this anthology are Priya Sood, Carol Pang, Timothy Yam, Lee Ee Leen, Wendy Jones Nakanishi, Ricardo Albay, and Aaron Ang, among others.

THE BEST ASIAN TRAVEL WRITING 2020

Percy Fernandez, Guest Editor • Zafar Anjum, Series Editor

Stories from the inaugural edition of *The Best Asian Travel Writing* offer you glimpses into the curious, strange and wonderful experiences in Asia through the eyes and words of our writers. They travelled to find the roots in Cherrapunji, discover the wonders of Bamiyan, volunteer in the high Himalaya, looking for Malgudi among others that offer a frisson of excitement and expectation.

For more titles from Kitaab, visit www.kitaabstore.com

Made in the USA
Las Vegas, NV
28 February 2022